Praise for Mimi Plus Two

"The marvelous Mimi is back and ready to face the next stage of her life with comedic grace and charm. A must read!"
— Barb Valentin, author of Key Change

"Utterly adorable! Whitney Dineen delivers a funny and heartwarming romantic comedy about having a wedding, having a baby, and having it all."
— Brenda Janowitz, author of The Dinner Party

"Mimi Plus Two races along with a snort and a giggle on every page. An appealing heroine, a great supporting cast…a perfect beach read!"
— Dee Ernst, author of Stealing Jason Wilde

"Mimi Plus Two is hilarious, entertaining and insightful—will keep fans of women's fiction and chick lit engaged to the end."
— Reader's Favorite

"Whitney Dineen has done it again! Mimi Plus Two is chick-lit at its best with a cast of characters not soon to be forgotten!"
— Susie Schnall, author of The Balance Project

"Wedding? With child? No sweat! Mimi's back with twice the humor, twice the zaniness and all the quirks we've grown to love about her."
— Book Mama Blog

"I didn't think it could get any better, after The Reinvention of Mimi Finnegan. I was wrong! Mimi Plus Two gives us a fantastic, candid look into the larger-than-life world of Mimi, one of the most endearing, hilarious characters ever created. She's the best friend I'd love to have in real life!"
— Sara Steven, Chick Lit Central

"Mimi Plus Two is a masterfully entertaining sequel sure to delight! Dineen has expertly crafted a piece that equally encompasses the charm of a romantic comedy and the empowerment of a coming of age saga!"
— Nicole Waggoner, author of Center Ring

"Dineen conducts another magic carpet ride! Mimi Pus Two tells the rollicking story of Mimi trying to adjust to life as a newbie millionaire, newbie aristocrat, and newbie mother ... all at the same time! And every word is comedic brilliance. From the hyperbolic hijinks of newlywed life to the very visceral vicissitudes of pregnancy, Dineen weaves her story with hilariously inspired prose that keeps you turning the page. You won't want to put this one down, except when you need a sec to catch your breath from all the laughing!"
— **Geralyn Corcillo, bestselling author of Queen of the Universe**

"Chick lit lovers will be entertained by Mimi and her foray into marriage and motherhood. Whitney Dineen delivers a warm and bighearted romantic comedy that makes for a delightful read!"
— **Marilyn Brant, NYT bestselling author of You Give Love a Bad Name**

"Mimi Plus Two will have you laughing out loud & and ignoring life until you read those dreaded words - 'The End'. Absolutely fabulous addition to the series."
— Aimee @ Hello...Chick Lit

"Mimi just gets better and better. Love weddings? Hate pregnancy? Mimi is a must on your beach read list!"
— Kim Gruenenfelder, author of Keep Calm and Carry a Big Drink

"With wit and imagination, Whitney Dineen takes her irrepressible heroine Mimi on another wild ride! I ran the emotional gamut with this book, laughing over some scenes and doing the ugly cry over others. Here's hoping the author is planning a trilogy!"
— Tracie Bannister, author of Twin Piques

"Mimi Plus Two is a wonderful, funny, entertaining, and heartwarming glimpse into Mimi's life as she becomes a wife, daughter-in-law, and mother. And she accomplishes all that with her great sense of humor and with the love of her family and friends. I really hope that that there will be more stories about Mimi's life—I feel like I have a beautiful friend who I need to visit again.
— Susan @ The Book Bag

Also by Whitney Dineen

She Sins at Midnight
The Reinvention of Mimi Finnegan

Middle Reader Books:
Wilhelmina and the Willamette Wig Factory

Mimi Plus Two

Whitney Dineen

This is a work of fiction. Any references to historical events, real people, or real places are used fictitiously. Other names, characters, places, and events are products of the author's imagination, as are any resemblance to events, places, or persons.

Copyright © 2016 Whitney Dineen

All rights reserved. No part of this publication may be reproduced, stored in a retrieval system, or transmitted, in any form or by any means, electronic, mechanical, photocopying, recording or otherwise, without the prior permission of the publishers.

Published in the United States by Kissing Frogs Publications an imprint of Thirty-Three Partners Publishing.

Library of Congress Cataloguing-In-Publication Data
Dineen, Whitney
Mimi Plus Two : a novel / Whitney Dineen.

First Edition

This book is dedicated to all the brave women who've become mothers. It's not only the hardest and most rewarding job you'll ever have, but studies have shown it can also cause insanity.

Acknowledgments

I have so enjoyed bringing Mimi back for her next adventures; marriage and motherhood. To me, Mimi is my dear friend and soul sister. I can't wait to spend time with her. While Mimi Plus Two is the second book in the Mimi Adventures, it also reads as a standalone.

As always, a book never gets written without the support of a great many people. First and foremost I'd like to thank my husband and parents for making my life run as smoothly as possible so I actually have the time to write; being a forty-something mother of two young children can be quite a thrill ride.

A special thank you to all my author and blogging friends who loved *The Reinvention of Mimi Finnegan* and encouraged me to continue her journey. I'm blessed to have such a huge support system!

My biggest gratitude goes to my readers. Without you guys buying my books, I wouldn't be writing them, so I thank you for helping make my dream come true!

Chapter 1

"A mucus plug?" I ask in horror. "What in God's name is that?"

My sister, Ginger, simply smiles and explains, "It's a necessity in pregnancy. It blocks any foreign matter from entering the cervix and introducing troublesome bacteria. It's really a wonderful thing."

I'm not buying it. "Pregnancy is way more disgusting than I anticipated. I mean seriously, it's like there's all this top secret information that doesn't get shared until it's too late."

My beautiful and brainy sister, only a year older than me, is also in the family way, with triplets no less. She and her husband, a.k.a. my boss, Jonathan Becker, tried in vitro fertilization after months of not being able to conceive. Three humans are currently forming inside her uterus. I'm only harboring one. But you'd think it was fourteen, such is the graceful way I've taken to breeding.

Ginger takes a sip of her "Mommyhood Tea," which near as I can figure contains every Chinese herb containing a dash of yin, a skosh of yang and a nice dollop of tranquilizer.

Ginger is positively glowing, not to mention peaceful. She looks like she's gestating the next Dalai Lama and his equally Buddha-like siblings. We're a week apart in the pregnancy game and both at the end of our first trimester. Ginger's first foray into childbearing has been ideal. She has not been plagued with any of the horrors I have. "Your eyes look a lot better, Meems. How's the vomiting?"

The eyes, of which she speaks, are blood red and look like I've poured blistering hot sand directly into them. My doctor likened them to the living dead. The nausea has been so bad and I heave with such wild abandon, I've been breaking blood vessels at an alarming rate. I've taken to wearing sunglasses whenever I leave the house so people don't suspect a deadly illness or fear that I vant to suck their blood. "Getting a bit better now that I'm taking Reglan for it. I just wish Dr. Fermin prescribed it sooner. Hopefully, they'll have a chance to revert to normal before the wedding."

The wedding would be mine, to the dashing and distinguished, Elliot Fielding. Elliot and I have only known each other for a few months but he snagged my heart the minute I saw him. Okay, maybe not the minute, but well within the first two weeks, possibly three. The PR company I work for signed on to launch Elliot's next book and in the midst of the proceedings, one thing led to another. We will be married in ten days and I'm more excited than I have ever been about anything. I'm not just marrying him because I'm in the "family way" either. I'm head over heels in love with the guy.

The only problem is that I haven't been feeling well enough to help plan the event. I know we will be saying our vows at

Our Lady of Peace Catholic Church in Pipsy, the same parish where my parents were married. The reception is going to be held in my sister Renée's backyard in Hilldale. Her grounds put the Haiku Mill in Maui to shame, so I've really hit the jackpot there. I have no idea what the bridesmaid dresses look like because truly, I could give a crap. As an ex-model and famous designer, I've left that particular detail up to Renée. My only request is they aren't brown, yellow or gray. Other than that, I'd rather sleep or vomit than have to be responsible for their wedding attire. Renée is also designing my dress and I have given her carte blanche.

My mother, Maureen O'Callaghan Finnegan, is choosing the flowers. She has an eye for floral arrangements and I trust her implicitly. She nearly shattered my eardrums when I handed the job over to her, "Meems, NO! This is the best job you could give me!! Do you have any favorites that you want me to include?" I was going to tell her that I would love lily of the valley in my bouquet but the very thought of their delicious aroma upset my stomach to the point I needed to cut the conversation short to puke.

The one task I was really, really looking forward to participating in was choosing the menu for the reception. The first two times we met with the caterer I became so ill we had to leave. Therefore, I reluctantly let Elliot and his English palate loose on them. I'm hoping he doesn't order fish and chips and warm beer. Not that it will matter much to me. If I don't get the retches under control by then, I don't suppose I'll be eating anything.

I am and always have been a wearer of double digits. All

three of my sisters hover around the size 6-8 mark. I have not been smaller than a size 12 since I turned thirty, five years ago. I am now a size 10 but only because I can't seem to keep any food down. It's the worst diet ever. In fact, I gave up on Weight Watchers on the advice of my doctor. "Mimi," she instructed, "you can gain 30-40 pounds and be well within the medical bounds for a healthy pregnancy. No dieting for this baby."

Another upside of losing weight is that my bunion has nearly vanished. Edith Bunker, so named because she has the same grating voice as Archie's wife, nagged me into successfully losing fifteen pounds before getting pregnant. Yes, I know a talking bunion doesn't make me sound very sane, but you have secrets too, so don't judge.

"Meems, are you listening to me?" Ginger inquires. "You look like you're about to pass out."

That's another thing. I'm exhausted all the time. I take at least two naps a day and sleep a good ten hours at night. "Aren't you even a little pooped?" I ask. "You know most women are dog-tired during the first trimester."

Ginger sighs, "I guess I have been a bit more sleepy than normal but I'm so excited to get the nursery ready and read everything I can about triplets, I really don't want to sleep. I just want to be prepared.

"Ginger, I may know squat about pregnancy but I do know there won't be much sleeping going on after those kids of yours hit the planet. You should try to store up."

My sister laughs, "I know, I know. Jonathan says the same thing, but after all those months of trying to get pregnant and then signing up with adoption agencies, I just want to be awake and enjoy every moment." Unlike me, I just want to go lights out and regain consciousness after the baby is born and possibly out of diapers.

"I'm just going to go upstairs and take a nap here if you don't mind. I don't think I can make it home safely." Ginger assures me it's fine so I take my shoes off and don't even try to get up the stairs. I just lie down on the couch and let the sandman take me.

I fall asleep so hard and fast that within seconds I dream I'm floating in the clouds, all snug and safe holding my baby in my arms. My hair looks fabulous, not the half red, half bacon grease I'm currently sporting. My skin is glowing and the bundle in my arms coos away. Somewhere, cloud adjacent, I hear Jonathan call out Ginger's name. In my vision, he hugs her for a long moment before saying, "Oh honey, I'm so sorry. Try not to worry." Then he asks, "Did you tell Mimi?"

Ginger replies, "How could I? She's having such a hard time with her own pregnancy. I don't want her to worry about mine."

Chapter 2

"Mimi, don't worry, they'll love you," assures my charming husband-to-be, as he announces the early arrival of his parents. "They're just like any other parents."

I interrupt, "Perhaps, if those other parents happen to be an earl and countess. God, Elliot, how could you not have told me this before now?"

He soothes, "Don't think of them like that. They're just my mother and father and they will adore you as much as I do."

Here's the thing. I know for a fact I would have loved Elliot and wanted to spend the rest of my life with him, regardless of his pedigree. I just haven't had much of a chance to come to terms with it. In my head, I was slated to fall in love with a regular sort of guy, maybe a high school football coach or plumber. At any rate, I envisioned him being locally born and raised. We would have pizza on Friday and meatloaf on Wednesday and watch sports at my parents' house on Sunday. Now, I'm not only marrying an internationally bestselling author but the future Earl of Houndstoothbury on the

Thames. That's not really his title. I've just forgotten what it is. Note to self, have Elliot write down his father's title so I don't come off like a completely ignorant American.

"They will be here late tomorrow night and will meet us for brunch on Sunday. So you have plenty of time to calm down." He looks so certain of himself.

"Oh my God, Elliot, my hair! My appointment isn't until Tuesday! I have to call Francoise and see if he can fit me in today." When I met Elliot, my hair color was not blonde and not brunette as much as baby poop in color. In my quest to catch his eye, my flamboyant hair stylist dyed it this fabulous shade of red. And by fabulous, I mean he unleashed the true me. But I'm not supposed to use dye on it for the first trimester. Something to do with my crazed hormone levels and the possibility the color won't take or will take incorrectly. But this is a crisis. I will risk pink roots so that the Earl and Countess of Upper Snob Hillery won't be horrified by the first sight of their future daughter-in-law.

Elliot kisses the top of my head and rubs my shoulders, "Forget about my parents for a moment and tell me how the little mother is doing."

Who says things like "little mother?" This is something else that takes some getting used to. While Elliot and I both ostensibly speak English, his is the queen's variety and mine is more closely related to a scullery maid. I smile and answer, "If by little mother, you mean the starving incubator of your seed, then I'm starving! I miss the cravings and all you can eat food fests. This nausea is for the birds."

"Dr. Fermin assures us it won't be for much longer. Once

you feel like eating again, I'll take you out for every meal and fill you up with whatever your heart desires. How does that sound?"

"Like heaven. I want to hit Burger City first and have a double cheeseburger with fries and root beer and …. Hold that thought, I need to throw up." Running to the toilet, I'm overcome with sympathy for anorexics. All this hurling is making my throat raw and irritated. Why in the world would anyone choose to do this on purpose?

Sitting on the floor with my head resting against the porcelain god, I start to cry. I am so sick and so happy and so overwhelmed and so delighted at the same time that the only escape for all these pent up emotions is tears. Gut wrenching sobs pour out of me as Elliot runs to my side, "Mimi, what happened? Are you are okay?"

With snot running down my nose and vomit on my shirt, I answer, "I'm just so happy. Thank you, Elliot, thank you for making my life perfect."

The look of shock and horror on his face make it clear he doesn't know if I'm being sarcastic or not. And while I am one hundred percent sincere in my gratitude, I can see where he might not be.

Elliot helps me into bed and covers me up, "Why don't I call Francoise for you while you have a little lie down? I'll wake you once you have an appointment time."

My eyes are closed and I'm fast asleep by the time he leaves the room. I dream about house hunting with my future husband. So far, we've put it off because we've been so busy getting ready for the wedding. Rather, everyone else has been so busy getting ready for it. I've been too sick and Elliot is hard at work on his next thriller, Double Jeopardy. Our original plan was to buy a house in Pipsy and an apartment in New York City. That way we could be near family and I could continue working for Parliament in Manhattan. But soon after discovering I was pregnant, it became clear I didn't have the necessary fortitude to grow life and hold down a job. For the first time in my adult life money isn't an issue, so with Elliot's persuasion, I agreed to leave my job until after the baby is born.

One of Renée's whoop de doo society friends hooked us up with her husband who is the premier real-estate agent in Hilldale. He's been sending preliminary listings for us to look at and I'm astonished by what he thinks our requirements are. My current little yellow house in Pipsy would be perfect for us and the baby, maybe a little snug but still, pretty darn ideal. Blaine, I swear that's his name, thinks we require at least ten thousand square feet and a pool. Elliot seems to agree with him. I was surprised by that until I learned he's 17th in line for the throne. If some unimaginable holocaust hits the royals, I could be living in Buckingham Palace. That's enough to make any middle-class girl from Pipsy sick to her stomach.

My pregnancy dreams have been fantastically absurd. Just last night I dreamt I was abducted by aliens that all looked like Prince Charles, at various ages. They all wanted to rub my bunion and feed me crumpets. That would have been fine and dandy, except when I threw up on one, he turned into a six foot lizard who licked me with a forked tongue.

Have I mentioned the smells? My nose has become bionic.

I can detect skunk before the malodorous aroma has even been released. Elliot's cologne, that I once found the most intoxicatingly manly fragrance in the world, is now up there with the stench of unwashed feet. He's been a good sport about not wearing it but I can tell he misses it. I've caught him taking a whiff every now and again out of the bottle.

My doctor assures me I will feel better than ever once I hit my second trimester. If that isn't true, I'm going to see what I can do about being put into a medically induced coma until this nightmare is over. No time to worry about that now though. My subconscious must start obsessing over meeting Elliot's parents and impressing them as the perfect vessel for their illustrious line. Crap.

Chapter 3

I don't know why, but I've started envisioning Elliot's mother looking like Patsy from that old sit-com Absolutely Fabulous. You know tall, painfully thin, beehive up to the heavens, cigarette perpetually dangling from her lips. I know this won't be the case and it's not.

Victoria Fielding, Countess of Derbyshire, looks no more like good old Pats than I do. There is nothing BBC America about her. She is solid Masterpiece Theater and I have the worst fear I'm going to soil her shoes, which are a feminine version of her husband's tasseled loafers. Much to my relief, she's not wearing tweed or carrying a shotgun for the hunt. She's sporting a lovely neutral cashmere twinset with matching trousers. Her deep auburn hair is so elegant and ladylike I feel like a hooker in comparison. A double strand of pearls hangs from her neck and her earrings probably cost more than my car.

Elliot's dad, the earl, appears to have just stepped off the set of Upstairs Downstairs. He's as handsome as Elliot but way more uptight in his bearing. He looks like he's just caught a hint of Limburger cheese. His name is Archibald and I haven't a clue what to call him. Archie, Dad, Your Lordship, Pops?

We're having brunch at The Hilldale Country Club, where until recently, my sister, Muffy, was the female tennis pro. Her ex-husband was the men's tennis pro until word got out that he was serving more than tennis balls to many of the members' wives. I don't think that's the reason they fired him as much as the fact that it became public knowledge. However, that is the reason he's Muffy's ex and not current other half. At any rate, I'm not a member of the country club, nor is Elliot, but they were more than happy to accept his brunch reservation in hopes he will join their renowned assemblage in the near future.

We're standing in what can only be described as the salon. Mere mortals might refer to it as the lobby but there is nothing mere or mortal about this setup. Huge chandeliers hang overhead from twenty-eight foot ceilings. Stuffed loveseats and winged back chairs are clustered together for various conversation areas. Fresh flowers abound and it is all I can do to keep my meager breakfast of dry toast and tea from coming up on me.

Trying to express my delight at meeting my future in-laws, I smile brightly and declare, "I'm so pleased to meet you both!"

The earl tilts his head to the side and murmurs, "Indeed." At the same time the countess offers, "Quite." What the hell? It's like meeting Elliot all over again. These Brits are so reserved and uppity I have no idea how to proceed.

Elliot kisses his mother's cheek then shakes his father's hand in greeting. It's like a Wild Kingdom episode. If you listen closely, you can hear the snooty voiceover of the show's host. "The animals at the top of the pecking order are only allowed to show the politest amount of interest in one other. Note, they do not embrace, that is for the more common of the species."

The earl allows a genuine smile to touch his lips upon laying eyes on his son and announces, "Elliot, we are delighted to see you." Notice he does not say, "We are delighted to see you and your charming fiancée." He says, "We are delighted to see YOU, period."

Elliot counters, "Let's see if our table is ready so we can catch up." While I have never dined at the country club before, I can tell you this, the staff is bending over backwards to make sure that we are given the best table and are seated with the proper amount of pomp and circumstance, enough to make any royal feel welcome. I'm ready to whip Edith Bunker out and suggest someone give her a nice rub but manage to hold back for fear of horrifying my dining companions.

The earl orders an Armagnac, the countess, a flute of champagne. Elliot requests black coffee and I simply ask for water with no ice and no lemon. Our server suggests we view the buffet before ordering off the menu. The tension is so thick you'd need a machete to cut through it. It's only after our drinks are served that my future mother-in-law deigns to speak to me. "So, Mimi, is it?" I nod to acknowledge that she's got my name right. "How is it that you and Elliot are on your way to the altar so quickly after meeting?" Then, just in case she hasn't made me uncomfortable enough, she adds, "We were expecting his betrothal to Beatrice. This is quite another matter."

What I want to say is, "For crap sakes, Your Highness, could you pull the stick out of your rump long enough to be civil?"

Elliot is wise enough to intercept and not give me free reign in my response. "Mother, Father, Beatrice and I are no more than good friends. I wanted to be there to help her during her breast cancer struggles, nothing more."

The earl answers, "Very noble of you son. How is dear Beatrice?"

Elliot tells them her cancer has returned and that she's back in London. He adds, "She's fallen madly in love with the chap who came out to fix her washer machine."

The countess gasps, "How unexpected! Well, I'm delighted for her that she's found companionship, no matter how common, in the midst of her ordeal." I swear to God, she glances my way when the second half of that sentence spews forth. Then she looks straight at me and asks, "How *did* you and my son meet, Miss Finnegan?"

Miss Finnegan? Is that what she's going to call me? It's like I'm interviewing to clean her toilets, not marry her son.

Elliot, in fear for his mother's life, answers, "Mimi and I met at her office. Her PR company is dong the press for Double Jeopardy."

The earl pipes in with, "How impressive to own one's own company at such a young age."

I choke on my water and reply, "It's not my company, sir. I just work there."

If you listen closely you can hear crickets chirping because the table has gone dead quiet. Elliot eventually contributes,

"Mimi and I travelled to New York City together and we fell in love there."

His mother wonders, "Didn't you want a longer engagement so we could have announced the occasion properly?" By properly, she must mean sending liveried servants to deliver engraved invitations for a party at the Royal Gallery, where the impending union would be announced by a troop of panty hose wearing town criers. That's when it hits me, Elliot's parents have no idea I'm pregnant!

Elliot and I share a glance that encompasses an entire telepathic conversation.

Me: What the hell? You didn't tell them?!

Elliot: Darling, you don't understand. This is big news for them.

Me: Listen, butt head, you're marrying me! Fix this, NOW!!!

Elliot: Yes, dear.

Elliot clears his throat, "Mother, Father, we have some wonderful news! Mimi is expecting our child."

This decree is received with the same degree of excitement one would expect if they had just learned their country home had been invaded by al-Qaeda and turned into a brothel. Lead balloon much? Yup.

The countess is the first to regain speech, "Oh, dear. Well then, I see where there's reason for some haste." She looks to her son and shares her own clairvoyant conversation.

Countess: Dear Lord, Elliot. Why on earth did you impregnate the girl?

Elliot: I love her, Mother.

Countess: But she's so common. And American! It's a dreadful shock of which I'm not sure I'll recover.

Elliot: You'll love her when you get to know her, I promise.

Countess: When pigs fly.

The earl seems to regain some decorum and raises his snifter in the air, "To my first grandchild."

Elliot raises his coffee cup, "Here, here." The countess doesn't even pick up her champagne.

I excuse myself to use the ladies' room, which translates into needing fresh air before I scream. By the time I return, our breakfast has been served and everyone seems to have moved on to discussing a rousing cricket tournament the earl is sponsoring at his old alma mater. I just pick at my fresh fruit bowl and count the minutes until I can go back to bed.

"I think that went well." Elliot offers once we get into the car.

I look at him like he's grown a second head and demand, "On what planet did that go well?"

"Mimi, darling, my parents aren't like yours. They're more…" he pauses while he searches for the right word, "reserved." What he means is they're more refined but he's smart enough not to say it out loud.

"Your mother more than insinuated she wished you were marrying Beatrice and not me. Then she made it clear she wasn't even happy about the baby. That's going well?"

"Yes," he replied, "but my father toasted his first grandchild. Certainly that's a nice gesture."

"Are they seriously going to stay here until the wedding? That's six whole days! What on earth are we going to do with them?"

Elliot responds, "They're my parents, Mimi. They understand we're getting ready for the wedding and don't expect to be entertained constantly. But we will include them for family meals and wedding preparations. It will give them a chance to get acquainted with your family as well."

Saints preserve us. No good can come from this. My family is Irish, after all. I can see my father pointing out the many sins of the English and maybe even parading out quotes from Angela's Ashes. My mom can show the countess how to make an Irish stew and then we can all sit and stare at each other like foreign bacteria under a microscope. This is going to be the longest week of my life.

Chapter 4

It's only five days until the wedding and today marks the end of my first trimester. It's like a switch has been flipped and I feel fabulous! I'm more refreshed than I've ever been. Rightly so as I've spent the better part of the last three months sound asleep. And I'm starving! For the first time since my sophomore year in high school, I weigh less than one hundred and fifty pounds, which if you ask me is quite impressive as I'm 5'11". No delicate flower here.

I roll over and give Elliot a wake surprise he hasn't had since the nausea took over. After a lovely hour of getting reacquainted, in the biblical sense, I hop out of bed and demand, "Take me to breakfast. I'm ready to make up for lost time!"

Elliot and I take a quick shower, get briefly sidetracked and don't get to The Cracked Egg until three minutes before they stop serving breakfast. I'm famished and ready to devour everything I've been missing out on. I can't decide what to order, so Elliot suggests I get anything that sounds good and eat whatever I want. His idea does not require a lot of persuasion.

We're snuggling together side-by-side in the red Naugahyde booth by the window, when who should we see walk by but my little sister, Muffy, and her new beau, my high school friend, Kevin Beeman. Kevin and I became reacquainted about five months ago when we ran into each other at a Weight Watchers meeting. Kevin's wife left him the year before, announcing she was pregnant with his business partner's baby. So in one fell swoop he lost his wife, his job and all meaning to life. He spent the next several months feeling sorry for himself and eating his body weight in Cocoa Puffs. You'd never know it to look at him now. He's lost forty-eight pounds under the guidance of my physically fit sister and looks a lot like his super cute high school self, only better.

Muffy and Kevin see us too and make their way into the restaurant. They get caught behind the waitress delivering our seven breakfasts. Elliot is having eggs Benedict and I'm having the farmer's omelet, pigs in the blanket, a short-stack, oatmeal, a bagel with cream cheese, and waffles with strawberry syrup and whipped cream.

Elliot explains, "The nausea has passed and we're celebrating. Care to join us?"

Muff and Kevin slide into the booth across from us and my sister asks, "Can we share yours or do we need to order our own?"

The look of panic in my eyes has Kevin holding up his hand to ask the waitress for menus. He knows me so well.

Muffy announces, "We just got confirmation, The Buff Muff will be open in time for Christmas!" In addition to being a couple, Muffy and Kevin are also business partners. They're opening a tennis club in Hilldale. She's the brawn and he's the brains, not unlike that old song by the Pet Shop Boys.

Kevin's smile is radiant as he grabs Muffy's hand, "We're on our way, baby!"

They couldn't be cuter or more deserving of one another. They've been together the same amount of time as Elliot and I. I'm hoping theirs is the next wedding.

Muffy announces, "After breakfast, I'm heading over to Renée's for my last fitting. Meems, you're going to love the bridesmaid dresses!" My bridesmaids are all three of my sisters and my old Weight Watchers leader, Marge. Marge appears to be a bit of an unlikely candidate as she's fiftyish and a bit matronly, but she held me together during a particularly rough time in my life and I wouldn't be where I am without her. I wanted to invite Elliot's sister to stand up with us as well, but he assured me it wouldn't be her thing. Having met his parents, I'm a bit relieved not to have her in the wedding party. I can just see her pinched face looking like she was trying to unsuccessfully pass a giant turd.

I ask, "What color are they anyway?" then mention, "I need to stop by Renée's later for my fitting, too."

"Oh Meems, they're so unexpected. Not at all the traditional bridesmaid dresses you see that are all one color and boring. They're a yellow and gray floral with a brownish background, totally stunning!"

I choke on my waffle, "What? I told Renée explicitly I didn't care what they looked like so long as they weren't yellow, gray or brown! Now you're telling me they're yellow, gray AND brown?"

Muffy's eyes start to dart around the table looking for reinforcements from the men but she soon discovers they're too afraid of me to participate. Then in a soothing voice, like she's trying to talk a mental patient off a ledge, she adds, "Don't make any judgements until you see them, promise?"

I promise, but I'm still pissed. I feel the beginnings of a real Bridezilla moment and realize with the wedding only five days away, I'll probably just have to live with it. But I'm not happy.

After breakfast, Elliot and Kevin decide to catch a workout while Muffy and I go over to Renée's house. Renée's home is exactly what our Realtor envisions for us. It's a three story brick edifice guaranteed to impress. With a large fountain in the center of the circular drive and ivy growing up the side of the manse, it's quite imposing. I pull my six year old red Honda up to the front and storm the staircase before Muffy can catch up. I don't ring the bell like a proper guest, either. I just slam through the front door and yell, "Renée Marie Finnegan-Bouvier, where the hell are you?"

Renée and Laurent turned half of their home into Renée's design studio and showroom for her exclusive clients and they still have more square feet to live in than a Romanian village. The grand French doors leading to her studio are opened by none other than Elliot's mother. I'm not sure why she's here but I couldn't be more delighted to have her witness my boorish manners, not.

With one eyebrow arched to the heavens and looking down the entire length of her nose at me, she inquires, "Mimi, are you unwell?"

I sheepish reply, "Yes, I'm not at all well. Is my sister in?"

Cue Renée. She glides in behind the countess and smiles beatifically, "Mimi, I didn't know Victoria was Elliot's mother! I'm not sure why I didn't put two and two together but I never did."

What in the world? "How do you know, um, er, Vic… rather, the countess?"

My sister responds, "I made her dress for Kate and Wills wedding." Of course she did.

Victoria intercedes, "Your sister is a genius, Mimi. I'm quite impressed by her." Well thank God she's impressed by someone in my family because Lord knows it's not me.

Just then Ginger yells out, "Meems, come on in. You have to see these dresses." It turns out I'm crashing quite the get-together.

When I walk into what used to be the grand ballroom, I see Ginger reclining on a chaise lounge looking a bit peeked. "Ginger, are you okay?"

She smiles, "I guess the exhaustion is just catching up with me. Wait until you see the bridesmaid dresses."

Muffy sneaks in like a stealth bank robber hugging the back wall while I shoot daggers into Renée with my eyes. "Yes, I'd like to see the dresses, Renée. I hear you've taken my suggestions to heart."

Not in the least worried, my sister waves a hand at me and announces, "Oh pish posh. Just relax and be prepared to be amazed." She has her little worker bees, LeRon and Fernando close the blinds and light about a million candles before they push in two mannequins sporting the infamous dresses.

I'm getting more and more agitated with every flick of the

lighter that passes until I see the final product. Dammit, I hate to be full of righteous indignation for nothing. The dresses are perhaps the most gorgeous things I've ever seen. They're a golden yellow and silvery dove gray floral pattern with a taupe and cream background. The material is a whimsical and fluttering silk and they have about a billion Swarovski crystal bugle beads sewn into the pattern that makes them appear to catch fire in the candle light. Holy crap, they're stunning!

I open my mouth to speak, then close it. Open and close, until I finally concede, "Wow! Maybe I should have been the designer. Who knew I could pick such an amazing color combination?"

Elliot's mothers interjects, "They're perfect for a fall wedding, very reminiscent of the changing hues of the foliage. You can positively feel the cool autumnal breeze as they flutter in motion." My God, she can't put two words together to say something nice to me but she's composed a full on sonnet to Renée's design capabilities.

Before I can say anything else, Fernando rolls in the mannequin wearing the bridal gown. Sweet Jesus, it's the most amazing creation ever! It's a strapless ball gown with a shimmering golden infused ivory, raw silk, crisscross bodice. The skirt is made up of layers of tulle over the same silk. And at the waist there are ivory silk sculpted flowers in a variety of sizes with golden crystals in the center. The gown is cathedral length and the veil is the simplest and sheerest layer of superfine English silk tulle ever spun. I express my only concern, "Renée, the gown is exquisite. There's just one problem."

My sister looks momentarily alarmed and asks, "What?"

"It's tiny. It has to be at least two sizes too small for me."

Renée laughs out loud, "Oh Meems, don't be ridiculous. I made it from the measurements I took off you last week."

What? How can that be? So I demand she help me try it on and low and behold, she's right. With my freshly retouched red hair, I look like the goddess of fall herself. I'm mute in awe of her talent and completely overwhelmed by how beautiful she's made me. Even Victoria can't pass up the opportunity to comment, "My word," she declares, "you look quite stunning, Mimi." I wish I had a tape recording of that. I'm sure there will be many occasions in the future where I will yearn for a compliment from that one.

Chapter 5

Two days before the wedding, our out-of-town guests begin to appear. Elliot has several friends and family members arriving from England today and I have an impressive number travelling to witness our union, as well.

While sitting on my mom's couch soaking Edith Bunker in a hot Epsom salt bath (apparently my bunion is making a return as she does not approve of the shoes I've been wearing this week), I ask what the plans are to entertain the troops.

My mom informs me she's made reservations for every meal leading up to and including the rehearsal dinner at various restaurants in town. She's decided eating out will be the lowest stress option for all. I couldn't agree more.

The doorbell rings just as I'm about to doze off for a mid-morning refresher. My mom answers it and I hear her say, "Yes, yes this is the correct address." And, "My word, really? Good heavens, come right in!" A delivery man, attired in what looks like an admiral's uniform enters carrying a magnificently wrapped wedding gift. My mother ushers him to the dining room, where he gently lays the gift on the table. Then she escorts him to the living room where I'm still soaking my bump. He bows before me and enquires, "Miss Finnegan?"

I mumble an affirmation as he hands me an envelope that must be at least five thousand pound card stock. Seriously, it's lush. I don't know much about elegant stationary but I assume this is the most expensive in existence. In an ornate calligraphy, it is addressed to Sir and Lady Elliot Fielding, KCVO. What in the hell? I thank the gentleman nicely and my mom shows him to the door. Sir and Lady Fielding? I pick up my phone to call Elliot. When he answers, I don't bother with niceties, I just demand, "You're a knight of the realm?"

I can actually hear him smiling into the phone, "Good morning, my love. How's Edith doing?"

"Don't you change the subject, just answer my question."

He clears his throat and replies, "Yes, dear. I was knighted by the queen five years ago."

"Why?" I demand.

Elliot laughs, "For being such a stellar British citizen, I assume. How did you find out? Did you finally decide to Google me?" Note to self: Google Elliot and find out what I'm really getting into.

"Noooooooooooooo, we just received the most extraordinary wedding gift addressed to Sir and Lady Elliot Fielding. Any idea who it's from?"

He asks, "Was it delivered in a postal box or simply gift wrapped?" I reply the latter. "Ah," he continues, "my guess is that it's from the queen."

"WHAT?" I swear I scream loud enough to be heard in the next county. "The Queen of England sent us a wedding gift?"

"I assume so, yes. Did you open it?"

I choke, "No, I haven't opened it. I mean, shouldn't I wait for you?"

Elliot chuckles, "I'll be right over." Then he warns, "I have Mother with me."

Oh great. I immediately remove Edith from her foot bath and put my sock and shoe back on, all the while babbling to my mom, "You're about to meet Elliot's mother. We've got to tidy up. The Queen of fricking England, can you believe it?" I just prattle on while running around like a chicken with my head cut off until the doorbell rings.

My mom answers it while I take a second to gather my composure. I hear her greet, "Elliot, come in. This must be your lovely mother."

I cringe to think how Victoria will respond, when I hear her reply, "It's a pleasure to meet you, Maureen." Just so we're clear, it appears the countess has decided to like every member of my family but me, which truthfully just stinks.

I hobble in and immediately go to Elliot's side. I feel safe there. He kisses me and explains, "Mother and I were out doing a little shopping when you called."

My mom pipes in with, "I hope you took her to the Hob Nob. They have the most wonderful little trinkets."

Elliot's mother smiles, "Yes, I do believe we poked around there." I'm full on dying. The Hob Nob is probably the most exclusive shop in Pipsy but I'm sure it's nothing like the shopping Victoria's used to. Of course I should thank my lucky stars he didn't take her to Walmart.

I lead the way into the living room and show Elliot the gift.

It is wrapped in a thick, dulled metallic pattern that looks like vintage wallpaper. The bow is probably a higher quality fabric than Renée uses in her designs. Then I hand him the envelope. He peruses the front before opening the back flap when his mother grabs it out of his hand, "Let me, darling."

I want to snatch it back and remind her who it's addressed to but I catch myself in time. The countess reads out loud for everyone's benefit, "Dearest Elliot and Mimi, We are sorry not to be able to attend your nuptials but offer you our most sincere congratulations. Elizabeth R and Prince Phillip, Duke of Edinburgh."

My mother trills, "How exciting! Hurry up and open the gift, I'm dying to see what they sent!"

Victoria hands me the card followed by a gift of her own. I thank her effusively, as I'm astonished she's bought me anything, when she orders, "Open mine first." I unwrap the small parcel to find that she has gifted me with my very own copy of Debrett's Guide to Modern Manners. She explains, "You will need this in order to send the proper thank you notes to our side."

What I want to say is, "Thanks, bitch. Can't you just let me enjoy the moment?" Instead I manage, "How perfectly wonderful. I'm sure it will come in handy." Then I proceed to unwrap the queen's gift. I do this as though the package is full of plutonium. I'm painstaking careful with the paper, not because I'm going to reuse it, but because I'm going to have it mounted in a museum quality frame and pass it down through generations of my own family. You think I'm kidding?

When I take the lid off the box I'm greeted with another

box. It's a simple and very handsome mahogany. I lift it out and open the lid. Nestled inside are eight sterling silver tongs and eight tiny forks. Elliot lets out a delighted burst of laughter. I'm confused.

The countess enlightens us, "When Elliot was a boy he was playing with the young princes, who were a good deal older than he was. They took Elliot out to the gardens to collect supper. Elliot thought they were going to pick vegetables but they wound up gathering a bucket full of snails. And wouldn't you know it, the queen ordered escargot to be served that night." Hahahahahhahaha. What's so funny about that?

Elliot explained, "We peeled them off the side of the spring house, slime trails and all. It was utterly nauseating. Of course I didn't know that you don't eat garden snails. Then snails were served for dinner and through the entire meal, Edward taunted me with images of mucus slithering down the wall. It was horrid. I haven't eaten them since."

I have never eaten snails, nor do I have any intention of doing so. As such, this gift smacks of an incredibly expensive joke. As soon as Elliot and his mother leave I get right onto Google and price sterling silver snail paraphernalia. Here's what I find. The English Royals spent several thousand dollars on a gift that we will in fact, never use.

Chapter 6

Tonight we are entertaining our out of town guests at a new Italian restaurant called Il Bucco. The smells drive me wild with desire. Elliot is picking up his parents from the hotel so I arrive alone. The first person I see is one of the most dashing and wonderful men to ever enter my life. His name is Richard Bingham. I met Richard when Elliot and I travelled to New York together on business. Elliot was still seeing Beatrice at the time, and Richard nearly swept me off my feet and right out of Elliot's arms. Elliot and Richard do not get along and see one another as competitors for my affections. Even though Richard conceded my heart to Elliot, my future husband is still a bit prickly that I demanded Richard be included in the wedding party.

I throw my arms around my friend and declare, "Richard, you're here!" I just hug and hug him, then announce, "I see you didn't use your plus one on the wedding invitation."

With his arm around my shoulder, he declares, "I told you I was leaving you in charge of finding your replacement and I'm holding you to it." Then he laughingly adds, "I suppose once you find my bride for me, I'll have to send your invitation to Mimi, plus two."

Richard doesn't know what he's in for. I've personally selected three women who I feel will fit the bill very nicely and all three are coming to the wedding. I lead my friend into the dining room and introduce him to my family. He knows Muffy and Kevin from their visit to New York but hasn't met the rest of the crew yet. I leave him in my brother-in-law, Laurent's, capable hands when I see Elliot arrive. He's with his parents, Beatrice and a very frightened looking man hanging onto Beatrice's arm. I assume he's the new boyfriend.

I greet Beatrice with a warm hug and declare, "You look wonderful!" The truth is she does. Even with the breast cancer back, it's apparent she's deliriously happy. Beatrice and I had a rough start. When I met her, she was about to become engaged to Elliot. Elliot loves Beatrice as a friend and when she announced she was sick again, he asked her to marry him. She said yes, which is why I almost wound up with Richard. But she backed out of the engagement when Kevin told her about Elliot and me. I went from hating her, to pitying her, to loving her at a breakneck speed.

Kevin spies Beatrice and comes over to meet her boyfriend and pull her into the party. Elliot is busy ordering drinks for his parents and I take a moment to stand back and enjoy the contentment I feel in my life. I am a thirty-five year old woman who just months ago was alone and suffering from the mother of all identity crisis. And now I'm deliriously happy, pregnant with my first child and about to marry the man of my dreams. How could life be any sweeter?

Victoria sidles up to me and announces, "Doesn't Beatrice look lovely tonight?" Ah, yes, life could be better if Victoria pulled the stick out of her butt and accepted me, but there you have it. I decide to ignore her attempt at an argument and agree. "She looks wonderful! Clive must be making her very happy." Then I wink.

The countess looks alarmed that I may have just insinuated Beatrice and Clive are spending all of their time doing the horizontal mambo and excuses herself posthaste. Don't let the door hit ya where the good Lord split ya, Your Highness.

I meet several of Elliot's friends from London, who all appear to be delighted to be attending our wedding. Elliot peels off to entertain his troops while I do the same with mine.

After a dinner of heavenly pasta dishes and my favorite eggplant Parmesan, it's time for a wicked tiramisu. I'm savoring every single bite when I notice a very odd character walk in. She's tallish and thin and what's the word, meek? Perhaps not so much meek as frightened looking. I don't recognize her so I nudge Elliot's arm. He immediately follows my gaze and jumps up to welcome her. They hug hello then Elliot leads her over to me. With his arm around her waist, he introduces, "Mimi, I'd like you to meet my sister, Philippa."

Philippa smiles shyly and holds her hand out to shake mine. In a whisper of a voice, she utters, "I'm so pleased to make your acquaintance, Mimi."

I want to devour her in a bear hug. How nice that someone in Elliot's family is delighted to meet me. Philippa is nothing of what I expected Elliot's sister to look like. I anticipated her to resemble a mini-version of Victoria, all hoity toity and snooty. She's a wonderful surprise.

I ask her to sit down next to me and demand that Elliot get the waitress to bring his sister some food. "You must be starved!" I declare.

She merely shrugs her shoulders, "I suppose I'm a bit peckish. It was a long flight."

"I wish we knew when you were arriving. We would have been happy to pick you up."

Philippa looks alarmed and replies, "Please don't worry. Father sent a car for me."

As if he heard her say his name, the earl stands up and walks over to his daughter. When he reaches her, he actually embraces her. No standoffish weirdness I would have expected, based on his previous stuck up demeanor. He holds her close and says, "Pip, I'm so glad you're here. How are you feeling?"

That's when I wonder if maybe she isn't meek as much as sickly. Poor thing, she doesn't appear to be very vibrant. She answers, "I'm fine, Father. How are you and Mother? Did you have a nice flight?"

He assures her they did when Victoria arrives. She takes her daughter's hand and commands, "Come, sit with me, darling. We'll get some food into you right away." I try to assure the countess that Elliot is already working on it but she ignores me and pulls her daughter away.

When Elliot arrives back, he inquires as to the whereabouts of his sister. I tell him his parents have rescued her from my wicked company and he quirks his eyebrow in response. "Not that again. Mimi, give them time. They'll learn to love you as much as I do."

I ignore him and ask, "Is Philippa sick, Elliot?"

"No," he answers. "She's just a bit frail. She has been ever since she had rheumatic fever as a young girl. She nearly died from it."

"She's okay now though, right?"

Elliot shrugs, "Medically speaking, yes." Before I have a chance to ask him what he means by that, he's up and bidding some friends good night. Hmmm, if she's okay medically, what could possibly be wrong with her?

Chapter 7

Against all odds it's my wedding day and I'm feeling great. I'm fit as a fiddle, in fine form and ready to boogy. I'm full on down with my bad self and only moderately worried my dress might be a bit snug after my week of binge eating. Elliot is getting ready at my house and I'm at Renée's with the girls. We're having manicures, pedicures and massages, a gift from my incredibly thoughtful husband-to-be. We have three full hours for these indulgences until the hair and makeup people arrive.

I've been pampered within an inch of my life and am currently enjoying a chocolate croissant when I spy Philippa coming up the front path. I immediately feel horrible. I didn't think to include her in on our wonderful spa treatments because she wasn't in the wedding party. What a dunce!

All I'm wearing is a plush terry cloth robe and cotton between my toes. I hurriedly make my way to the front door and answer just as she rings. She jumps when the door swings open so quickly and looks like a scared rabbit. "Philippa, I'm so glad you're here! I'm so sorry I didn't think to ask you to join us. Come in, come in."

She follows me rather meekly and mumbles, "I don't want to intrude on your preparations. I'm just here to deliver a message."

"A message from whom?"

Poor Philippa looks like she's about to be sick, "Can we go and sit down somewhere quiet?"

Uh, oh, this can't be good. I wonder if Elliot has opted not to go through with the wedding. I decide that's ridiculous. After the sendoff I gave him last night, there's no chance of him bailing. Then I wonder if maybe Victoria has had second thoughts about showing up. Now that's more likely. Philippa and I sit down in Renée's library and I gird my loins for the bad news.

Philippa tentatively takes my hand in hers and takes a deep breath for fortitude, "Mimi," she starts. Dear God, this is it. Well screw Victoria, if she's such an ill bred cow that she'd boycott her only son's wedding, she can kiss my Aunt Fanny! Elliot's sister continues, "Your grandma Sissy would like you to know she's thrilled for you. And she's asked me to give you this." Philippa hands me a rubber frog.

First off, you should know that my grandma Sissy has been dead for ten years. Dead, as in not breathing, as in six feet under, for ten years. So I'm pretty sure that she did not, in fact, wake up this morning, claw her way out of her grave and go shopping for a rubber frog. I'm beginning to see what Elliot meant when he said *medically* Philippa was alright. Apparently, mentally, she's a real piece of work.

"Um, thank you?" Really, what else can I say? I briefly consider picking up a rather large vase sitting on the end table next to me and cracking it over her head. What if she's unglued and is about to do me bodily harm? It would be considered self-defense then, right? Oh my God, what would Elliot say? And Victoria! She'd never speak to me again if I bonked her daughter unconscious. Not that that would be an entirely bad thing.

Philippa watches as every one of these thoughts crosses my mind before she stands up and shouts (shouts!), "Fecking, bloody ballocks of thing, isn't it?"

Now I'm the one cowering. Sweet Jesus, is she going to pull out a gun and shoot me? I think of my baby and whimper, "Please don't hurt me."

Philippa dives full on into the deep end and screams, "Hurt you? Why in the world would I hurt you?"

I have absolutely no idea why she would hurt me, but I also have no idea why she would hand me a rubber frog and say it's from my dead grandmother, either. I choose not to answer lest my response anger her and force her into more dire actions.

"Mimi, for heaven's sake, do I look like a person who would do you bodily harm?" she demands.

"No?" I can't make my answer sound surer than that because I think she might do just that.

"Mimi, I'm not going to hurt you. I'm just here to share a sentiment from your grandmother." And a rubber frog, she doesn't mention the frog.

"Um, Philippa, thank you for that, but my grandma Sissy has been dead for several years." I'm not sure how explaining this to her is going to make her sane but it's worth a shot. It's that or concuss her with crystal.

"Of course she's dead. How else would I have spoken to her?" she asks.

I'm just going out on a limb here because I don't know what's happening and because I really, really want to get married today and not murdered. So I ask, "Philippa, are you dead?"

She looks at me like I'm the one who's lost her marbles and fires back, "Of course I'm not dead! Are you an idiot?"

Here we go again. I either assure her I'm an idiot in hopes that she won't kill me or I tell her I'm not and sign my own death warrant. When all of sudden it hits me, "Philippa, do you see dead people?"

"Finally!" she huffs. "Yes, that's it. I see dead people and I pass on their messages to whomever they tell me to. I've had this hellish responsibility since I was a child. If I refuse to pass on their messages, you know to save face and not appear completely unhinged, I break out in spots, great big, godawful red spots that make me look like I'm allergic to the air."

All of a sudden I burst out into hysterical giggles. "But that's wonderful! I understand now!"

"Wonderful? You've been acting like I'm Jack the Ripper. Do you think you're the only one to react like this? I get this response ninety-nine percent of the time I go up to a complete stranger and give them a communication from their dead loved one. This is not wonderful, let me assure you."

I'm still giddy with relief I'm going to live and console, "But what an amazing gift to have. Being able to pass on messages of love is just incredible."

"They're not all words of love," she assures me. "Once I

was compelled to approach a man in the tube and tell him his uncle knows he's the one who killed his dog and he was going to seek retribution from the great beyond." She rolls her eyes and continues, "I had to run for my life after delivering that message, let me tell you."

"But Philippa…" I start.

She interrupts, "For heaven's sake, just call me Pippa or Pip. We're going to be family after all."

"Okay, Pip." I stand up and give her a big hug. "Thank you for Grandma Sissy's message. I find it very comforting to know she's here and knows about Elliot and the baby." Then I inquire, "So what's up with the frog?"

Pippa explains, "She says when you were a little girl you bought yourself a rubber frog to kiss in hopes that one day it would turn into your handsome prince. It's just a little joke."

And then I really do laugh. I've never told anyone about Rufus. This is going to be the best wedding ever. I sidetrack Pip and speak directly to my grandmother, "Gran, will you walk me down the aisle?" Pip doesn't have to answer for her. My whole body becomes flooded with the most wondrous sensation of light and love. I know the answer is yes.

Chapter 8

I'm in a glow all afternoon after Pip leaves. I don't profess to know how this whole life after death thing works, but I've always believed in it. After all, what would be the point of all the joy and suffering if it weren't for a greater purpose?

My sisters and Marge leave for the church ten minutes before I do. I'm going to put on my dress and do all the final touches there. But for now I'm at Renée's all by myself while I wait for my dad to pick me up.

I'm the last Finnegan girl to get married and I've dreamed of this day since I was a little girl. Do I need a man to survive? No. Do I want one? Yes. And Elliot is all I could ever hope for in a mate. I'm not thrilled that he appears to be an entirely different species from me, darn those aristocrats, but defying all the odds, he loves me and that's enough.

My dad honks the horn twice before jumping out of the car to escort me. Even though I'm wearing jeans and flip flops, he grabs his heart when he sees me, like I've taken his breath away. A lot of men wouldn't have done well with four daughters but my dad thrives on it. Even the continuous teenage drama didn't seem to bother him. Although when we got a dog, he insisted it be a boy to dilute some of the estrogen in the atmosphere.

When he gets close enough to offer me his arm, I can see there are tears in his eyes. "Meems, you're a site for sore eyes! I can't believe I get to walk you down the aisle."

"Thanks, Dad." I reply, "Bet you never thought this day would come, huh?"

He pauses a beat before answering, "Truth be told I thought you'd be the first of my girls to marry, not the last."

I'm speechless for a moment before asking, "Why in the world would you have thought that?" Then I announce, "I am by far your least impressive daughter."

"Just between you and me," he confides, "you have the biggest heart. You're the most giving of my daughters and you're by far the most humble. In many ways, you are my *most* impressive child."

I can't speak because tears are clogging my throat. I merely squeeze his hand and focus on not crying so my mascara doesn't run.

When we arrive at the church, I'm ushered through the back door into the basement where the rest of the bridesmaids are waiting. Somehow my dress is thrown over my head and the final fussing takes places without my even being conscious of it. The first real moment of awareness I have is standing in the vestibule with my wedding party. The beginning strains of Pachelbel's Canon in D start and that's when I realize Elliot hired a live orchestra to perform it.

Tingles of joy flood through me as Camille starts the

procession. She's like a little fairy princess tossing her petals. However, once she's half way down the aisle, she turns around and comes back toward us, picking up the petals as she goes. This is some unexpected choreography.

Laurent gets out of his pew and tries to scoot her forward when she announces rather loudly, "Mommy says I have to pick up my messes!"

Renée gestures for her to keep going but her daughter doesn't seem to trust this is okay and keeps turning back looking for assurances.

Renée is the first up the aisle after her daughter, followed by Ginger, Muffy and Marge. It's surreal as I watch them process. The candlelight in the sanctuary reflects off of the beads on their dresses causing them to sparkle like a million pixies are lighting the way. I'm having an out of body experience. How can all this grandeur really be for me? If you would have told me I'd be marrying the man of my dreams six months ago, I would have never believed you.

Once everyone is up the aisle, the whole church stands and faces me. The orchestra switches to Purcell's Trumpet Voluntary and I ever so dramatically begin my journey to Elliot. I know I look better than ever. I'm certainly happier than I've ever been. I also know this is a magical moment that only happens once in a lifetime. I want to sear it into my brain so I can relive it again and again.

My dad holds my arm on one side and I can actually feel my grandmother on the other, just as she promised.

Elliot and I wrote our own vows instead of going with a more standard fare. So after welcoming everyone and going through all the proper steps, Father Brennan motions to Elliot to begin.

My wonderful Englishman clears his throat and takes both of my hands in his. "Dearest Mimi, It's my greatest honor that you have chosen me for your life's mate." He gives a little glance to Richard which I'm sure is as much of a dig as it is relief I didn't choose him instead. Then he continues, "I've walked through much of my life wondering if there was such a thing as a true love and then I saw you. I loved you on site, even though you accused me of pushing you into your sister's pool."

The congregation snickers in delight at this peek into our first meeting. I laugh, too. It's hard to believe I ever thought Elliot was anything less than perfect.

He continues, "And now here we are." He lifts one of my hands to his mouth and gives it the most tender of kisses before continuing, "I pledge my life to you. I vow to love you, cherish you and sometimes even obey you, as long as your demands aren't too unreasonable." The crowd giggles again. "I give you my heart, my hand and all of my worldly possessions. I will carry your burdens as my own and I will love you until the end of time."

I open my mouth to say my vows in return but all that comes out is a sob of raw emotion. I finally go completely off script, because I've totally forgotten the promises I wrote and manage, "Elliot Fielding, you are it for me. All those years of wondering if I'd ever find my mate, all those god-awful blind dates and first dates left me thinking, if I ever wanted to get married, I'd have to settle." You can tell who the writer is and it's clearly not me; having said that, all of my words are heartfelt if perhaps a bit less than poetic.

"Then you came into my life and literally knocked me off my feet." The congregation laughs. So I add for their entertainment, "Right into Renée's pool." Elliot squeezes my hands and I realize he must really love me because my awkward speech has elicited tears.

I finish, "Elliot, I give you my heart, my ear and my hand. I will support you, partner you and love you until I draw my last breath."

Father Brennan clears his throat as if to clear away some emotion of his own and blesses the rings before we place them on each other's fingers. The rest of the service is a blur. I half expect to wake up and find it's been no more than a beautiful dream. But before I know it, my priest announces us to the congregation as husband and wife and we are running down the aisle to the applause of our loved ones.

Chapter 9

Renée and Laurent's backyard is fit for a royal ball. Normal humans, lucky enough to have a pool, often lay boards on it to make a room for a dance floor. Renée and Laurent have such vast property they've built the dance floor next to the pool. On the other side, a tent large enough to house the entire Ringling Bros. and Barnum and Bailey Circus has been erected. That's where we will be dining. Even with all the wedding paraphernalia, there's still enough land left over to house an entire city block.

The heaters blow enough hot air to launch a fleet of balloons, which is how I'm so comfortable wearing a strapless gown outdoors in mid-October. The trees are filled with sparkling white lights and Japanese lanterns are dangling from their branches. The stars twinkle overhead, promising an enchanted life. I know there's no such thing, but it's my party, I can dream if I want to. A bridge has been erected over the pool which has been turned into a magical pond straight out of a fairytale. Candles float by on lily pads and are those koi? Holy heck, they've drained and refilled their pool to turn it into a koi pond! I'm shocked until the swans float by. I expect a unicorn or two to trot through at any moment.

Had I been feeling well enough to plan my own wedding, none of this would have happened, because in all honesty I couldn't have dreamt something this magnificent. As I'm standing on the bridge gazing out into the location of Elliot's and my first encounter, the same pool he claims he didn't push me into, my new husband comes to join me. "Penny for your thoughts," he croons.

Smiling, I answer, "For your information, sir, my thoughts are worth more than a penny. I mean really, they've got to be worth at least a dollar."

"In that case, my love," he reaches into his pocket and hands me a five spot, "what's going on in that beautiful brain of yours?"

"What's going on is that I can't believe this is all real. Never in my wildest dreams did I expect my wedding to be anything like this. It's a bit overwhelming, you know?"

Elliot kisses my forehead. "You're worth all of this and more. Tonight is for us to mark the beginning of a beautiful life together." Had he just stopped there it would have been the perfect sentiment. But no, he keeps going and I'm filled with dread as he adds, "Nothing can ever go wrong for us, Mimi."

I want to scream, "Oh my God, you've just jinxed us! Take it back, take it back!" Yet I realize that would ruin the moment so I don't say a word. But just so you know, it is my truest belief that the instant you think your life is so perfect nothing can ever go wrong, is the same one an army of fairies or leprechauns or trolls carry the news to the underworld to unleash a terrible catastrophe upon you. I believe in gratitude and I believe in humility. I do not believe that any person or couple gets through life unscathed. Even though I don't consider myself superstitious, I'm still going to think long and hard about what I can do to undo Elliot's proclamation that we're golden. Because we're not. No one ever is.

I let Elliot lead the way into the dining tent and I'm stunned by what I see. There are honest to God crystal chandeliers dangling from the support structure, at least fifteen of them. There must be ten thousand yards of filmy fabric draped down the walls in an elegant sweep, leaving you with the sensation that the room is floating in the clouds. My mother has done a bang up job with the flower arrangements. They're all shades of red, yellow, orange and rust with just enough greenery to add the necessary backdrop. And there are enough candles illuminating the tent to make you believe you're in the middle of the most amazing dream and not in reality at all.

The wedding coordinator sees us and cues the band director who grabs his microphone and belts out, "May I present Mr. and Mrs. Elliot Fielding!" The crowd roars their approval as we glide in. I'm glad no one thought to tell her Elliot has been knighted. That would seem a bit pretentious even given the current opulence.

Elliot takes the microphone, "Mimi and I are so honored to have you all here with us to celebrate our marriage. Please, eat, drink and be merry!" He doesn't add, "For tomorrow we may die." but I hear it none-the-less.

While the warm goat cheese salad with beets and toasted walnuts is served (kudos to Elliot on that one), I look over the room to survey our guests. Renée's children, Camille and Finn, look like sprites running around in their finery, my parents are beaming with joy and even Elliot's parents appear to be having a wonderful time. Richard is ensconced at a table with five single women and two other single men. He appears to be quite engaged by whatever my friend, Ellie, is saying to him. Muffy and Kevin are whispering secrets to one another and Ginger, for the first time in her pregnancy, looks totally wrung out. She has her head on Jonathan's shoulder and he's tenderly rubbing her back. I make a mental note to spend some time with her soon to see how's she's feeling.

Elliot's sister, Pip, is standing in the back of the tent by herself. She's not talking to anyone and is looking quite miserable to boot. I point her out to Elliot and tell him to go get her. I see him encouraging her to follow him but she's rooted to her spot. When Elliot comes back alone, I give it a whirl.

I approach her and ask, "Pip, what's wrong? Why aren't you sitting at your table eating?"

She looks at me miserably and groans, "I have another message to deliver."

Excitedly, I ask, "Oh, yeah, who's the lucky guest?"

She rolls her eyes, "Only you would think this is a good thing. I'm not sure which one he is, but his name is Richard Bingham."

"Richard?" I gasp. "Who wants to send Richard a message?"

Pip responds, "I'm not allowed to tell you and before you

ask, I can't tell you what the message is either. It's part of the rules."

I hadn't considered there might be rules regarding this talking to the dead thing, but I guess it makes sense. "What happens if you tell someone?"

Elliot's sister visibly shudders, "You know the spots I get when I refuse to share a communication?" I acknowledge that I do. "Well, if I convey the message to someone other than the person it's meant for, I get the most uncontrollable diarrhea you can imagine, explosive really. Remind me to tell you about the time I found that out." She adds, "The worst first date of my life." Then she asks, "Would you mind pointing out Richard to me?"

I smile, "I'll do better than that. I'll take you to him."

I lead the way to his table and Pip recognizes him immediately. "Oh yes, he's the one who stood next to Elliot's friend Rupert at the altar." Her voice takes on a bit of a gravelly tone.

"Now, how do I cull him from his crowd of admirers?"

"I have an idea," I say as a thought comes to me. I walk over to my friend and whisper in his ear, "Richard, there's someone special I want you to meet."

He looks up, mid-bite and asks, "Now?"

"Yes, please," I respond.

He puts his fork down, takes a sip of water and wipes his mouth. Then he stands up and lets me lead him away. I take him over to Pippa and introduce, "Richard, I would like you to meet Elliot's sister, Philippa." Then to Pip, I add, "Pip, this is my dear friend, Richard Bingham."

They greet one other rather awkwardly, which I get on Philippa's part. She's about to tell a complete stranger that his dead loved one has a message for him, and we know how well that can go. I almost hit her over the head for her effort. But Richard looks very uncomfortable and nervous. He's so much smoother and more gallant than his current demeanor indicates. Instead of taking her hand and beaming his thousand watt smile or bowing before her and clicking his heels, he rather uncomfortably mumbles, "It's nice to meet you." That's it. No, "May I have the honor of escorting you to your table? Would you care to join me at my table? How 'bout a V-8?" Nothing.

So I'm going to have to try a little harder to get them alone. "Richard, would you please be a dear and show Pip up to the house? She needs an aspirin."

Richard looks at me like he wants to know why I'm asking him. It's not like he's ever been to Renée's before. But he's polite enough to offer Elliot's sister his arm and say, "I would be delighted."

Pippa takes his proffered appendage and reluctantly follows him out of the tent. When I get back to Elliot he demands, "What's that all about? I hope you're not trying to play matchmaker between my sister and Richard." He spits out Richard's name like he's trying to spew poison out of his mouth.

I laugh, "The thought hadn't occurred to me." Then I add, "Pip has a message for him." Then I wiggle my fingers, shrug my eyebrows and spooky up my voice for effect, "You know, from beyond the grave."

At that Elliot actually chokes on his wine. "How in the world do you know about that?"

My husband and I haven't had the opportunity to discuss my earlier meeting with his sister so I enlighten him. "She came by Renée's earlier today with a communication for me from my grandma Sissy. It was quite lovely, actually." I don't mention the near beaning of his only sibling.

"Dear God, Mimi! I don't know what to say. We try to keep this business private, you know, so as not to bring Pippa more embarrassment."

"But it's what she does, Elliot. I guess it's part of her deal with the other side. You know, 'We'll let you recover from rheumatic fever but now you work for us,' kinda thing?"

My husband gasps, "You're not telling me you actually believe this nonsense, are you?"

It's my turn to be shocked. "Nonsense? What nonsense? How could Pip even know about my grandma Sissy yet alone about a private joke between us? My own sisters don't know about that." Elliot doesn't reply so I ask, "Elliot, are you telling me you don't believe your own sister? That you think she's been mentally ill since childhood?"

He grabs at his neck to loosen his tie as though it's choking him and answers, "I don't know what to think. I just know hers is not normal behavior and it's brought a lot of discomfort her way."

I want to add, "And your way too, apparently." But I don't. I have years to figure out how Elliot ticks and to explain the real world to him. Thank goodness I've got multiple seasons of the New Jersey Medium on Netflix. This is not an argument I need to take on right now.

Our server arrives to clear our salad plates and right behind him another appears with our entrées of beef Wellington and French green beans. Let's not forget the bread basket filled with an assortment of artisan breads. Elliot has outdone himself selecting our menu and clearly doesn't have the boring British palate of some of his countrymen. Yum, yum, yum, I'm eating for two!

My husband seems to have lost his appetite but I'm not letting this meal go to waste. Midway through, I see Richard return to the tent alone and he looks fit to be tied. He's not only disheveled but he looks steaming mad. Uh, oh. As soon as Pippa returns I'm going to have to find out what happened.

When our plates have been cleared, the wedding coordinator taps her microphone to get everyone's attention and the orchestra begins the intro of Nat King Cole's song, *Love*. Elliot takes me in his arms and pulls me close. It's the most beautiful moment of my life, waltzing with my husband under the starry October sky. When our song ends we switch partners and I dance with my dad while Elliot glides around the floor with the countess to Frank Sinatra's, *Cheek to Cheek*.

We head back to our table and it's time for toasts. Kevin is Elliot's best man. I didn't even have to suggest this to my husband. It was his idea to ask my friend. Without Kevin clearing the way with Beatrice, this night would have never taken place. Without Kevin there would have been no Lady Fielding. Just plain old knocked up Mimi Finnegan raising her bastard child all alone. Doesn't have the same ring to it, does it?

Kevin stands up, gently taps his champagne flute and then he bellows, "I have something to say! Listen up, folks!" Everyone quiets to a dull roar and he continues, "I have known Mimi since Mr. Phipps chemistry class in high school and let me tell you, she's only gotten better with age!" Pause while the crowd enjoys his compliment. Although it makes me feel like a slab a beef hanging from a hook.

He continues, "The day I ran into Mimi six months ago was the best day of my adult life."

I haze him, "Yeah, because it got you and Muffy together." The crowd chuckles.

Kevin continues, "Well, there is that. But truthfully Meems," then he gets serious, "you are one of the most remarkable women I have ever known and I love you like my own sister." My eyes tear up a bit when he turns to Elliot, "Elliot, you are one lucky man. Take care of her and I promise your life together will be magic!" He doesn't elaborate what kind of magic, bunny out of the hat, wicken wonders or perhaps the old eye of newt, wing of bat variety.

I giggle at my own little joke when I realize Muffy has taken over. She stands still while everyone settles down after cheering Elliot's and my impending charmed life. Then she announces loudly, "Mimi has a bunion." What the heck? Well that sure quiets everyone down. "That is the very worst thing about my sister." Thank God she's turning this around. I briefly worried her next line would be, 'and you should see her blackheads!' But instead she says, "Mimi has a full heart and an open door to everyone who needs her. She's always put her family's needs above her own. I'm thrilled she's found her handsome prince and is going to be able to put her energies into her own family now. She and Elliot deserve only the best." Then with her glass held high, she wraps it up, "May they never have any bumps in their road and may their lives always be perfect!"

Dammit, this wedding is turning into a jinx fest! Why don't people get it that this kind of happily-ever-after they pontificate about doesn't happen outside of fairy tales? And in order for those to occur, you need to endure an evil stepmother, wicked queen bent on murder or gnarly old witch who wants to fatten you up before turning you into stew. People, DO NOT TEMPT THE GODS with your crazy 'Nothing bad can ever happen to you,' talk. Please! But of course it's too late. They've done it and all that's left to do is move on.

Chapter 10

The post wedding brunch is being held at the country club. We've invited all of our families, out of town guests and dear friends to this meal and they are the only local venue big enough to handle our group effortlessly. Elliot and I are planning on leaving for a week to Lake Geneva straight from here. We didn't want to travel on a plane or go any great distance because we had no idea how I was going to be feeling. All-in-all, I'm glad we're staying so close to home. It's less stressful that way.

I cannot believe how many people I didn't have a chance to talk to last night. I greeted everyone but had almost no opportunity to delve into any real conversation. Take Pip, for example. She never came back to the reception after talking with Richard and Richard made himself rather scarce as well. I'm dying to find out what happened.

But before I can, my new mother in-law corners me. "Mimi, I understand you've been made aware of Philippa's abilities." I nod my head as she continues, "Please keep her talents to yourself and don't broadcast them. This is something we keep in the family."

So two things, one, apparently the countess believes Pippa's got something real going on here, kudos to her for that. And two, what kind of gossipy Nelly does she take me for? Of course I'm not gonna prattle on about Pip to all and sundry. She senses my offense and offers an olive branch of sorts. "You're a Fielding now and I just want to make sure you understand how our family operates." Then she kisses me on both cheeks and I wake up in bed with a dead horse. Fingers crossed I'm joking.

After Victoria leaves, I realize I'm still not sure what I'm supposed to call her. I search out Pip. She's sitting at a table by herself picking at her kippers, an English dish we've added to the menu for Elliot's side. It is singularly the grossest thing I have ever smelled. I mean pickled fish, yuck. Thankfully it's not enough to make my nausea return, but just barely.

I sit down next to her. "So, you didn't come back to the party after talking to Richard. What happened?"

Pip rolls her eyes. "I can't tell you everything but I can tell you this. He doesn't believe me."

I beg to differ. "He looked furious when he came back into the tent so I'm willing to bet he believes enough to be angry about it."

She agrees, "Oh, he was mad alright."

I'm dying to know something so I beg, "Come on Pip, can't you give me a hint, anything?"

"Mimi Fielding," oooooh I like how that sounds, "I will defecate in my pants the very second I allude to anything to do with the message Richard received. Is that something you want to witness?"

I immediately scrunch up my face in disgust. "Not really, no. How 'bout this, can you tell me why Elliot doesn't believe in your gift but your mother does?"

"Mother believes because she's been the recipient of some messages I could have known nothing about. She believes because she has not been given the option not to. Elliot on the other hand hasn't had anyone beating down his door with communications, so he chalks it up to female hysteria or brain damage. Either way, it's not particularly flattering."

Richard walks into the dining room and I immediately signal him over. He starts to head my way until he sees I'm sitting with Philippa. Then he turns at a ninety degree angle and strides straight for the buffet. What the heck? I excuse myself in an effort to find out what's up.

I grab a white dinner plate and get in line right after Richard, "Hey you, what's going on?"

Richard stiffens and simply answers, "Mimi."

"Richard, are you mad at me or something?"

He replies, "Mimi, when I asked you to find my replacement, I told you I wanted the woman to be quirky and unique, an individual. I do not remember asking you to find me a basket case."

"Richard, what are you talking about? I sat you at a table with several unique and lovely women. I gave you exactly what you asked for." I want to stick out my tongue at him but I'm aware this will only make me look petulant.

He turns to me and answers, "What about Elliot's sister? What in the world was that all about?"

"I have no idea. I only know that she wanted to talk to you, not what she wanted to talk about."

He snorts, "I don't believe you. I think you know exactly what she said to me."

"I haven't a clue! Why don't you tell me and then we can work it out together?" Do you see how I'm slyly trying to gather intelligence?

He scoops up scrambled eggs and simply replies, "I'm done talking about it. Just so you know you've been relieved of your matchmaking duties."

What could have possibly happened between the two of them? I try to make nice to Richard after our discussion about Pip but he's not having any of it. Before he leaves, he comes over to say goodbye and promises to be in touch. Then he just walks out the door.

I have a little bit of time to talk to Beatrice and her friend, Clive. He seems nothing like the type of man I would have seen her with but he obviously makes her very happy and I'm thrilled for them both. Kevin and Muffy are taking them out to dinner tonight on the way to the airport. I think Beatrice would have totally gone for Kevin if we hadn't misled her into believing he was gay. But again, that's a story from another time.

My parents are busy entertaining their friends and Elliot is "chatting up some mates from university," so I sit down with my plate of meat and relish a nice moment of contentment. I think the baby must be working on growing something important because I'm all about the protein this week. I'm currently enjoying six sausage links, four strips of bacon and a thick slab of ham.

Two hours later, we make our way through the crowd and say goodbye to everyone. Elliot's parents promise to come back in time for the birth. I hadn't expected that and I can't say I'm too thrilled, but I am pleased by their excitement. Pip says we'll be hearing form her soon, as well. Many hugs and kisses to my family later and we're off for our first week together as husband and wife.

Chapter 11

After the wedding, life settles into a nice routine. Elliot is hard at work on the edits for his next novel and I've taken to nesting with wild abandon. I've even allowed Blaine (hear that name with the disdain in which it's intended) to show me a few houses. As a tony suburb of Chicago, Hilldale is home to many of the movers and shakers of the Chi-town's business world. It's Pipsy adjacent and a world away from my little yellow house on Mercer Street. I'm having a hard time understanding why we have to move at all. Yes, a bit more room would be nice but these estates are big enough to house a large African village. Elliot claims he would like a home far enough removed from the road where random stranger can't peek inside the windows to get a look at him (yes, that does seem to happen quite frequently, but let's face it, he's the biggest thing that's happened to Pipsy in, well, forever) and in a neighborhood that does not boast huge pedestrian traffic. That probably goes back to not wanting the Misses Kravitz of the world to have a free show. That is why I'm currently driving through Hilldale with the preppy and holier-than-thou, Blaine Harrington.

After the second house, I broach the subject, "Blaine, Elliot and I are only two people. When the baby arrives, we'll only be three people. You're showing me homes big enough to host the Super Bowl. What gives?"

Blaine turns a condescending eye to me and replies, "Mimi, may I call you Mimi?" He has previously been calling me Mrs. Fielding, which at least garnered me a modicum of respect in his eyes.

I smile tightly and suggest, "Let's start with Lady Fielding and see where we go from there, hm?"

The title catches him up for a moment. "I had no idea your husband was part of the aristocracy!" He's mightily impressed by this, the prick. "Lady Fielding," he oozes, "I'm showing you homes that are expected of people in your husband's position. Surely, you want him to live in a dwelling he'll be proud of."

"Listen here weasel, I'm proud of my house because I earned the money for it myself and it's darling; small, yes, in Pipsy, yes, but darling nonetheless, you douchebag!" What I really say is, "Blaine, please don't assume to tell me how we're expected to live. That's my call, not yours." Smack, smack, smack. I appear to enjoy being as condescending to him as he does to the middle class as a whole.

Blaine pulls into the gates of the next estate, rather tight-lipped. "I don't suppose we should bother looking at this one then. Perhaps you'd rather wait until I can find something in a more pedestrian neighborhood." He regurgitates the word pedestrian like he's actually vomited in his mouth when he said it.

I heartily want to point out to Blaine that he is in fact not an independently wealthy lord of the manner. He's a Realtor, working for the people he tries so hard to impress. Yes, I'm sure he's worth quite a bit of money, but he has as much class as a monkey's butt.

I open the car door. "We might as well look while we're here."

Blaine rattles off the houses features, "This is a six bedroom, seven bath home boasting both a tennis court and swimming pool. The property is on 5. 9 acres and abuts a forest preserve so there can be no more building behind it." Of course he's insinuating the riff raff are barred from ever getting near this property and erecting homes on a pathetic half-acre. He continues, "The entry is Italian marble, the kitchen is travertine and the rest of the house is Brazilian cherry." Blah, blah, blah.

As we walk up the manicured path leading to the front door, I'm expecting to feel the same loathing I've had for the other homes I've seen. So far, this one is much less McMansion-esque, which is a huge plus. It has the feeling of old world elegance. No faux turrets and overly fussy architecture all smooshed together on a tiny lot. It has all the characteristics of the Georgian architecture I love, even though it's a much more recent build. There are eight, twelve-paned sash windows on the lower floor, the same amount on the second floor and half again as many dormered windows on the third floor. Because three people living in a house each need their own floor, don't you know?

I'm rendered speechless when we walk in. The entryway is as big as my entire house, yet it's so warm and charming I'm hard pressed not to love it. Instead of being all white, sterile and pristine, the walls have been painted a warm toffee color and the period dentil molding sets it off in a rich creamy satin. There's a truly enormous staircase that curves up to the second floor, but even that doesn't intimidate as much as it tempts you to climb up so you can slide down the banisters.

If I ever lived in this home, which I won't (because jeez, who the heck would clean it?), I would move into this kitchen. It's massive but so warm and welcoming I just want to get right to work baking something. There is a six-burner Wolf stove with warming oven, a massive commercial refrigerator, double ovens and even double dish washers. The island is big enough to easily fit a king-sized mattress, so I could sleep in here as well. Breathe, Mimi.

Blaine can tell that I love the house and I make a mental note to try to dial back my enthusiasm. The bedrooms, one more fantastic than the next, are all en-suite except two of the smaller bedrooms which are a Jack and Jill set-up. I'm guessing those are used for young children or servants. God knows.

The pool is extraordinary and the grounds are other worldly. Large mature trees, both hardwood and fruit abound. The tennis court is an impressive, albeit unnecessary beast. I don't think I've ever even lifted a tennis racket. I'll have to ask Elliot if he plays. The pool house is lovely and small and manageable. I could live there in a heartbeat. There is a golf cart available if I want to further peruse the land, which I simply cannot. I've hit my capacity to absorb all of this grandeur and tell Blaine I've had enough for today. I'm sure he thinks it's because I want to go home and tell Elliot all about it so we can make an offer, not. I have to fall asleep immediately; I am so overwhelmed that people live this excessively. Overwhelmed and dare I say, in love?

Before pulling out of the drive, Blaine hands me the brochure on the house. It's twenty glossy pages of the most amazingly gorgeous photographs of the estate in various seasons. It probably cost thirty bucks just to print the thing. In one photo, the entry houses a hundred and eighty-seven foot Christmas tree (yes, I exaggerate but barely), then there is one of the formal dining table set up for twenty-four diners (I kid you not) and my favorite is the one of the kitchen with a full breakfast buffet laid out on the counter. All for the bargain price of $5,469,000, a steal by anyone's estimation.

Chapter 12

I'm on my way to pick up Ginger for a cup of tea. We've both given up coffee in an attempt to be as healthy as possible during our pregnancies and have replaced our caffeine addictions with the passion fruit/verbena blend at The Tea Room. Ginger meets me in her driveway and she does not look well. "Heya, get in." I say as I open the passenger's door from the inside.

She climbs aboard and groans, "I feel like I'm ready to deliver any minute." Ginger is only sixteen weeks pregnant to my fifteen but she looks like she's at least eight months gone.

"You're huge! Of course I'm sure you love hearing people tell you that." I laugh. She doesn't even crack a smile. "Ginger, how are you feeling? Everything going okay?"

Without any notice whatsoever, my sister bursts into tears, big, ugly, snotty tears. I immediately pull my car over. "Honey, what's wrong?"

"I didn't want to burden you, but we, we…" snort, hiccup, sniffle, "we haven't heard baby three's heartbeat since before your wedding."

Holy crap! I ask, "Why haven't you told me this before now?"

She blows her nose before answering, "I didn't want to ruin your big day."

I unbuckle my seatbelt and wrap my sister in my arms. "Oh, Ginger. I'm so sorry. What does this mean? Is the doctor sure the baby is…" I pause to figure out how to phrase this sensitively and settle on, "gone?"

She shakes her head. "There are a couple possibilities. One is that baby three is dead." She sobs before continuing, "The other is that the heartbeat is beating in sync with one of the other babies. So every time I go in, they listen for an echo, which could be baby three's heartbeat. We have an ultrasound appointment tomorrow to try to get confirmation one way or another." She adds, "Unfortunately, it's very common for one of the fetuses to die early with multiples."

My sympathy isn't enough. "I'm so sorry. Would you rather just go home? I would totally understand."

"No way!" she assures me. "I need to get out of the house and out of my head for a while. Let's get tea and then find something else to do to fritter away the day, maybe a pedicure?"

But after tea and a nice sampling of pastries (because we're gestating and we need the extra calories—that's our story and we're sticking to it) we decide to forgo the pedicures and head over to my house to look at housing brochures.

Elliot left for New York yesterday. He'll only be gone two days but it's weird not having him home. When I woke up alone this morning, I briefly panicked thinking the last few months were just a dream. My relief was palpable when I spotted a pair of his loafers sitting next to the wall.

I tell Ginger about all the colossal homes Blaine has been trying to push on us as I hand over a stack of brochures. She laughs. "What does Elliot say?"

I roll my eyes. "Turns out his highness grew up in houses like these and he finds them 'perfectly acceptable domiciles.' His words, not mine. I had to Google "domicile" to know what he was talking about."

Ginger flips through the stack and pulls out my favorite. "Holy cow, look at this one!"

My breath catches a little. "It's even better in person."

Ginger brightens up immediately. "Let's call Blaine so you can show me."

I shake my head. "We're never going to buy the thing. It would be a complete waste of time." That's when it hits me, it would be a complete waste of Blaine's time and I immediately jump on board with the idea. That little twerp needs to be brought down a peg or two. As I have nothing else on my schedule today, I'm happy to work towards that end.

Ginger and I spend three hours at the castle I'm never going to call my own. We plot and plan all kinds of parties and adventures, including the possibility of hosting a small circus for our children's joint birthday celebrations. Then we set about figuring out how to decorate each room. After we're done, we take the golf cart out to explore the grounds. Blaine stays back at the pool where I'm sure he's calculating how many hundreds of thousands in commission he thinks he's going to make selling us this ridiculousness. I can't wait to tell him it's a no go, but think I'll enjoy letting him imagine it's going to happen for a while longer.

We drive through the grounds quietly, both lost in our own thoughts when I break the silence and say, "I know you're worried about baby three and I'm not trying to make light of that, but have you guys started talking about names yet?"

Ginger confirms, "You bet, we have. Jonathan thinks we should use names of famous artists, you know, with me being the director of the museum and all. So far he's suggested Picasso, Leonardo, Salvadore, Jackson and Hieronymus for boys."

"Impressive list," I choke, hoping to God they have all girls, although I do like the name Jackson. Of course as an artist, I find Jackson Pollock's work highly overrated and reminiscent of blood spatter, but what do I know? "What about if you've got girls in there?"

"Freda, Georgia and Moses."

"Moses? Who do you think you are, Gwyneth Paltrow?"

Ginger giggles, "God knows I'm not trying to emulate her. It's short for Grandma Moses."

"Wow." I mean what else can I say? For once, words escape me.

Ginger asks, "What about you guys? Any ideas?"

"We're kind of going along the lines of you guys, thinking in terms of writers we love."

"Oh, what fun!" Then she starts to ramble off possibilities, "You could name a boy Henry or Earnest or Charles. And if it's a girl, you could name her Louisa, Charlotte or Jane. Which are you considering?"

Of course my sister has picked names from highbrow authors of the classics. So I sheepishly respond, "We're thinking Sophie or Stephen."

Ginger pauses for a moment, looks confused and confesses, "I'm drawing a blank. I cannot think of any authors with those names."

Confession time, "Well, Elliot, believe it or not, idolizes Stephen King."

Ginger gasps, "You're kidding!"

I shake my head and say, "Of course you know my love of all things, Sophie Kinsella."

Ginger nearly busts a gut laughing, "Oh my God, that's hysterical!"

A bit offended I declare, "Well at least the names are classic. It's not like I'm jumping on the bandwagon to find the most farfetched thing in the world to call my kid." Of course I'm thinking Hieronymus and Moses, but now doesn't seem the proper time to make fun.

My sister agrees, "Totally. I want our babies to have good solid names that won't be a hindrance to them in life." Ahem, Hieronymus and Moses? But again, I don't say it out loud. "I was going through baby books the other day and almost choked when I saw what people were naming their kids today. I picked up a book called Name Your Child for Their Star Sign, freaky stuff in there."

"Tell me about it. Renée's been regaling me with names her friends are sticking their kids with and I feel like calling child protective services on them. Camille has friends named Bluebell, Margarita and Vienna." I continue, "I get naming your kid after a flower, but Bluebell? That's something you'd name your cow!"

Ginger snorts, "And Margarita? Why not just name her Daiquiri or Mud Slide?"

I'm laughing so hard I'm in jeopardy of running into a tree. "And Vienna! If you're going to name your daughter after a sausage, why not Bratwurst or Kielbasa?"

This is just the kind of distraction Ginger needs today. After we finish the grand tour and head back to Blaine, I offer, "Ginger, if you ever want me to go to a doctor's appointment with you or you just need to talk, please let me know. I'm always here for you."

Ginger reaches out and takes my hand. "I know you are, Mimi. Thank you."

This crazy life is full of such ups and downs it's amazing more of us don't drop dead from the sheer shock of living. Here Ginger never even thought she could give birth to her own children. She accepted it and signed up with adoption agencies only to wind up pregnant with triplets. Now she finds out that she may have lost one of her babies. It's been the most wonderful and horrific rollercoaster ride of her life. Yet I'm willing to bet she wouldn't change a thing.

Chapter 13

For five solid weeks, starting the week before my wedding, I'm the picture of health. I've never been more rested and radiant. I am a veritable goddess of well-being. Enter this week. My boobs ache like the heavy weight champion of the world has mistaken them for his boxing bag. My nipples are the size of my head and the veins running through them are so dark, you'd swear my blood was as blue as Elliot's. And that's just my boobs.

My baby bump is as cute as ever but all the stretching and pulling of the skin, to make room for this kid, is making me itch like I have a virulent case of chicken pox. I'm in line at the grocery store the other day and all I want to do was lift up my shirt and scratch till my skin comes off; which of course I don't do. Although I do bend over to pick up a quarter only to pass gas on the person behind me. It was no delicate little poof of air either. That expulsion could have been a contender.

I've still been craving all things meat. Meatloaf, meatballs, pot roast, pork, if it's meaty, I want it. As a result, I have not been eating enough fruits or vegetables and am constipated.

I'm currently full of baby, meat and crap, the trifecta of discomfort. After gassing the person behind me in line, I call my doctor and ask for help. She prescribes a prenatal vitamin with a stool softener. So far so good, I'm still a gaseous time bomb but at least I'm not stopped up.

Being a newlywed, Elliot and I have not yet achieved the comfort level of old married couples who understand cutting the cheese, burping and other bodily functions are par for the course. I think we were hoping to ease our way into this. Yet, nature is not allowing me the dignity I crave. Just this morning I went into the spare room where Elliot is editing in order to bring him a fresh cup of coffee, when what should happen? I sneeze. That's right, I sneeze, wet my pants and release stinky fumes all at the same time. My face turns red with mortification and Elliot pretends he doesn't notice. While he might be able to imagine I'm not the most disgusting thing on the planet, I can't. I've never been good at ignoring the elephant in the room so I simply announce, "That's right, Elliot. I just sneezed, farted and wet my pants."

He looks up at me over the rim of his glasses and smiles, "Yes, I know."

I demand, "Then say something! Don't pretend this ugliness isn't happening!"

"What would you like me say?" I roll my tear-filled eyes and prepare to cry when he offers, "Can I get you a towel?"

Then I really do cry. I'm so humiliated by my body's duplicity and irritated by my stuck-up English husband's reaction to it; I don't know what to say. I just stand there.

Elliot tries to console me, "Mimi, everyone, um, err... you

know, passes wind, even me. It's a natural function of the human body. And given that you're creating life, I assume there might be a good deal more in there than normal."

Through my sobs, I manage, "Shut up, Elliot. Yes, I know even *you* fart, but do me a favor. If you want me to feel better, you better start doing it in front of me. Understand?"

Elliot looks like I've just asked him to urinate in public, which I did not. Although it's clear that's something I'll be inclined to do if I sneeze, cough, or God forbid, laugh outside the comfort of my own home. He tries to console me. "Mimi, if that will somehow help you, I'll endeavor to try." That's all I ask.

While we're on the subject of horrific body betrayals during pregnancy, I'd like to issue a warning: not all gas is just gas, so be careful. Sometimes, especially when you're taking a prescription strength stool softener, this trapped air is traveling with a friend. If you forget and try to push it out anyway, don't be surprised if you fill your pants.

I grill Renée on all the disgusting things yet to come and she assures me there are many. Hurray! I can look forward to hemorrhoids, acne that would put a teenager's complexion to shame and excessive sweating. If that isn't enough there's heartburn, leg cramps and not being able to sleep for more than an hour at a time without having to go to the bathroom. Dear God, we'd better love the heck out of this baby as it's destined to be an only child. Elliot is never going to want to touch me again once this one pops out. Oh, and about that, Renée assures me her fifty-plus hour labors are atypical. Let the good times roll.

Today is our sixteen week appointment even though I'm seventeen weeks pregnant. The doctor was booked solid last week and apparently it's not considered an emergency when the mother is desperate to find out the sex of her child. So here we sit, me in my stylish paper gown with my butt hanging out and Elliot looking as dapper and English as ever. Seriously, he's wearing tweed.

Dr. Fermin comes in all bright and perky and wants to know, "How are we doing today?"

Elliot answers, "Lovely." at the same time that I offer, "Gassy." That about sums it up.

She opens my gown and globs the warm gel on my stomach before rubbing the ultrasound wand over it. I'm staring intently at the monitor trying to figure out what I'm looking at when I see a wonderful, perfect little foot staring back at me. The doctor asks, "Do you want to know what you're having?"

I yell out, "Yes!" before Elliot even has a chance to weigh in.

The doctor smiles and asks Elliot, "Do you want to take a guess?"

He looks closely at the monitor and breaks out into a huge grin and exclaims, "We're having a boy!"

My obstetrician wonders, "How do you figure?"

Elliot points to long straight part of our child and replies, "Right there. That's his manhood, no?"

Dr. Fermin bursts into laughter before answering, "Uh, no. That's the baby's leg." Then she looks at me as if to suggest, "Someone thinks highly of himself."

I just smile and say, "I'm guessing a girl."

She replies, "And you would be the winner." Then she points to a straight line on the monitor and announces, "This is the baby's vulva. There is approximately a .002 chance that this isn't accurate and there's really a penis in there somewhere." For Elliot's benefit, she adds, "Which if so, would be incredible tiny."

Elliot doesn't even react to her slight but just gazes at me with tears in his eyes. "Mimi, thank you. You're making me a daughter."

I choke up, too. His declaration is so heartfelt and touching that I don't point out I'm making this child for both of us, not just him.

On the way home from the doctor's appointment I announce, "I want watermelon."

My husband points out, "It's Halloween. I think it's highly unlikely we'll be able to find you watermelon."

I command, "Let's stop at the market and see what they have. When I say I want watermelon, what I mean is, get me watermelon. Understand?"

Elliot nods in confirmation of my desperation and blazes a path to the nearest Jewel, where in fact they don't have any watermelon. What now? We search the aisles and come up with watermelon flavored Jell-O, yuck, watermelon flavored bubble gum, double yuck and watermelon flavored Jolly Ranchers, yum! With a bag in tow and the produce manager's confirmation that fresh watermelon isn't going to happen anytime soon, we go home so I can peruse the Internet. Certainly, someone, somewhere has to have something watermelon that will fit the bill.

I find a source for fresh watermelon in Central America and show it to Elliot. He calls the number, as he speaks Spanish and I do not. He discovers that while yes, they would be happy to ship watermelon to us; they have a minimum order of a full carton, which holds between 40-50 melons depending on the size. We're talking two hundred and seventy-five dollars for the melon alone and about a thousand to ship it. Elliot doesn't even ask me, he just places the order. He is getting so lucky later.

Renée and Laurent are bringing Camille and Finn over to our house tonight to trick-or-treat. In their neighborhood, they'd be lucky to hit three houses in an hour. The homes are way too far apart for a decent haul. Ginger and Jonathan, Muffy and Kevin and my parents have all decided to come as well. I make it clear it's going to be potluck so I don't have to do more than throw a cloth on the dining room table and pour a jar of processed cheese spread on tortilla chips. Nachos, I've been craving them almost as much as watermelon.

Ginger and Jonathan are the first to arrive. My sister throws herself into my arms and declares, we heard number three's heartbeat! It's softer and slower than baby one and two's, so we're not out of the woods. But she's still alive."

I burst into tears. "Baby three is a girl?"

Jonathan answers, "Baby one and three are both girls. Baby two is a boy."

And with that announcement we all sit down for a moment of gratitude that Jonathan and Ginger's little girl is a fighter.

Chapter 14

Camille is dressed up as a wedge of Brie cheese. I blame her father for this. Laurent is French and loves his fancy fromage. I assume she wanted a costume that would make her daddy proud. Laurent also brought a round of delicious smelling baked Brie with cranberries and walnuts which Ginger and I aren't allowed to eat because Brie is one of the forbidden foods for pregnant women. It contains listeria bacteria. So does goat cheese. Something I didn't know when I ate it at my wedding reception.

Finn is dressed as a baked potato, full on with shredded cheese in the form of orange felt and bacon bits masquerading as crumpled up brown construction paper. Now if they'd only brought stuffed baked potatoes as well as the Brie, I'd be pretty darn jazzed to see them.

My mom arrives toting her famous tuna and cashew casserole and my dad hauls in a case of Guinness. Muffy and Kevin bring a crudité platter with enough vegetables to keep me regular for the duration of my pregnancy, except they don't bring any ranch dressing so I'm not interested.

While Renée and Laurent take their little ones out to trick or treat, the rest of us descend upon the food like starving castaways. By the time we break into the Halloween candy, I'm feeling quite content. Renée and Laurent have returned with enough candy to keep their children on a yearlong sugar high and we all settle into the living room to unwind from the festivities.

Elliot's rubbing my bunion when he announces to one and all that his family will be joining us for Thanksgiving. Everyone but me is delighted to hear the news. I inquire, "Really? When did you find this out?"

He smiles sheepishly and replies, "A couple of days ago."

In response, I remove Edith Bunker from his grasp to make it clear he is no longer allowed to touch me or my bump. Imagine, knowing this exciting news and keeping it from your wife until you can use her family as a buffer, dirt bag.

Renée senses the tension and immediately announces, "Let's have Thanksgiving at our house this year! There's plenty of room." She immediately adds, "And Laurent and I would be delighted to have your parents stay with us, Elliot. We have a lovely guest suite that almost never gets used."

I brighten at both ideas when my husband replies, "Thank you Renée, that's very thoughtful. But I thought we could host the meal and of course my parents will be staying with us." He stares straight into my eyes as he announces this. Then adds, "I'm sure Philippa will be delighted by your hospitality though." That's one ray of sunshine in the whole Fielding storm. Having Pip here will be a nice distraction.

My reaction to Elliot is to scoot as far away from him as

possible while still sharing the same couch. He appears to be asserting some kind of husbandly dictate, so I counter, "Why don't they stay with Renée and Laurent? After all they would be so much more comfortable there. And we can host Thanksgiving dinner." Then I graciously offer, "And let's have Pip here with us."

Elliot smiles calmly and looks around the room at my family then replies, "No, I think they should stay with us. After all, they are my parents."

Damn him and the horse he road in on. He's making a show of letting me know we live in the same town with my family and therefor this is not an unreasonable request. In truth, it's not an unreasonable request. If the earl and countess were normal people or just liked me for that matter, I'd be more than happy to have them in my home. But now I'm not only expected to house and feed them, I'm also expected to prepare a Thanksgiving feast for them. It's enough to put me right off the Twix bar I'm munching on.

My mother pipes in with her two cents, "Meems, you make the turkey and your famous cranberry relish. I'll make the green bean casserole and Jell-O mold."

Renée adds, "Oh and let Laurent do the mashed potatoes and stuffing, you know what a great job he does with those!"

Laurent joins the conversation by adding, "Mimi, I'll just need the giblets and neck once you remove them from the bird." I throw up in my mouth a little at the thought. Those darn French do not have the proper respect for animal guts that they should, as in throwing them away. They like to chop them up and serve them to people. Note to self: avoid the stuffing.

Muffy suggests, "Kevin and I will bring a tossed salad," then shoots a look at Ginger, who's still looking a bit peeked and adds, "And Ginger, why don't you bring the crescent rolls?"

Ginger, who normally loves to cook, and when not pregnant would have offered to make the whole feast complete with chestnut dressing, just smiles and replies, "Sounds good."

I glare at Elliot like, "Put that in your pipe and smoke it, Mr. I'm gonna tell you how it's going to be." I'm not making this whole thing myself no matter what you say.

He merely nods his head and responds, "It sounds lovely. Thank you all."

I manage to avoid my husband for the rest of the evening by handing out candy to trick-or-treaters and then tidying up after dinner. I'm glad I didn't try to confront him sooner because after some consideration, I've decided to take this one on the chin and appear the proper and doting daughter-in-law. I'll show Elliot I have what it takes to be a gracious hostess, even if it kills me, which it might.

Of course, I'm not taking this totally lying down. The next morning I get on the phone and call Richard to invite him to Thanksgiving, as well. That'll show Elliot two can play at this game and in the future he'd be better off talking to me first. Then I call Renée to see if Richard can stay with her, totally forgetting that Philippa will be there. I don't know what went down with the two of them at the wedding but I'm sure hoping to find out on turkey day.

Chapter 15

Elliot picks his parents and sister up at the airport two days before Thanksgiving. While he's in route, I run around the house like the Energizer Bunny on crack. I clean everything until it sparkles and even replace the comforter in our bedroom, where Elliot's parents will be staying. This way they have an attached bathroom which will offer them a bit more privacy. I've bought new towels, put out fresh bars of soap and have strategically positioned bouquets of flowers throughout. I've gone above and beyond. I am the epitome of the perfect daughter-in-law.

As the Fielding party won't be arriving home until dinner, I have plenty of time to take a little snooze before putting the meatloaf in the oven and getting dinner on the table. So I lie down on the couch, snuggle under the afghan and proceed to fall asleep for an unprecedented three hour nap. I only awaken when I hear the front door open. At which point I've totally and completely entered the Twilight Zone and I'm still working out where I am not to mention who I am, when I see Elliot and his parents standing over me. Of course I have a trail of saliva hanging out of my mouth. Hurray.

Elliot smiles, "Did you have a nice nap, love?"

Dammit. I was going to have the fire and candles lit when they walked it. The house should be filled with the aroma of my Italian meat loaf and fresh bread. I'm supposed to be in one of my beautiful new maternity dresses from Pea in the Pod and instead I'm lying on the couch in old sweats, drooling. Cheers to me.

I manage to sit up and smile. "Oh dear, I must have slept longer that I thought." Then confess, "I haven't even put dinner on."

Elliot comes to the rescue and offers to make reservations after he shows his parents to their room. I take the opportunity to run upstairs to change clothes and brush my hair and teeth. By the time they come down, the fire is lit and I graciously offer an aperitif.

Elliot announces our reservation is in an hour so we all settle in to chat for a while. Victoria manages, "You have a charming little house, Mimi." Then to her son adds, "Don't you think it's about time to move into something more suitable, Elliot?"

I immediately take offense and am about to say something when I see the brazen face of Mrs. Mifflin, from next door, staring into the living room window. The earl sees her too and announces, "My goodness, you have a peeper." Mrs. Mifflin runs off when we all turn to look at her.

I try to mitigate the scene by offering, "Elliot is a bit of a celebrity in our little neighborhood."

The countess replies, "He's a bit of a celebrity throughout

the world, Mimi. But he shouldn't be subjecting to being spied on in his own home."

I don't disagree. It's gotten a bit much lately with all the lookiloos. A short bus from one of the senior homes pulled up last week and let the old folks get out to see where the one and only Elliot Fielding was living. We didn't realize this until Elliot ventured out front to get the newspaper only to be applauded by twenty of Pipsy's elder population. I know it's time for us to find a new house so we can be settled by the time the baby arrives, but I can't convince Blaine to show me something I'm comfortable with. He continues to drag me to one behemoth McMansion after another. The only place he's shown me that I truly love is so far above our needs it's ridiculous.

Elliot assures the countess, "Don't worry, Mother, Mimi is hard at work finding us a new place."

Victoria raises an eyebrow and suggests, "Why don't I give you a hand while I'm here? I have a very good eye, you know."

With the promise of help I don't want, we head over to Renée's to pick up Pip. By the time we get to the restaurant I've stopped participating in the conversation with Elliot's parents in lieu of chatting with his sister.

Pip assures me she's doing well and hasn't had any ugly scenes whilst relaying messages to strangers. In fact one older woman took her to tea and thanked her profusely for the words from her departed husband. I assume the earl and countess pay Pip's bills as her only job seems to be surprising strangers with news from the dead. I learn that she lives in the family townhome on Hans Place in the Knightsbridge area of

London. This means absolutely nothing to me as I've never been outside of the U.S.

Pip says she has a lovely group of friends who understand her proclivity for approaching unknown persons with her messages. I discover she's thirty-six and her beaus have been few and far between. There has been an overwhelming disregard for her gift amongst them. I feel dreadful for her and immediately feel worse that I haven't told anyone about Richard yet. I only invited him to get even with Elliot. It didn't even occur to me I'd be causing his sister any discomfort. As apparently Richard has made it clear that he too, doesn't believe in her gift.

This is the right moment to clear the air, but I dread telling the Fielding siblings. I wait for a lull in conversation before announcing, "I have some news to share." All eyes turn to me. I clear my throat before plastering on a vibrantly fake smile and announcing, "Richard Bingham has decided to join us for Thanksgiving. Isn't that wonderful?"

The earl and his wife make all the appropriate sounds. Pip goes dead quiet and Elliot asks, "Really? How long have you known about this?"

Shamefacedly, I reply, "Just a couple of weeks."

Elliot immediately realizes I did this in retaliation of his announcing his parents visit in front of my family. He's not pleased. Yet he knows enough to keep his yap shut and carry on with dinner. Pip appears to lose her appetite entirely and I feel positively dreadful for my act of spite. It's not like I'm not looking forward to seeing Richard. I adore him. But Elliot and Pip do not share the sentiment.

Chapter 16

I give up reading books about pregnancy after the dreaded mucus plug chapter. I now subscribe to a weekly email called Bun in the Oven to keep me posted on where my baby is in her development and what changes to expect in my body. Today, I've hit the twenty week mark and Mistress Sophie Fielding is a whopping six-and-a-half inches long and almost eleven ounces, which in no way justifies the fourteen pounds I've gained in the last five weeks. Dr. Fermin has warned me to quit the party and start eating like a normal human being again, which I will do as soon as Thanksgiving weekend is over, really.

Kevin is picking up Richard at the airport this morning and Elliot is speaking only the minimum number of words. It's been a whole morning of 'yes,' 'no,' and 'perhaps.' Throw in a couple of grunts of acknowledgment and you have our conversations in a nut shell.

I finally approach Elliot in his office/our room (while his parents are here) and announce, "Elliot Fielding, there is no reason in this world to be mad at me for inviting Richard to

Thanksgiving. I married you, not him."

Elliot initially looks like he wants to yell but then seems to think twice as he pats his lap for me to take a seat. This is a good sign. I hop aboard and he rubs my back and then nibbles at my neck before declaring, "I know I shouldn't be jealous of Richard. But I came a tad too close to losing you to him and he brings out my insecurities."

I place Elliot's hand on my rounded stomach and reply, "This is your little girl in here, Lord Fielding and don't you forget it. Richard has been a very good friend to me and supported my decision in marrying you, so don't you think it's time to bury the hatchet?"

Holding me tight, my arrogant, wonderful, sexy British husband agrees, "For you, I'll do it." Then he adds, "Just don't get any ideas about matching him up with Pip. I may accept him as a family friend but I'm not yearning to have him in the family."

I explain, "You have nothing to worry about there. Richard is very put out with your sister and I'm not quite sure why."

That brings out my husband's protective instincts and he demands, "Why in the world would he be piqued with Pip? She' a lovely, sweet-natured girl and if you ask me Richard Bingham couldn't do any better for himself."

"Except he's not allowed to entertain romantic thoughts about her," I tease.

Elliot exclaims, "Absolutely not!"

I laugh, "No need to worry. After Pip's message to Richard, he doesn't want anything to do with her."

My husband demands, "Why?"

"Because," I explain, "he doesn't believe her."

"What? How dare he not believe her! Who does he think he is?"

I just smile and remind him, "You don't believe her either, Elliot."

He looks chagrined for a moment and tries to defend himself, "I don't have to believe her, I'm family."

"Do you realize how idiotic that sounds?"

Nodding his head, Elliot laughs, "Yes, yes I do. I just want to protect my sister from ridicule and judgement, that's all."

I suggest, "Then why don't you lead by example and quit ridiculing and judging her yourself?"

Elliot agrees to give it a shot. I offer a gentle lingering kiss, promising a fun night ahead, if he behaves himself and announce, "I need to get into the kitchen and get the turkeys and cranberry sauce ready for tomorrow."

"How many birds are you making?"

"Just two, one for us and one for the homeless shelter. Don't forget, we need to be there by one with the food and we start serving dinner at one thirty."

Elliot nods, "What time should I tell my parents we'll be back for our celebration?"

"We should be sitting down to eat at four."

With that I take off to the kitchen to start my preparations. It's been a practice in my family ever since I was a little girl to make a double Thanksgiving feast, one for us and one for the Catholic Church's soup kitchen. We've continued this tradition into our adulthood. Whatever part of the meal we're responsible for; we double it and meet the rest of the family to help serve our fellow man. We try not to restrict out charitable contributions to just the holidays but there's no better time to share the wealth than on a day of gratitude.

Kevin brings Richard straight to my house from the airport and I'm thrilled to see him. He's brought a gorgeous bouquet of flowers that I set down straight on the dining room table. My dining room seats eight comfortably so we're going to have to attach another table to the end and continue seating into the living room to fit all sixteen of us. Again I wonder why we couldn't have just had Thanksgiving at Renée's house, but for some reason it's important to Elliot to do it here.

I put Richard and Kevin to work prepping ingredients for my famous cranberry relish. Kevin grates the fresh ginger root while Richard pulps the oranges. As I'm assembling it in my grandmother Sissy's crystal salad bow, I mention, "Richard, I don't know what happened with Philippa at my wedding…"

Richard gruffly cuts me off, "Mimi, I've told you I don't want to discuss it with you. In fact, there's no reason to ever mention it. It's not like I ever have to lay eyes on the woman again."

Uh oh, now I'm in for it. "Richard," big breath, "I'm afraid you are going to have to see Pippa again. I mean, rather, crap. It's like this. She's in town and she'll be joining us for Thanksgiving."

Kevin decides to join in by adding, "She's staying at Renée's, too."

I turn to glare at my friend and accuse, "Are you trying to make this worse?"

Kevin turns red and fidgety, "No, but I think Richard

should know that, don't you?"

Clearly, I don't, but I can't say that so I turn to Richard and offer, "You know how big Renée's house is. You never have to see her if you don't want to."

In an act of pure sullenness, Richard grabs his phone and starts to look up hotels in the area. Strangely, there's nothing available so he finally decides, "Fine, I'll stay there but I don't have to like it."

Renée and Laurent have invited us all over to their house for a casual pizza party. With all the preparations for Thanksgiving, this will allow us to enjoy each other's company without a hassle or mess.

Once we get there, Richard escapes to his room, pleading exhaustion and we don't see him for the rest of the night. Pip seems relieved, but this tension between them is making me nervous about tomorrow. Ah well, with sixteen of us, they don't even have to speak to each other, right?

Chapter 17

I am forever befuddled that a world as technologically advanced and inherently wealthy as ours has not been able to solve the homeless problem. We're so out for ourselves and our own pocketbooks that it's become too easy to turn a blind eye to human suffering in this world. I am by no means the queen of charity, but darn it, at least I try to make a difference.

Elliot and I are on the way out the door to the parish when his mother calls out, "Don't leave yet! We'll be ready in two minutes."

I look at Elliot and ask, "They're coming with us?"

He nods his head and responds, "They offered to help last night at Renée's."

I'm not sure what to make of this. I mean heck, I'm wearing jeans and a sweater, I have my hair tied up and I'm prepared to get sweaty while helping serve my fellow man. I can imagine the countess showing up in cashmere, sticking her nose in the air and breathing into a scented hanky so she doesn't pass out from the stench of the unwashed masses.

When Elliot's parents join us at the front door, they look as regal as always, but somehow seem more human in casual attire. I'm sure their clothes still cost enough to feed a family of four for a month but they've made an effort to fit in. The earl is carrying a shopping bag with him and the countess has forgone her usual Hermès tote in lieu of a less pretentious model. They really do appear to be trying, although I have no idea what's in the shopping bag.

We meet my family in the parish parking lot and begin to unpack all the goodies we've brought. Jonathan has four hotel pans full of crescent rolls and enough butter to grease the Hippodrome. He notices my surprise and announces, "Ginger went to the market hungry and craving crescent rolls. She came home with forty-eight tubes of them."

I reply, "I hope you saved some for us."

Ginger winks, "I saved nine for us which will make seventy-two rolls." Doing the math, I smile. Seventy-two crescent rolls for sixteen people sounds just about right.

Father Brennan pops his head out of the kitchen door to hurry us along. "Let's go, Finnegan family! I need your food on the buffet right away."

With that dictate, we pick up speed and immediately jump in where needed.

Laurent enlists Elliot's help in putting the final touches on his stuffing and mashed potato contributions. Kevin and Muffy assemble their salad and start pouring sparkling cider in the church's all-purpose glassware. A special touch Father Brennan has insisted upon is the use of the church's dishware and glasses. The only disposables are the napkins. He's adamant, "Every one of the fine folks dining with us today remembers a Thanksgiving during better times. Let's encourage the hope that those times will come again."

My parents slip on aprons and start carving the turkeys and Richard and Pip wind up side by side serving on the buffet. Neither looks very pleased but before they can scramble to get farther away from each other, the diners start to pour in.

This is one of those moments that overwhelms me every year. These are not nameless, faceless, soulless beings. These are people down on their luck for one reason or another. Yes, some of those reasons might be a product of their own making, but many are simply the result of circumstance.

My eye is drawn to a ragged looking woman who seems to be about my age. She has two small children huddled at her side and they all appear to be malnourished. I immediately put my hand to my stomach as if to shield my unborn child from ever knowing this reality. My eyes fill with tears and I am hard-pressed to control them.

Elliot sees me and comes to my side, "Do you need to sit down, love?"

I assure him I don't and send him back to his duties. Then I find my mother, "Mom, where are the clothes we collected?"

She gasps, "Drat, I left them out in the car. Here, take over for your father and he'll go get them." I take up the carving and my dad disappears to retrieve the items I've requested.

When he returns, I hand his knife back and go into the kitchen to find what I'm searching for. Inside one of the shopping bags are children's boots and coats. I go out to the dining room and find the woman with the small children and ask if any of these items would be useful to her.

She smiles shyly as tears run down her face. "I'm so embarrassed to be here in this situation." She adds, "You know, three years ago I was helping to serve this same meal in my parish."

I ask her what happened and she confesses, "My husband got sick. The medical bills were staggering." With a sob, she adds, "He died last year and the kids and I have been doing everything we can just to stay together. We lost our house at the end of the summer."

Every year I talk to the people who come into the soup kitchen for Thanksgiving dinner and every year I hear stories that tear me apart. But this year, this story hits so close to home I know I have to do something. I find out the woman's name is Faith and she and her children are staying at the shelter in Pipsy. I tell her that I'd like to find a way to help her and ask if it's okay for me to come and see her. She sobs in heartfelt gratitude and I assure her I will be there Saturday morning.

By the time everyone is sitting down to eat, I'm wrung out physically and emotionally. I just want to collapse and thank God for every last gift in my life. I don't know how I, Mimi Fielding, turned out to be the most blessed person in the world, but I am. I'm so overwhelmed with abundance; I can never show my gratitude enough.

As I sip on some apple cider I notice Pip making her way around the room. It's like she's encased in a bright light. I know that sounds fanciful but I really can see it. She's radiant and so self-assured and composed as she sits down with people. Several hug her and many others are just drawn to watch her.

Pip doesn't hurry or rush. She just takes her time and offers a message to every person that waits to hear one. It's like watching Jesus walk amongst the masses. These people are drawn to her. They are hungry for any word she has for them.

I notice Richard watching her too and he appears to be as enthralled as I am. I think maybe my friend might be seeing the error of his ways. I hope so anyway.

I also find out what's in the earl's shopping bag. No wonder none of the Pipsy hotels had any vacancies. Upon arriving in town earlier in the week and hearing of our soup kitchen plans, Elliot's father bought out every vacant room in the area. He's handing out gift cards to each person or family in need of a warm, clean hotel room. The rooms are booked for four nights so they will have ample time to rest and enjoy some basic comforts like heat and running water. Apparently, he's planning to meet with Father Brennan to help find a more suitable long-term solution for our town. I have the strongest urge to jump into old Archie's arms and hug him for all I'm worth, but I'm afraid the shock might kill him.

Chapter 18

By the time we get back to my little yellow house on Mercer Ave. I'm totally done in. Elliot sends me upstairs to lie down while he and my family get our dinner ready. The house is overflowing with noise, people and love. Even though Renée's house would have been a million times more comfortable, given its size, I like the feeling of all this happy energy in my home.

As I come down the stairs, I stop for a moment to take in the contented scene before me. The earl and Elliot are adding the folding table to the end of the dining room table so we'll all fit, my mom flits about tidying the silverware, Kevin and Muffy are snuggled on the couch. Elliot walks in wearing my grandma Sissy's apron. My cup runneth over.

I don't hear the countess creep up behind me until she begins to talk. As soon as she speaks, I jump, let out a rather large scream and wet my pants, simultaneously. Once I gather my composure, she says, "What a nice day, Mimi. Thank you for including us in your celebration."

I murmur the appropriate response and go change my

underwear before joining everyone. By the time I get to the table there are only three vacant seats, two together and one across from them. I take the single seat next to my husband, leaving the other two for Richard and Pip who are not yet seated. They show up at the table moments later, from opposite directions only to find out they're sitting together. After seeing Richard's admiring looks towards Pip at the soup kitchen, I'm less inclined to break them up. I'm actually rather looking forward to seeing what will happen between them.

As soon as I sit down, my mother stands to offer a word of gratitude, as is our tradition. She rises and remains quiet until the table settles and then starts, "Every year I'm overwhelmed by all the gifts life brings. This year we've added a new son-in-law and four grandbabies on the way." She stops to collect her emotions before continuing, "In addition to that, we've joined Elliot's family to ours, Kevin has come into the fold and Mimi's dear friend, Richard, has become a cherished friend to us all." Then she looks to the earl and countess, "Archibald and Victoria, we are all so grateful for all you've done for our town's underprivileged and we thank you for your generosity." To Pippa, she adds, "Philippa dear, the lovely message you shared from my mother this morning was so meaningful, I can't find the words to thank you. You have an amazing gift and I'm humbled you shared it with me."

I take a quick peak at Richard to see how he's receiving that bit of gratitude and notice his face redden. I can't tell if it's from shame, anger or embarrassment at not believing in Pip.

My mom continues, "It is my goal through life's ups and downs to always remember that the gifts outweigh the troubles." Then she raises her wine glass, "To all of you, thank you for being part of my family and thank you for gracing our holiday table."

Everyone lifts their glasses to toast before my dad stands up to offer the prayer. "Oh Gracious God, we give you thanks for your overflowing generosity to us. Thank you for the blessings of the food we eat and especially for this feast today. Thank you for our home and family and friends, especially for the presence of those gathered here. Thank you for our health, our work and our play. Please send help to those who are hungry, alone, sick and suffering war and violence. Open our hearts to your love. We ask your blessing through Christ your son. Amen."

Chapter 19

My bionic emotions hit on the way to my meeting with Faith. I'm already feeling fragile, grateful and weepy (three of the gestational seven dwarves), when I decide to turn on the radio hoping for some classic eighties rock to take my mind off the arbitrariness of life. Why do some people wind up with real struggles while the rest of us with invented ones? That's when I hear it, Shannon, sung by Henry Gross. It's a song my parents used to listen to and I remember dancing around the yard singing it with my sisters when we were kids.

I immediately flash back to my carefree childhood and think of Faith's kids and the real struggles they're facing. Life without a father and dreary days in a homeless shelter, with a mother doing her best to get her family back on their feet. The song ends and the DJ announces, "I bet you didn't know that Shannon was Brian Wilson's Irish setter. Yup, the Beach Boy was nearly suicidal in his depression when a friend brought him the dog to cheer him up. And boy howdy, did it work! Brian and Shannon were inseparable, running and playing together on the beaches of Southern California until the day a big wave came and washed old Shannon out to sea. Brian never saw his beloved pet again."

What the hell? OMG, this is too much sadness for my hormonal body to handle. I pull off to the side of the road and burst into uncontrollable tears. I sob until I'm nearly dehydrated. My eyes are almost swollen shut and my nose is so stopped up I can barely breathe. Apparently I can't handle pregnancy *and* the tragedies of life because there's no sign of the waterworks abating.

I must be parked at an alarming angle because the next thing I know, a police officer is tapping on my window. I look up, unroll the window and manage to utter, "Y-y-yes, sir. How, how, how can I h-h-h-help you?"

Alarmed, the young officer answers, "Ma'am, are you okay? Do I need to call the paramedics?"

I'm thinking, the paramedics? Yes, I'm sad but it's too late to save Shannon now. Then it hits me all over again and I burst into another round of uncontrollable weeping. I try to assure him that I'm fine and just completely off my nut due to the very natural thrill ride of pregnancy, but he's already taken note of my rounded tummy and is beating it back to his squad car. The next thing I know, the cop is opening the passenger side door and he climbs into the seat next to me. He says, "Ma'am, please relax, I'm here. The paramedics are on their way." Then he pats my hand and soothes, "Try to stay calm."

To say I'm totally alarmed would be the understatement of the century. This well-meaning officer of the peace has just called an ambulance because he thinks something is wrong with me or my baby. I've got to set him straight before this scene turns into a circus. So I shout out, "Shannon, Shannon, oh my God, she's d-d-d-dead!" This isn't quite what I was going for, but it's all that I can manage.

The officer grabs my phone and asks what my husband's name is. I manage, "Elliot, E-E-Elliot Fielding." The officer finds Elliot's name and calls him. When Elliot answers, I hear him say, "Sir, this is Officer Ben Malone of the Pipsy Police Department. I'm sitting here in the car with your wife and I'm sorry to tell you, she appears to be miscarrying."

"WHAT?" Now I absolutely have to get ahold of myself before Elliot freaks out and gets killed on the way to picking me up. Then I remember Faith's dead husband and I'm history again. Great big, ugly, sobs escape me and I moan, "Shannon, oh Shannon..."

Officer Ben tells Elliot to meet us at the hospital because the paramedics have just arrived. How can this be happening to me? I cannot let the ambulance take me to the hospital because Brian Wilson's dog died forty years ago. But I'm helpless to stop it. I can't control my outburst long enough to make it clear I'm just a lunatic and not in any real danger. Although they might just lock me up in the psych ward by the time this is over.

Two burly paramedics come to check me out. They take my blood pressure and other vitals before the one with blond hair asks, "Are you bleeding heavily?"

Of course I'm not because my baby is fine but I only shake my head and weep, "Oh Shannon..."

The EMT's strap me to a gurney and roll me into the ambulance which arrives at the same time Elliot does. Elliot runs to meet me and cries, "Mimi, my love, are you okay?"

I scream, "No, Shannon is dead!"

I know Elliot's thinking, "Who the hell is Shannon? I thought we were naming the baby Sophie." But all he says is, "I'm right here, darling. We'll have a dozen more babies. I love you so much. Hang in there; we'll get through this together."

Holy crap I have got to get control of myself long enough to tell everyone that I'm fine. I finally succeed in yelling/sobbing, "Shannon is a dog!"

That stops everyone in their tracks. Officer Ben asks, "Shannon's a dog? Did you hit a dog?"

"No, she's Brian Wilson's dog."

Elliot inquires, "The Beach Boy?"

I smile through my tears, "Yes, exactly!"

Blond paramedic adds, "Brian Wilson is dead."

Nodding my head I agree, "Y-y-yes and s-s-so is Shannon."

All four men stand and stare at me like I've totally gone off my gourd. Brunette paramedic inquires, "Ma'am, is your baby dead?"

I shake my head, "No, S-s-s-s-ophie's fine."

Elliot throws himself in my arms and starts to cry before exclaiming, "Thank God! You're both okay then?"

I nod my head and answer, "Of course. It's just Shannon who's dead."

Office Ben apparently needs some more clarification and asks, "Shannon, Brian Wilson's dog?"

Blond paramedic hands me a bottle of water to sip which is just the ticket because I finally stop the emotional hiccupping. I look at the four very confused faces surrounding me and tell my story, "I was on my way to a meeting when the song Shannon came on the radio and the DJ said it was a song written for Brian Wilson's dead dog. It was just so, so, sad!"

The paramedics finally grasp what I'm saying. They explain they legally have to take me in and get checked out by the emergency room doc before letting me go, even though this is just a horrible misunderstanding. Officer Ben mumbles something about how he'll never understand women and Elliot is so relieved he remains glued to my side the whole time.

Thank God the ER doc is a woman and a mother to boot. She totally comprehends how my emotions took over and agrees that Shannon is one of the saddest songs of all time. She confesses that during her third pregnancy, Mr. Bojangles was her undoing, although she never wound up being transported to the hospital, via ambulance, because of it.

Elliot takes me home and he and the earl go to meet with Faith. They find out that her parents live in Tacoma and they purchase plane tickets for her and her children to go home. They also give them enough money to help them get back on their feet. I'm starting to think this being rich thing is going to be fun. I could have never helped Faith so much on my own.

Chapter 20

The frigging countess and I are on our way to see my favorite house with Blaine, the Realtor boy wonder. To say I hate the guy would be incorrect. I do not know him well enough to hate him, thank God. But I do dislike his demeanor. He acts like he's better than 99.9 percent of the free world and he kisses the other .01 percent's asses like their bum's hold the secrets of the ages. I loathe Blaine's arrogance, his fawning and his superiority. And quite frankly, I hate his sweater. Heterosexual men should not wear sweaters flung over their shoulders like they're afraid of catching a chill. Man up, dude.

Blaine is so far up the countess's hind quarters I haven't had to contribute much to the conversation. I do insert pertinent facts like, "No small family needs fifteen thousand square feet to live in." And ask insightful questions like, "Who's going to clean all these bathrooms?" They both ignore me, which is exactly what I expect given the circumstances.

When we pull up to the house, my insides perform a secret, spastic jig. I know this isn't the house for us but it's still magnificent to behold. The fountain is bubbling away and the grounds are hanging on to their crisp autumnal colors. This would be the perfect backdrop for a feminine hygiene commercial from the eighties. Remember how elated those chicks were with their new slim maxi-pads? They felt such freedom to be active they were always filmed running through nature, blatantly expressing their joy.

Blaine gives Victoria the same spiel I got upon my first visit here. She seems to think the bedroom to bathroom ratio is quite normal and wants to know if the kitchen hosts a bun warmer. I wrestle against suggesting she just sidle up to the oven if she wants her buns warmed and actually win the war against my inner devil by staying quiet.

I let my mother-in-law take a tour with my eager Realtor and opt to sit out by the pool. Against all conscious desire, I can see Sophie learning how to swim here. I imagine golden retriever puppies running around the water, barking at her and eventually jumping in to join her. It's a picture right out of a fairy tale. Why can't I just make the leap and say, "What the heck, let's buy this castle and call it home?" Probably because my definition of home has always been something more intimate and quaint, something this manor could never be.

I must have dozed off because the next thing I know I wake up to find the countess and Blaine standing next to me talking numbers. The countess inquires, "Do you feel the listing price on this property is appropriate for the area?"

Blaine, nearly drooling on his Italian loafers, responds, "Most definitely! This estate will be snapped up in a heartbeat!"

I can't help but interject, "Blaine, "I've been looking at this house for a month and it hasn't sold yet. In fact, you've told me there haven't even been any offers on it."

My mother-in-law arches one of her perfectly groomed English eyebrows and informs Blaine, "While we are interested in the property, we're not interested in being taken advantage of."

Blaine assures her the right couple simply hasn't come along yet. But as soon as they do, they will happily pay full asking price. Victoria seems to be no more enamored of my Realtor than I am, so she simply turns her back on him and asks me, "What do say, Mimi, shall we make an offer?"

No one, I repeat no one in my previous acquaintance could or would so cavalierly suggest purchasing a five million plus dollar home as easily as proposing a Grand Slam breakfast at Denny's. I fight against choking on my own saliva. Hoping to buy time, I answer, "Elliot hasn't even seen it yet. I really think he should before we buy it."

The countess shifts her attention to Blaine, "I assume you have no problem waiting while my son stops by?"

I can't pull myself together fast enough to call a halt to this farce. Elliot's mother has smoothed out all the wrinkles and is on the phone with Elliot before I can scream, "NO!!!"

She's arranged for him to drive himself over to meet us so I will have zero opportunity to convince him not to love it. And of course he's going to love, I mean, I love it. And he grew up like this so it will in no way intimidate him like it does me. And you know Elliot is never going to worry about who's going to clean all these bathrooms. I'm sure he's never so much as held a toilet brush, assuming he even knows what one is.

I am so overstimulated and nervous at the thought that I can't stop this thing, my bladder goes into overdrive. I'm in real jeopardy of having an accident so I excuse myself without any explanation and run through the French doors leading to the kitchen. I make it in the nick of time and after completing my mission, take a moment to realize this is the singularly most comfortable toilet seat I have ever been on in my life. Why is that I wonder. I mean a toilet seat is a toilet seat is a toilet seat, right? Unless, of course, you happen to be sitting on a heated toilet seat. That's right. My posterior is being kept toasty warm while I complete my business. This is unadulterated luxury. I may never be able to go back to the unwelcoming embrace of a cold toilet seat now that I've know this splendor.

I detour through the kitchen to drool at the appliances on my way back to the pool, which is how Elliot and I arrive next to his mother at the same moment. My husband's smile is in jeopardy of taking over his entire face. "Mimi, I adore this place! It's everything I imagined for us." And that's before he's even seen the inside.

I know when I'm beat. There is no way to convince Elliot this house is too much for us when he, his mother and Blaine, are all of the opinion it's perfect. Once Elliot finishes the grand tour, he announces, "We'll take it."

Blaine appears to be having spasms of joy and Victoria actually steps away from him as though his distasteful behavior might be contagious.

I seize the moment to declare, "Don't do a happy dance yet, Blaine. We aren't offering full asking price."

Elliot asks, "We're not, why?"

The countess interjects, "Mimi mentioned the estate has been on the market for over a month and there have been no offers." She says this almost admiringly, like she might actually realize the value of money and isn't one to give it away for no reason.

My clueless husband inquires, "But if we like it and want it, why not pay full asking price? We don't want someone else to snatch it out from under us."

Accepting my fate, I reply, "Don't worry. We'll get it."

Our greedy real estate agent turns to Elliot and advises, "Sir Fielding, you are a man of the world and understand how these things are done far better than your wife. I think paying the full asking price is the prudent way to go."

Oh Blaine, you idiot, now you've done it. First off, don't ever cross a Finnegan, yet alone a hormonally challenged one. I lean into my husband and give him "the look." You know the one that says, don't you dare open your mouth under pain of death or you will regret it for all-time?

Then I share a knowing glance with the countess before turning my attention to Blaine. "Blaine, are you or are you not representing us in this sale?"

He bristles a bit and his face takes on a definite flush before answering, "Of course I represent you."

Then Victoria, bless her heart, appears to have had a thought, "You aren't perchance the listing agent as well, are you?"

Blaine shifts back and forth, looks at his shoes and mumbles, "Well, yes, yes I am."

Elliot seems to have grasped the significance of this and raises a supercilious brow in question. With a nod to me and a glance to his mother, he offers, "Why don't I leave this up to you ladies?"

God save the queen! He knows I hate Blaine and up to this point has felt my disregard was unwarranted. Now, he sees what a scum sucking worm he really is and is letting me have my revenge. As far as I'm concerned, this lets him off the hook for every birthday and Christmas gift for life. I'm about to have some fun.

"Blaine," I start, as sweetly and condescendingly as I can. "What percentage of the sale are you expected to get as both the listing and selling agent?"

If Blaine was even one iota less egregious a human being, I might have felt sorry for him at this moment. His face turns bright red and he appears apoplectic. He clears his throat before answering, "Six percent."

I ask, "Have you by any chance only shown me properties you are the listing agent of?"

Now it's his turn to look indignant. "Not at all! I don't know what kind of man you take me for, Mimi, but I'm not Machiavellian. I have shown you all the homes I've felt were right for you, regardless of who has the listing."

I believe him, dammit, but I'm not done with him. "First of all, Blaine, I have not given you permission to call me by my Christian name. I believe we settled on, Lady Fielding." Watch out, I appear to be channeling Downton Abbey. I may have a real future in this countess business. In fact, Victoria looks rather proud of me at the moment. So I continue, "Secondly, you are not only representing us and the seller, but apparently yourself, as well." Blaine looks like he's about to throw up so I pause for a moment to give him the opportunity. "Therefore, I feel that you cannot possibly be giving us the best advice."

Blaine stumbles over his words, "Mimi, rather Mrs.... Lady Fielding, I'm not at all trying to take advantage of you, truly..."

I don't let him finish, "As such we are offering $5,200,000, not the asking price of $5,469,000." Before he can interrupt me, I add, "And we are offering a Realtor fee of 4.5% instead of the standard 6%."

Poor Blaine seems to be absorbing the fact that if the seller takes our offer, his commission will be reduced by nearly $100,000. I can't say I pity him too much though as he has brought this on himself. He seems to be wrestling with telling me to go take a hike and being grateful that he'll still walk away with nearly a quarter of a million dollars for his month of work.

After a few moments of consideration, our Realtor responds, "Of course I would be willing to reduce my percentage if that would help you out, but I don't think the seller is going to take such a lowball offer. In fact, I think they'll be insulted by it." With a gleam in his eye, he adds, "And when sellers get insulted, they often refuse to entertain further offers from that particular buyer."

I'm about to yell my reply with an, "Asshole!" and a swift kick to the shins, when Victoria steps forward. "Blaine, I think you're mistaken. I would direct you to present Sir and Lady Fielding's offer with haste." Then she adds, "Before my son and his wife choose to find another Realtor who would better suit them."

Go Victoria! I want to grab her in a bear hug and dance her around the pool but realize this might turn her against me for all time. After all, if I've learned one thing from the countess, it's that she isn't hip to middle-class displays of emotion.

Blaine wisely chooses not to provoke any of us further and declares he will present our offer that very day. Trying to undo some of his earlier damage he manages, "There is a small chance they'll accept it as it's a cash offer with no contingencies."

Chapter 21

I'm in the doctor's office with Ginger when I find out the good news. I'm a home owner. I knew Elliot and I would get the house and have been trying to prepare myself for this moment. I'm torn between conflicting emotions. I have no idea how I am possibly going to adapt to such grandeur, yet I'm thrilled at the same time. I want to share the news with my sister but decide against it until after her appointment.

Jonathan has been to every one of Ginger's doctor appointments but couldn't make this one as he's visiting the New York office for a few days. He offered to try to get out of the trip, but Ginger told him not to be ridiculous, she would be just fine. The truth is she isn't fine, she's a nervous wreck. She told me on the way over that she expects to find out baby three is no more every time they step through the clinic doors.

She looks positively terrified and painfully vulnerable lying on the table in her paper gown waiting for her ultrasound to begin. I try to take her mind off her troubles with humor. "Every time I put on one of those God awful things, I try to imagine a Parisian fashion show with emaciated models strutting their stuff up and down the runway." No response, so I amp up my attempt, "You know with their hair slicked back, sporting giant diamond chandelier earrings, six-inch stilettos and peacock feathers for hats…"

With the barest glint of a smile, my sister reaches for my hand and responds, "Only you, Meems. You are the only other person in the world, other than Jonathan, I'd want here with me for this." I've spent the majority of my life under the false impression that my sisters were always trying to show me up with their perfection. Until recently, I thought my claim to fame in our quartet of sisterhood was that I had the prettiest feet. Of course now I have Edith Bunker and prettiest feet is off the table. Bunions are many things but pretty isn't one of them.

Muffy recently shared that my sisters view me as the heart of our family, the emotional rock. She explained I was the first one they all shared their news with, good and bad, because I was the one they could count on to care the most. To say she totally rocked my world with her declaration would be the understatement of the century. All these years I thought I was the family disappointment, the one that didn't live up to the rest of them. It just goes to show our version of reality is often the farthest thing from reality.

The doctor chooses that moment to come into the exam room. She's all smiles as she announces, "Ready to take a look at the Becker triplets?" With no further ado, she squirts a glob of pre-warmed gel on Ginger's tummy and begins. Ginger has her eyes closed and isn't even looking at the monitor when the doctor asks, "Mimi, can you tell Ginger what you see?"

In sheer delight, I answer, "I see three little squirmy worms wiggling around and three heartbeats!"

Ginger opens her eyes and reluctantly looks before bursting into tears. "Oh my God, look at them!" Then to the doctor she asks, "Does this mean we're out of the woods?"

The doc smiles and answers, "We're not totally out of the woods as multiple births can always result in complications. But if I were a gambling woman, I'd say you better set up all three cribs and prepare not to get much sleep for about six months."

Ginger seems to be playing out my "Shannon" scene with tears streaming down her face and her whole body shuddering in release of emotion. "I don't care if I ever sleep again. I'm the luckiest woman in the whole world!" While I might normally fight her for that honor, I decide to let her win this one.

The doctor reminds Ginger that triplets generally only gestate for 32-36 weeks and in order to keep them in the womb for as long as possible she needs to continue to take good care of herself. "Keep up your intake of fluids and remember to have protein at every meal." She leaves after receiving my sister's promise.

Ginger and I decide to go to The Cracked Egg for an early lunch. She's craving quiche and I'm jonesing for Belgium waffles. Once we're seated and place our order, I share the news about the house. "Remember that house I showed you?" With a nod in the affirmative I continue, "Well, it's my house now."

Ginger squeals, evoking looks of alarm from nearby diners and exclaims, "Meems, this is turning into the best day ever!"

I concur. Ginger is no longer interested in my concerns over the size of the house. She promises to give me the number of her cleaning lady, as I have recently decided to quit fretting over the upkeep of my new behemoth dwelling. I've embraced the fact that I'll need help and as long as said help doesn't reside in servant's quarters and wear uniforms, I think I might just be able to manage it.

I share with Ginger that the house will close in thirty days as the sellers need to relocate to San Francisco ASAP so we'll move in the day after. I confide, "I'm very excited, but I'm totally sad to leave my little nest on Mercer St."

Ginger laughs, "I bet Elliot's glad to leave though." Ginger is of course referring to the neighbor girls attempt to sneak into the house in order to catch Elliot in the shower. I have known Tiffany since she was in junior high and never thought her the sort to do such a thing. But now that she's eighteen, full of teenage hormones and has recently fallen madly in love with my husband, I can see that she's become a bit of a wild card. Elliot will no longer shower unless I'm home to protect his modesty.

Chapter 22

Happily, for me anyway, Elliot's parents leave shortly after our offer is accepted on the new house. Of course they'll be back for Sophie's birth and while I'm not terribly excited to see them again so soon, at least our house will be big enough for me to avoid them if I choose. Even though Victoria and I bonded over our distaste for Blaine, I'm leery of thinking she's decided to embrace me with open arms.

Pip is planning to come for the birth as well, so I told Richard we should make a party of it and invited him along. I thought for sure he'd turn me down once he learned Elliot's sister would be there, but he didn't. In fact he sounded quite pleased by the news. Things progressed nicely for them at Thanksgiving and while Richard doesn't seem to be ready to drop his previous anger completely, he's definitely softening. I can't help but speculate about what information Richard received from beyond the grave that made him so mad. But alas, neither he nor Pip will talk, so speculation is all I have.

I've developed an alarming new symptom in my pregnancy. I've become claustrophobic, but not for myself, for Sophie.

I've decided she can't possibly be comfortable all squashed up in my womb and I've begun panicking for her. I haven't told this to Elliot because it makes me sound insane. I'm sure I'll give him a million reasons to question his choice in marrying me in the years to come, but I'd like to put that off for as long as possible. Doctor Fermin assures me, while this is not a common occurrence; women react in a slew of different ways to gestating and she's encouraged me to join a group that originated with her practice. The group started as a support for women experiencing postpartum depression, but has grown to include pregnant women as well as new mothers. My first meeting starts in thirty minutes. Elliot knows I'm going to a gathering of expectant mothers, but he doesn't know why I'm going. I'm sure he assumes it's some sort of pregnant-palooza and I'm letting him.

The assembly is twenty women strong give or take, depending on the week. They meet in the back room of Giovanni's Trattoria in Hilldale, so I figure the worst thing that can happen is I'll have an awesome meal. The best thing would be I quit freaking out for Sophie.

In my excitement, I'm the first one to arrive. As the other women start to show up, I'm astonished by the wide array of types. They range in age from twenty-something to forty-something and appear to span a cross section of socio economic situations. There are moms sporting tattoos and multiple facial piercings and others that appear to have just left a junior league meeting. Some are wearing ripped jeans and some are tricked out in designer maternity gear, while others appear normal like me, in yoga pants and a sweater.

A tall, slim, blonde woman about my age stands up and introduces herself. "As most of you know, my name is Adele and I'm the founder of this group." She seems to be saying this for my benefit as well as one or two others as we are the ones she's addressing. "We're a group for women who have experienced difficulties during and after pregnancy." She shares, "After the birth of my third child I experienced such debilitating postpartum I felt like I couldn't carry on and became suicidal."

I let out an involuntary gasp. I'm not nearly as bad off as that and worry Dr. Fermin thinks I'm a total fruit loop. Adele smiles as me, "Not everyone gets as depressed as I did. In fact some aren't depressed at all. They just come for the support of other mothers. My personal journey was so bad that I needed a lot of help. I continue on with the group, even though I've been through with postpartum for a of couple years now, because I want to encourage other women and let them know they aren't alone." Then she looks right at me and asks, "Why don't you stand up and tell us your name and why you're joining us this evening?"

Before coming, I decided to use a fake name to protect Elliot's identity. People, in our area gossip about him enough without adding a crazy wife to the mix. So I stand up and say, "My name is Miriam Murphy and I'm twenty-four weeks pregnant with my first child. I'm here because I've recently developed claustrophobia." I don't tell them it's for Sophie, yet.

A young woman named Jen, sporting a nose ring and pink hair, replies, "The same thing happened to me! I can't stand to be in a room and have the door shut. I just totally start to wig out!"

A couple of other women contribute that claustrophobia is actually a pretty common sensation in postpartum.

I'm comforted to know I'm not alone and start to feel safe enough to explain further. "You see, I'm not the one I'm claustrophobic for." All eyes turn to me for further enlightenment so I plow forth, "I'm claustrophobic for my baby."

An uptight looking mother-to-be named Laura furrows her brow and questions, "What do you mean you're claustrophobic for your baby? You're not thinking of trying to get it to come out early, are you?"

I force a smile and respond, "No, no, nothing like that. I'm just worried she doesn't have enough room in there and she might start to panic."

An unassuming young woman named Jessica adds, "I don't think fetuses can feel panic. I don't think they've formed any self-awareness yet."

This is something that hasn't occurred to me before now and I plan to do some serious cogitating on it once I get home. If I can convince myself that Sophie isn't even aware she's there, I might just be able to believe she's not suffering from any space issues.

A thirty-something wearing a designer suit with mega high heels contributes, "This is the way humans have always gestated and there's no other option for you, so you should probably just get over it."

Jen, the pink haired mom with the hooped nostril defends me by replying, "Get over it? Gee, Taylor, do you think we should have told you to just get over it when you came unglued worrying you'd never fit back into your pre-pregnancy clothes? I don't think one person called you out for being a shallow bitch." She hesitates a moment to take a breath and continues, "So why don't you quit being a stuck-up cow and be as supportive of Miriam as we all were of you?"

As soon as she says, Miriam, I wonder who they're talking about. While my given name really is Miriam, I have gone by Mimi for so long I no longer identify with my real name.

Taylor the "uptight bitch" reddens and fires back, "I didn't mean it like that. I meant that babies have always incubated the same way and as far as I know, no one has ever come forth in adulthood to say they were panic stricken in the womb."

I clear my throat and suggest, "Just because they don't say it or remember it doesn't mean they weren't."

Taylor replies, "But what can you do about it? Why worry, if you can't change it?"

And while this actually sounds like reasonable advice, I don't think I can be reasoned with. It makes sense, but I'm hard pressed to convince myself to just stop feeling this way.

For the rest of the meeting I focus on my eggplant Parmesan and iced tea. I'm happy to just listen to others and fade into the background.

Adele, our leader, asks various members how they're doing with their different problems. She inquires if Taylor is doing any better with her body issues.

Taylor, who is clearly back to wearing her tiny pre-pregnancy clothes answers, "I'm struggling."

I learn she gave birth three months earlier and recently

stopped trying to breast feed because her body wasn't making any milk. Laura, the one who worried I might try to free Sophie early suggests, "Well, clearly you're not eating enough to make any milk."

Adele asks, "What does your doctor say, Taylor?"

Taylor seems to physically melt in front of us. With her head in her hands she answers, "She says the same thing Laura said. I need to eat more." Looking a bit wild-eyed, she continues, "But I can't! Every time I put food in my mouth and try to swallow it, I feel like I'm going to choke."

Jen sighs, "We all have these control issues. They just manifest differently. Taylor can't eat, Laura's worried she can't protect her family from a terrorist attack and I can't get my floors clean enough. We're all crazy because we've lost control."

Adele replies, "It's true. Becoming a parent is all about redefining our concept of control. It's one thing when it's just us. But when these helpless creatures enter our lives and depend on us for every little thing to survive, it can become overwhelming. One of the first things we have to do is learn to release our grip a bit."

Jessica, the shy young brunette who gave me such food for thought about fetuses and self-awareness, starts to cry. "I'm just so tired all the time. I feel like I could handle everything if I could just get some sleep."

The other women console her and commiserate. Everyone is tired, overwhelmed and trying to navigate this journey without a map. It's not at all what I was hoping to find. I came tonight with one problem and have been made aware there are a million more lurking just around the corner.

Chapter 23

When I get home, Elliot cuddles up with me on the couch. He pulls my foot up on his lap to give Edith Bunker a nice rub and asks about my meeting. I don't want to discuss it so I tell him it was enlightening and change the subject. "Have you given any real thought about what we're going to do with six bedrooms?"

My darling English husband laughs at my continued disgust that our new home has so many rooms. So he explains, "We need a bedchamber, so there's one down. I thought Sophie could use the Jack and Jill set-up as a bedroom and playroom combination, two more down. One room will be a designated guest suite for when my parents come to visit." He adds, "Which I hope is often. So that only leaves two spare bedrooms. One can be for the nanny and you can use the other however you wish until Sophie's sibling comes along."

He seems so pleased with himself until I gasp, "Nanny? You don't really expect us to have a nanny, do you?"

Elliot looks confused and answers, "Well, of course I think we'll have a nanny. In fact, we should get busy looking for one soon so we'll be all set up when Sophie arrives."

I'm immediately overcome with anger. "We are two people bringing one child into the world, Elliot. Don't you think we can handle that on our own?"

"It's not a matter of handling it. It's a matter of comfortable adaptation." Witnessing the steam pouring out of my ears, he adds, "Pip and I had a nanny. It's not uncommon."

Not uncommon if you're from a blue-blooded family with your own coat of arms. I stand up in indignation and try to breathe deeply to calm myself but find it rather hard as Sophie is kicking her feet up into my diaphragm. The more I struggle for breath, the more light headed I become until I feel like I'm going to faint. As I wobble, Elliot grabs hold of my arm and sits me back down on the sofa. "Darling, what's wrong?"

"Elliot, I love you immensely, but it occurs to me that we don't know each other that well."

Rubbing my shoulders, he sooths, "We have the rest of our lives to get to know each other, sweetheart."

I respond, "While that might be so, we have some decisions we need to make now, for example, the nanny. I didn't grow up with one. My mom and dad managed to raise four daughters and we never had more than a babysitter. Why in the world do you think that two reasonably intelligent adults like us can't handle one child on our own?"

My husband truly appears to be pondering his answer before saying, "Well, I work from home but I'm on the road an awful lot researching and promoting my books. I won't be any help at those times and I don't imagine we'll want to take

Sophie on the road with us."

"What do mean us? Why do I have to go with you? I just assumed you'd travel when you had to and I'd stay home with the baby."

Elliot looks shocked by this. "You mean you don't plan on coming with me? I just thought we were a team. It didn't occur to me you wouldn't be by my side."

"Figuratively, I'll always be by your side, Elliot, but sometimes I'll have to be by Sophie's side. Don't you think?"

His Lordship really seems to be struggling with this when he suddenly asks, "But what if you want to go back to work? Who will watch Sophie then?"

I hadn't really thought about that yet, but suggest, "What about my mother?"

Elliot replies, "You're mother is going to have her hands full with four brand new grandbabies, not to mention her own life."

Damn, that's a good point. I can't expect my mom to drop everything for us when Ginger and Jonathan are going to need a lot more help than we will. So I counter, "I don't plan to go back to work for at least a year, so that shouldn't be an issue until then."

My husband looks thoroughly exasperated with me when he suggests, "Mimi, darling, why don't we just go ahead and interview a few people to see what we think? We don't have to make any decisions now, but at least we'll know what's available should we decide we want a nanny."

I know he's thinking he's going to win this one, but he's not. I'm just too worn out after my night out with the other moms to keep arguing. So I agree to meet with some Mary Poppins' wannabes to placate him, knowing full well we aren't going to hire any of them.

Elliot and I form a sort of truce as he leans over and kisses me behind the ear. The sensitivity of my neck is the real reason I could have never been a spy. Forget waterboarding or thumbscrews, all they'd have to do is kiss me behind my ears and I'd spill all of my country's secrets. Of course there's also the small problem that I have no ear for foreign languages and I'm about as inconspicuous as Mt. St. Helens. I believe I mentioned I'm 5'11" in stocking feet. And now that my hair is red, seriously, no one will be scouting me as the next Mata Hari.

The Englishman and I retire to our bedroom to further canoodle. I'm glad I decided to quit arguing with him about the nanny business and pretend to be flexible. We wind up having a way better time this way than we would have if we'd gone to bed angry.

Chapter 24

The first thing the next morning, I call Ginger and demand, "Are you and Jonathan looking for a nanny?"

Ginger gasps, "I wish! I'm afraid that luxury won't be happening any time soon." She continues, "We'll be going down to one income when the babies get here and there will be three kids to keep in diapers, food and clothes. Sadly, a nanny isn't in the budget."

"What if money weren't an issue? Would you get one then?"

My sister exclaims, "In a heartbeat. Why, are you and Elliot looking for a nanny?"

"I would say no, but the truth is we're currently battling about it." I add, "My aristocratic husband thinks they're a normal part of a child's upbringing and I'm trying to introduce him to life on planet earth. He's fighting it."

Ginger laughs, "We would have killed to have a nanny growing up. Imagine another adult to listen to us, help us with craft projects and pick up our messes. What a dream!"

"Maybe," I concede. "But there were four of us. Sophie is

one baby. How much trouble can one baby be? If the time ever comes when Elliot and I have four kids, I might seriously consider getting help. Or," I add, "If I were having triplets. But for one kid? No way."

"I have an idea. Why don't you get a nanny and I'll move in with you and she can take care of all of the babies?"

Poor Ginger, I shouldn't have called her with such an insensitive question. Of course she would love some full time help and here I am turning my nose up at it. I still don't want a nanny but I need to be more considerate of what she's going through. What I should do is tell Elliot to hire his precious nanny and send her to my sister but I know Ginger and Jonathan would never go for it.

My slightly older sibling asks, "What do you have on your agenda for today?"

I sigh, "I'm meeting Renée over at the new house to pick out paint colors." I explain, "Elliot wants to refresh everything before we move our furniture in, although truthfully, my whole house would fit in the entry hall."

She asks, "Is he planning on sending for his things from England?"

"He's already had some stuff shipped, but he doesn't want to get rid of his flat in London yet. I promised as soon as Sophie is old enough to fly, we'd spend a couple weeks there to sort everything out."

"Mimi Finnegan-Fielding, you have an enchanted life. Do you know that?" My sister doesn't sound at all envious, she simply sounds thrilled for me. From my eyes, her life has always looked perfect. It's kind of novel for her to be the one thinking that of me for a change.

I wish I was as excited as she is though. I have a new understanding of how overwhelming it must be to win the lottery. One day you're saving all your latté money for a new water heater and the next, you're paying cash for a mansion big enough to fit the water heater factory. In many ways it's a dream come true, but it comes with a huge adjustment factor. I suggest, "If you feel like getting out, why don't you join us?"

Ginger jumps at the offer, "I'd love to! I'm getting sick of being stuck at home. Pick me up on your way?"

My lovely sister has been ordered to stop driving because her mammoth stomach no longer fits between the driver seat and the steering wheel and if she moves her seat back to accommodate her girth, her arms aren't long enough to reach the wheel. It's a bit comical actually, but she's starting to feel like a caged animal. I agree to fetch her in an hour before hanging up the phone.

I'm trying to tie my sneakers when Elliot walks in and laughs, "Mimi, don't you think it's time to forgo shoes with strings?" He sits down on the couch next to me and takes my foot into his lap to tie for me.

"I'd love to but have you seen the size of my feet lately? I'm hoping the extra support of tied shoes will keep them from spreading further. You know, a moderate form of foot binding?"

He takes a good look and gasps, "They're huge! What happened?"

I'm too realistic to be offended by his reaction. So I simply answer, "Sophie happened. Apparently it's not uncommon for feet to grow a full size when pregnant. I think mine might be on the way to two sizes."

With a smile, he responds, "The good news is Edith Bunker looks positively petite in comparison."

His words hold truth. My bunion does look like a shadow of her former self. Of course there's a lot more foot to support the load now that I'm a size ten instead of a nine. I give Elliot a kiss goodbye and heave myself off the couch. "I'm on my way to pick up Ginger and meet Renée at the new house to choose paint colors. Are you sure you want to trust me on this?"

"Of course, my love, you've done a wonderful job decorating our little house here. I'm sure you and your sisters will do a bang up job with our new home. Plus, I have a phone interview with In Style magazine this morning. I've put it off twice already so I should really get it over with."

The closest I've ever come to In Style magazine is reading it at the hair dressers. Now my husband is going to be featured in an article within its hallowed pages. This is one crazy, crazy life.

On the way to pick up Ginger, I'm overcome with a craving for French fries. So I let my little red Honda take me to Burger City. I order four large fries, as I have every intention of sharing them, and low-fat milk. Gone are my Diet Coke days and I miss them tremendously. Alas, caffeine and fake sugar aren't on my pregnancy plan.

I hoover down one order of fries on my way to Ginger's in hopes of quelling my mad desire for them. My sister is waiting in her driveway when I pull up. She gets into the car with as much ease as a forty month pregnant woman can. Seriously, she's huge. The first words out of her mouth are, "You have fries!" She digs through the bag and inquires, "Three orders?"

I smile, "I thought we'd bring one for Renée."

Ginger snorts, "Don't be ridiculous. She won't eat them. We'll just have to split them ourselves." Which is how I came to eat enough French fries to feed an entire kindergarten class.

My new address is 1492 Magnolia Lane. As we pull through the gates, I let out a sigh of wonder. "I cannot believe I get to live here."

Ginger smiles, "It sounds like you've come to terms with being lady of the manor."

I reply, "Not at all! I mean I love this house but I'm still totally overwhelmed by it."

My sister laughs, "I think it might be even bigger than Renée's."

I'm sure she's right. And speaking of Renée, she's already arrived and is sitting by the front door with a couple of boxes at her feet.

My oldest sister jumps up and helps Ginger out of the car. She laughs, "This looks like a joke. How many pregnant women can fit in a Civic?" She announces, "I had the boys pick up my favorite paint samples and I've narrowed it down to forty-eight."

"Forty-eight?" I gasp. "I thought we'd just pick two or three different colors and paint the whole house with those."

Renée rolls her eyes at me. "Mimi, don't be ridiculous. We can pick two or three basic colors and then use different shades throughout but two or three colors alone would reduce your home to commonplace."

As a former super model turned designer, Renée has been wealthy a lot longer than I have and therefore I bow to her expertise. God forbid my five million dollar home be construed as common. This is the first time I've seen the house without the former owner's things in it and the entry is no longer warm and comforting. It's vast and unwelcoming.

Renée announces, "I'm glad you decided to paint before moving in." She indicates dark rectangles on the walls where pictures once hung blocking the paint from fading evenly. "Now in here," she spokesmodels with a sweeping wave of her arm, "I was thinking you could keep the same earthy tones but maybe darken the color a bit to give the feeling of intimacy, something along the lines of this, Mushroom Bisque." She opens a small plastic jar of paint and slathers some on the wall. She continues, "It's a silvery grey, slightly hued with taupe and just the slightest mossy tinge."

I'm experiencing the same sensation I have when a self-proclaimed wine expert expounds upon the wonders of a particular chardonnay; a ripe melon bouquet with undertones of freshly mown grass and sunlight; great legs with a full nose of roses. Ginger lets out a giggle as I roll my eyes.

Renée looks between us and demands, "What are you laughing at?"

I reply, "You're pretty poetic about a color I'd call greige, that's all."

Renée huffs, "I'm a designer, for God's sake! So shoot me for knowing my colors and being able to express subtlety and nuance." She continues, "What do you think? Do you like it?"

I reply, "I do, but now I want some mushroom bisque."

Gingers exclaims, "Me too. Why don't we go out for lunch when we're done here?"

I willingly agree and it's Renée's turn to roll her eyes. She agrees, "Fine with me but can we try to stay focused?"

Renée quits telling us what the paint colors are after Ginger and I get into a debate over whether we should paint the powder room Raspberry Mousse or Pistachio Cream. Neither one of us care if the room gets painted hot pink or green, we're just focused on what we want for dessert after we have our mushroom bisque at lunch.

But Renée's plan backfires. Once she stops telling us the colors we start inventing them. When the eldest of our sisterhood brushes a yellowish cream on the kitchen walls, Ginger declares, "I'd call that one Crème Brulee!"

I counter with, "No, no, I'd call it Banana Cream Pie."

Renée demands, "If you don't stop and get serious about picking colors, I'm going home."

Her threat is enough to shake me up and get down to business. The thought of having to choose paint for the whole house is beyond daunting. In the end, I wind up picking colors with names like Chai, Pavement, Siren and Wharf. Serendipitously, the ones I decide on for Elliot's office are called Editor's Grey and Paperback, and I did that without even knowing their names!

Chapter 25

Over lunch with my sisters, I broach the subject of weird pregnancy symptoms. I don't tell them about my claustrophobia for Sophie for fear Ginger might glom onto it. What with three buns in her oven, I run the risk of wigging her out and I don't want to do that. So I keep things generic and ask Renée, "What's the weirdest sensation you had when you were pregnant with Finn and Camille?"

She thinks a moment before answering, "Hot flashes."

Ginger asks, "Like menopausal hot flashes?"

Renée replies, "God, I hope not. But I'm guessing the answer is yes. I would be freezing cold one moment and the next I'd feel like I was on fire. Seriously, I would have lain naked on an iceberg if given the option."

Thank God I haven't experienced that one yet. Of course the fun isn't over. I have another thirteen weeks to go. I ask Ginger, "How 'bout you? What's the weirdest feeling you've had?"

She exhales slowly and answers, "I have six feet, six hands, and three heads in my uterus. It's a wonder my lungs haven't been shoved up through my throat."

Curiously, I prod, "How does that make you feel?"

Ginger looks at me like I'm an idiot, "Crowded. It makes me feel crowded. How do you think it would make me feel?"

I venture, "Do you wonder how they feel?"

She answers, "The babies? I assume they feel warm, cozy and pissed off they don't have any room."

Aha! This is the perfect opening to come clean about my insanity, so I say, "I've started going to a sort of support group."

Renée turns her head toward me so quickly she may need a neck brace for whiplash. "What kind of support group?"

"You know, the regular kind. It's just a group of women from Dr. Fermin's office who are having prenatal and postnatal issues."

Ginger worriedly inquires, "What's your issue?"

I look between my sisters and answer, "I've recently begun to get claustrophobic."

Renée nods her head, "That not that uncommon, actually. I had that after Finn was born. I couldn't close the bathroom door without feeling panicky."

"Well," I start, "I'm not claustrophobic for me as much as for Sophie."

Ginger ponders her response before saying, "Listen Meems, I don't want to make light of what you're going through but Sophie is one baby inside a tall mother. She's got enough room. Imagine what she would be feeling if she was one of three."

I stare at my sister and begin to breathe too rapidly. Sweat breaks out on my forehead and I become woozy. I must look a sight because Renée wets her cloth napkin in her ice water and holds it to my forehead. It helps but I'm still inhaling too quickly. So she tells me to cup my hands together and hold them over my nose. She explains, "You're hyperventilating, Meems. You have to slow down your oxygen or you're going to pass out."

I try to do what she says but I can't get over the image of Sophie being one of three babies instead of the only one. Holy, holy, holy crap! I cannot take on panic for kids that don't even exist, can I? What would you even call that, insanity by proxy? Finally, after several minutes of breathing into my hands and creating a small scene, I start to feel more normal.

Renée pats me on the back and says, "Oh Meems, I'm sorry." Then looking at both me and Ginger, she adds, "Parenthood is the craziest thing you're ever going to experience. And I hate to tell you, but just as one thing gets easier another fun-filled adventure takes its place."

Ginger looks a bit alarmed, "But you love being a mother!"

Renée smiles, "I do love it and I wouldn't trade it for anything in the world, but it's a damn hard job."

Ginger and I both look like we want to cry. If Renée, who makes motherhood look like a walk in the park, is coming clean about how hard it is, we're screwed. I mean, heck, Ginger will have three babies to take care of and I can't seem to keep all of my marbles in place just being pregnant with one. Suddenly mushroom bisque doesn't seem nearly as tempting a large sedative.

I offer, "There are quite a few women in my group with

some odd postpartum issues."

Ginger asks, "Really, like what?"

"Well, there's this one gal who seems to be on the verge of mental breakdown over fitting into her size two power suits again. She's even had to stop breast feeding because her body doesn't have enough fat stored to create milk."

Renée says, "I ate like a cow while I was breast feeding and still dropped weight. That's the beauty of the thing. You're giving your babies a rocking start by building a healthy brain and immune system and you get to eat burgers and lose weight at the same time."

Ginger laughs, "Says the supermodel. I know plenty of women who breast fed and gained weight."

Renée smiles, "Happily, I wasn't one of them." Then she asks, "What else, Meems?"

I briefly wonder if I'm breaking any confidences by sharing these stories but justify it by the fact that my sisters don't know these women and I'm not using their names. "Well, this one woman is afraid of terrorist attacks. She's worried she can't protect her kids from ISIS."

Ginger gasps, "In Hilldale? The chances aren't too great of a terrorist attack here."

I answer, "She was supposed to take her oldest son to New York City on a class trip and told him he couldn't go at the last minute. Apparently, he's threatening to run away from home in retaliation."

Renée says, "I can't wait until you two are done breeding so we can have these conversations over cocktails. Do me a favor though? Let's not talk about any of this in front of Muffy.

There's no sense in worrying her about a future she isn't even thinking of yet."

I respond, "Oh, I don't know about that. I'm guessing Muff and Kevin might be entertaining the idea of marriage and babies."

My eldest sister allows, "I'm sure they are. But she's probably not taken her day dreams so far as including the roller coaster ride of parenthood."

I confess, "I'm a little worried about going back to Dr. Fermin's support group."

Ginger asks, "Why? It sounds like a great place to vent. In fact I might go with you sometime."

I answer, "You're more than welcome to join me if I go back. The problem is I'm very susceptible. If I'm making spaghetti for dinner and then see a commercial for pizza, all of sudden I need pizza. Spaghetti be damned!"

Renée nods, "That's true. You've been like that as long as I've known you. Are you worried you're going to take on other people's worries?"

I nod my head, "I've already started thinking about ISIS way more than I should." With a smile, I add, "I'm not so worried about getting back into my size twos though."

Both of my sisters laugh. Being that I was in third grade the last time I was a size two, we all know that ship has sailed.

Chapter 26

We have five potential nannies coming by for interviews this morning. I feel terrible wasting their time but it's the only way to keep Elliot and his rabid patrician sensibilities at bay. We've begun packing up the Mercer Street house so the dining room is stacked floor to ceiling with boxes. His Lordship suggested having the movers pack us but I put a stop to that nonsense. Not only do I want to go through my things and get rid of the junk in my life, but there's only so much I'm willing to have others do for me. I have a disturbing vision of Elliot's nanny pre-chewing all of his food so he didn't have to wear himself out masticating.

Elliot is currently at Parliament meeting with Jonathan about his new book release, so I'm supposed to start with the nannies until he gets home. This is totally absurd, if you ask me, because I'm the one who doesn't want a nanny. My husband has completely mislaid his trust if he thinks I'm going to give him an honest account of these interviews.

The first applicant to arrive is exactly what I would expect a nanny to look like. She's wearing some kind of archaic gray uniform and her hair is short and shot through with silver strands. If I had to guess, I would peg her at fifty and hailing from some Eastern Bloc country. She's built like a German swimmer and her name is Elka.

When I open the door, Elka nods her head once and announces, "I am the nanny." She says it in such an authoritative way, like it's a done deal.

I invite her to sit in the living room and offer her a cup of coffee or tea, but she declines. So I ask, "How long have you been a nanny?"

She responds curtly, "Twenty-four years."

"And what aspects of the job do you like the most?" I'm totally winging it here, but this is something I used to ask hopefuls at Parliament who desired a future at our PR firm.

She stares at me like I've just asked her what size bra she wears, before responding, "I like the order."

Not the answer I was expecting. One would think a prospective caregiver of young life would try to impress the parents with their love of children. Not Elka. I imagine she and Colonel Von Trapp would have hit it off like a house on fire. She could have probably taught him a couple toots on his whistle even he didn't know.

I'm not planning on giving Elka much time but I don't feel right about dismissing her after only two questions, so I soldier on, "What is the longest you've stayed with a family?"

"Seven and one-half months." Responding to my look of surprise, she adds, "I find most Americans do not like order."

Well, then, okay. What now? I throw out of couple more inquiries before informing Elka, "We'll let the agency know once we've made our decision. Thank you for your time."

Elka does not take the hint and stand up to vacate the premises. Instead, she declares, "I will speak to your husband now."

Excuse me, what? "I'm sorry, Elka, Mr. Fielding is at work and won't be home for a while. Rest assured, I'll tell him all about you." Again she doesn't budge, so I prompt, "We'll let the agency know."

Elka demands, "I will wait."

I have a vision of having to physically eighty-six this battleax from my house when Elliot strolls through the front door. I turn to greet him and announce, "I'm so happy you're home! Elka, here is refusing to leave until she speaks with you."

Elliot takes my tone and looks to the nanny with surprise. "Is there some reason you need to speak to me? I assure you my wife is perfectly capable of interviewing you."

Elka replies, "She asked me why I enjoy my job and I told her I like the order. Being a disorderly American, she did not appreciate my answer. So I wished to speak with you. You are British and therefore understand the necessity of things being kept in their proper place, children included."

Elliot looks surprised by her candor. "Thank you for the vote of confidence, Elka, but I don't think you're the right fit for us."

At that she stands up abruptly, nods her head once and let's herself out the front door. I shake my head at Elliot and demand, "This is the kind of person you want living in our home and taking care of our daughter?"

He looks surprised by my anger. "Clearly not. I dismissed her. I want someone who is going to love Sophie as much as we do. After all, she's our child, not a military campaign."

With that declaration, I throw myself into my husband's arms. "Thank God! I was a bit worried Elka was exactly what you have in mind."

Elliot kisses me on the head and gives me a little squeeze. "Mimi, my love, my nanny's name was Mrs. Hedgegrove and she was a sweet, lovely old gal who adored me and Pip like we were her own grandchildren. She made us tea every day, cleaned us up after rolling in the mud and made up stories about African safaris. She was a delight and I relish that she was a part of my childhood." Then he pats me on the fanny and adds, "That's the kind of experience I'd like Sophie to have. Not a drill sergeant who blathers on about order."

I reach up and give the Brit a tender and thoroughly impressive kiss. These are the moments when I'm sure we're going to overcome the hurdles of our vastly different lifestyles. I can just picture a Mrs. Doubtfiresque, Mrs. Hedgegrove, fussing over Elliot and his sister and I admire him for wanting the same thing for our children. After all, if I had the countess for a mother, I'd crave someone to love me with unrestrained joy, too. Victoria does not bring about thoughts of tender maternal moments. She was probably too busy lunching with the queen and killing cute little foxes on the hunt, probably bare-handed.

The next three women we meet don't inspire a lot more confidence than Elka. They are a cross section of boring middle-aged women who seem to lack excitement for their chosen careers. By the time the fifth applicant shows up, I'm sure I can convince Elliot the error of his thinking. Then the doorbell rings.

I jump up to answer, eager to put the great nanny debate to bed. I pull the door open and there she stands. She looks like the cross between a 1970's hippy and a new millennium hipster. She's wearing a long jean skirt with patches sewn into it, cowboy boots, a flannel shirt tied at the waist and a derby hat, covering what looks like a pile of curly brown hair. She's completely unexpected.

I greet, "Hello, you must be Abigail."

With a huge grin on her face, she replies, "How'd you guess?"

"Well," I smiled, "you're the last person we're meeting today and I haven't crossed Abigail off my list yet." I lift my list and wink, "Pretty ingenious of me, huh?"

She laughs, "Totally." Then she walks in, puts her hand out and introduces herself to Elliot. She exclaims, "I love your house. It's so cute!"

I'm guessing our final candidate is about twenty-five or so, though her energy feels a lot younger. She's appealing without being obviously pretty, but it's her aura I find so compelling. She's sparkly and effervescent. If she was a drink, she'd be champagne.

I offer her a cup of coffee but she refuses, instead she pulls out a bottle of something green and chunky looking. She lifts it up and announces, "Kale and pomegranate smoothie, so delicious and unbelievably nourishing."

I gag a little at the thought, yet I'm kind of jazzed that she's into health food. I ask, "Do you make things like that for the kids you take care of?"

Abbie, as she asks us to call her, responds, "Oh, well, this would be my first gig. I haven't done any professional nannying yet."

I find I'm disappointed by her response. While I'm not really looking to hire a nanny, she would have been my vision for the perfect one, had she been experienced, that is. I ask, "What in the world made you want to be a nanny?"

Abbie laughs, "I never really thought I'd be one but I have to survive, right?"

Elliot interrupts, "What have you been doing to make money up until now?"

Our guest answers, "Recycled art collages." Noting our confused looks, she explains, "You know like scrap metal, sea glass and assorted trash all fashioned together into art. It's a totally invigorating way to express yourself."

I can't relate to this at all, but I still find myself infected by her excitement. "So what made you change your direction to being a nanny?"

Abbie explains, "I'm the oldest of nine children. Taking care of kids just comes naturally to me. So I figure I can be a nanny and make money to create my art when I'm off the clock. Cool, right?"

Elliot smiles, nods his head and replies, "Cool."

I offer, "You know this is a live-in position."

Abbie answers, "I didn't, but that's awesome!" Looking around, she says, "This would be a great house to live in, too." I don't know why but I don't tell her we're leaving this house behind and moving on up ala George and Weezie Jefferson. "I'd be able to rent an industrial space for my art so I wouldn't crowd us with it." Looking at my stomach, she asks, "What number are you working on there?"

I answer, "Number one."

She looks shocked and turns between me and Elliot before asking, "I don't mean to be dense or anything but why do you need a nanny for one baby?"

My husband raises an eyebrow, "Mimi might go back to work after Sophie is born. Surely we'd need a nanny then, yes?"

Our prospective employee looks confused before answering, "Actually, you'd just need daycare, not a nanny." She explains, "I thought you'd have three or four kids for me to take care of, at least." Then she adds, "I'm not sure this is the job for me. I don't like to be bored." Then she adds, "And babies sleep, a lot."

I'm a little disappointed even though I don't really want a nanny or rather didn't want one until meeting Abigail. So I say, "Well, if we hire you, we could use you in other areas, like light housekeeping and maybe cooking once in a while." Why I'm saying this I don't know. I don't want a nanny and I certainly don't want a housekeeper or cook. But I really like this girl. She seems like she'd be fun to be around and I bet kids love her. Also, if she likes kids so much, maybe I could get her to keep an eye on Ginger's brood every now and again.

Abbie announces, "I love to cook! I made most of the meals at home growing up and I make a killer whole wheat tofu mac and cheese with pine nuts and kale." Kale seems to be a staple in this girl's life. She shrugs her shoulders, "What the heck, I can do anything you need me to do. I don't mind cleaning and I'm brilliant at mowing lawns. I could be your gal Friday!" She amends, "As long as you give me enough work to earn my keep."

After another ten minutes of small talk, we learn that Abbie's family lives on a farm in rural Oregon and that she's not seeing anyone, but if she does, she promises to keep all nocturnal activities off the premises; we bid her goodbye and promise to be in touch with her agency soon.

Once she's gone, Elliot and I snuggle in front of the fire and he teases, "So, you don't want a nanny, huh?"

I smack his arm. "No, I don't. But I think I want Abigail."

Chapter 27

I continue to debate whether we really need to hire a nanny until the week before Christmas. Elliot talks me into giving it a six month trial and as I already like Abigail, I agree. I figure with a house as big as Fielding Abbey, that's right I've named it, we never have to see each other if it's not working out.

I call to inform the agency of our decision and learn that Abbie can't wait three plus months for our baby to come before she's employed, which is how I wind up hiring a nanny for me and Elliot. My hubby has a good laugh when I tell him our childcare provider will be moving in with us right after the New Year, months before there's a child to care for. But I figure I can use her to help get the house in order.

We're going to get our Christmas tree today. I find the whole thing bittersweet. This is my first Christmas as a married woman and expectant mother, which makes it as sweet as can be, but it's also the last one in my house. I love my little yellow house and all the memories I've made here. Sure, I was single and lonely most of the time, but I bought this place all by myself and I don't want to say goodbye to it yet.

Elliot suggests we don't sell it but offer to let Muffy and Kevin move in as caretakers. Muff moved out of her house after she divorced Tom, her cheat of a husband, and moved in with Kevin, who's leasing a condo ever since *his* philandering wife left him. With their new business venture, The Buff Muff, just starting out, neither wants to buy a place until the market turns a bit. It sounds like a brilliant idea to me and we're going to put it to them Christmas morning.

The holidays are going to be a low key affair this year. Renée and Laurent are taking the kids to Paris to visit Laurent's family. So Mom has decided she and Muffy will cook Christmas Eve and New Year's Eve dinners at her house. We'll have everyone over Christmas morning for assorted goodies that I'll be buying at the bakery and Ginger and Jonathan will make an egg casserole and ham for New Year's Day brunch.

The earl and countess are going to be spending their holiday in London, which makes me happier than you can imagine. Even though we came to a bit of a truce over Thanksgiving, there's only so much of her ladyship I can handle. I feel like I have to be on my best behavior when I'm around her and that can be rather exhausting.

We are officially moving into Fielding Abbey on December 27th. It's all a bit harried, but I suppose there's no point in waiting. The painters are finishing up this week and there isn't another thing that needs to be done to the place.

I am officially 27 weeks pregnant and Miss Sophie has expressed a real love of jazzy Christmas music. Every time Rockin' Around the Christmas Tree or Holly Jolly Christmas comes on the radio, she kicks up her heels like she's auditioning for the Rockettes. It's by far the coolest and strangest feeling in the world.

Ginger's abdomen is so full of babies that when she lifts her shirt you can see various hands and feet pushing out as if trying to escape. Speaking of which, my panic attacks over Sophie feeling confined have eased up since starting a gestational yoga class last week. There seems to be something about the breathing that helps me win the mind over matter fight.

Ginger comes with me to class and pretty much just lies on her yoga mat and does nothing else. There are no movements that come easy to her right now and the doctor recommends not starting any new exercise at this stage in the game. She tags along to get out of the house and because we go out for frozen yogurt after every class. White chocolate raspberry mousse with eighty-three assorted toppings is a temptation few could resist.

The triplets are all doing well and the doctor expects no complications as long as she can keep them in for another month. Although, they're hoping to get as close to thirty-six weeks as possible. There are no guarantees with multiples though, so she's taking it really easy.

Jonathan has given up traveling until after the babies come and our mom has taken over their grocery shopping and other sundry errands as Ginger doesn't drive anymore and Jonathan is working around the clock.

Their nursery is all set up with three cribs, three mobiles, a changing station and more stuffed animals than you can shake a stick at. She's gone with a gender neutral owl theme that I tried to talk her out of. My reasoning is that owls stay up all night and you don't want to send the wrong message. She told me owls were cute and babies weren't smart enough to grasp the subtleties. It's her funeral.

The only real reason I'm excited for our move is to start getting Sophie's room ready. The painters covered the walls in a whispery pink called Cotton Candy Clouds and the crown molding offers a crisp white in contrast. I haven't ordered any of the furniture yet because I've been a little preoccupied getting everything ready for the move, which turns out to be more of a chore than I remember.

As I pack up my house I realize I'm something of a hoarder. I have five boxes full of recipes I've clipped over the last fifteen years, one crammed with wedding ideas that I started in high school and fourteen-and-a-half bottles of sunscreen varying in age from 1998 to just last summer. I've throw away nine tubes of ancient lipstick, all clothes older than five years and six bottles of hairspray with the nozzles glued shut. I've also gone nuts and pitched all the spices that moved in with me seven years ago. Note to self, have Abbie shop for spices in the New Year. Oh, and mention my aversion to kale.

Chapter 28

Christmas was relaxing and thoroughly delightful. It was also extremely quiet with Finn and Camille in Paris. We missed them dreadfully but know that next year will more than make up for it with six grandchildren under foot. Everyone was on their best behavior and the stress levels were in the negatives. I can't help but think it was the calm before the storm.

I think back to all the proclamations of an enchanted life that were bandied about at our wedding and occasionally worry the pendulum is destined to swing back. But for now, I'm just going to enjoy everything going in our favor.

Today is moving day and I'm very emotional and a touch grumpy. Elliot suggests we go out for breakfast before the men come to uproot my whole life. I burst into ugly tears and accuse him of wanting to rob me of my last meal at home.

When he proposes he go out and get us breakfast and bring it back, I yell, "And never use my stove again?"

Somewhere around the time I call him an uppity aristocratic, thoroughly unprovoked, he decides to humor me and not fight when I poke him. This just pisses me off more.

Yes, I know I'm totally irrational but I'm itching for battle. The least he can do is accommodate me.

It turns out the only person willing to indulge me is the head mover, Bob. Every time I bark at him to be careful with a box, he stops and yells, "Lady, this isn't the first house I've moved! If you don't trust us, fire us. Otherwise, get out of my way."

I turn bright red with fury when he insults my dining room set by commenting that he and his wife bought one just like it at a yard sale when they first got married. Don't get me wrong, I love a good garage sale but there's something in his tone that seems judgmental.

At the new house I show Bob where the kitchen is and instruct that I'd like all the boxes piled on surfaces, not the floor, so I can reach them when I unpack them. Miss Sophie is seriously getting in the way of my even seeing the floor, yet alone bending to reach it. So much so, I'm back in loafers because I can't finagle the pose necessary to put on tennis shoes.

When he nearly drops the first box of dishes on the counter, I admonish, "Be careful! We didn't hire you to break things."

That's when he suggests, "You might want to take your shoes off."

"Excuse me, what?"

He laughs snidely, "Well, you're already pregnant, now you just need to be barefoot to get the picture right."

What in the hell? Steam starts to rise out my ears and I'm ready to pummel the stuffing out of this moron. Instead, I yell, "Elliot, get in here!"

The future earl hightails it into the kitchen to find me with my hands on my hips, my jaw clenched in fury and panting like I've just run a marathon. "Darling, what's wrong?"

"This, this, maggot," I thrust my hands forward in a very Italian gesture to indicate I'm speaking about Bob, "has been insulting me and our things all day." Then I demand, "I want you to fire him, now!" That's right, Bob, put that in your pipe and smoke it.

Elliot looks from me to Bob and after a significant moment of silence, bursts into laughter. He finally manages, "You've played your part very well, Bob, thank you."

Wait, what? Why is my husband thanking this offensive beast?

Our mover shrugs his shoulders and joins into the laughter. "I did my best, Mr. Fielding."

I'm totally confused, so I demand, "What in the hell is going on here?"

My husband explains, "Darling, you seemed to be looking for a bit of a fight this morning."

"Yeah, so? I'm leaving my house. I'm a tad emotional," I offer defensively.

"Well," he continues, "I don't want to fight with you. But I thought having someone to clash with might take your mind off your sadness. So I told Bob what was going on and he offered to be your target."

I don't quite know how to respond to this. I know I've been a handful today, but this seems like a betrayal. Elliot couldn't deal with me so he tells the mover what a pain I am and the two of them conspire to keep me mad. At the same time, fighting with Bob has totally taken my mind off moving and truth be told, it's been kind of fun. I'm torn between anger and gratitude. Much like a thunderstorm is the result of two opposing energies, so is my reaction to this news. I burst into tears.

Elliot rushes to my side and wraps me in his arms. He apologizes, "I'm so sorry, darling. I just didn't know what to do."

A chagrined Bob offers, "Geez Mrs. Fielding, please don't take it so hard. I'm sorry, too. My wife gets just like you when she's pregnant and I know she would love someone to give her a reason to scream." He continues, "I only wanted to help."

I decide to let them both off the hook. My temper did take my mind off the move and now that we're in the new house I find that I'm thoroughly wrung out and explain all I want to do is lay down.

Bob offers, "I had my boys put your bed together first thing."

With a watery smile, I excuse myself and go upstairs to the master bedroom. I'm currently so overwhelmed by this vast new house that I want to drive back to Mercer St. for my nap. Although, there's no bed there now so I'd have to sleep on the floor.

What is the opposite of claustrophobic? Because that's what I'm feeling right now. Every room on the second floor is totally vacant with the exception of our room and the furniture in there is so dwarfed by the space, it feels pretty close to empty.

I fall into a restless sleep and wind up having the same

dream I had when I was first pregnant, the one where Prince Charles wants to rub my bunion but turns into a lizard and licks it instead. I haven't consciously thought the future king of England looks like a reptile but after these recurring reveries I've started Googling pictures of him and there is some resemblance. No offense meant.

I finally wake up at dusk and I'm starving. I don't bother with shoes and opt to pad down the hall barefooted. I know we'll eventually get some rugs but the cool of the hardwood is very comforting for Edith. You might have noticed that even though she's still around, my bunion has stopped talking to me. It makes me wonder if she ever really did talk or if I was presenting with early signs of insanity. Either way, I don't miss the nagging.

Elliot atones for his earlier sins by bribing me with Chinese food. He's ordered all of my favorites including Kung Pao Shrimp, Cashew Chicken, Won Ton Soup and Pork Eggrolls. So I decide to forgive him. It should come as no surprise to you that I can be bought with food. It's my Buddha nature.

My table looks like doll house furniture in this dining room. The ceilings are twelve feet high and the huge picture window overlooking the rose garden makes the already palatial dimensions seem twice as big, thusly, causing everything in it to look twice as small. Elliot has suggested I go furniture shopping to fill the house out a bit. He doesn't think he has the time to join me, so I'm waiting for Abbie to move in. This will be her first order of business as my nanny/decorator.

Chapter 29

Our first few days in the new house make me feel like I'm in the Twilight Zone. I expect Rod Serling to peak around corners and offer, "You are about to enter another dimension; a dimension not only of sight and sound but of mind. A journey into a wondrous land of imagination. Next stop, the Twilight Zone."

On day two, my mom and sisters show up unexpectedly. I answer the door wearing one of Elliot's old button down shirts and a pair of pregnancy yoga pants. My hair is in a ponytail and my feet are bare. Ginger greets, "You look adorable!" Then pushes me out of the way, "Let us in."

Their arms are loaded with flowers and bags of groceries. My mom announces, "We know you haven't made it to the store yet so we thought we'd bring in a few staples." Their idea of staples includes extra-sharp cheddar cheese, Triscuits, pancake mix, Nutella and the whole cookie aisle. They know me well.

Once seated in the living room, Muffy says, "You need some furniture, Meems."

Ginger adds, "You need more than some. You need a lot."

Renée contributes, "You actually need more than furniture. You need a decorator."

I'm about to poo-poo such a ridiculous notion, when Elliot strolls in and replies, "We *do* need a decorator. Can you recommend someone, Renée?"

She beams, "You know I can. I've already called my friend Andrew, and he can get started this week."

I groan, "Renée, I was planning on going furniture shopping. I'm sure we don't need a professional."

My sister responds, "Really? You were going to do the drapes, window treatments, carpets and walls too? Mimi, decorating is more than just furniture. It's creating a mood." She continues, "Andrew decorated for the previous owners of this very house."

Startled, I ask, "How do you know that?"

"The pictures were in his portfolio."

Well crap, I love how this house looked before the last occupants moved all their stuff out. Andrew turned an obscene amount of space into a very warm and welcoming home. I'm not sure I can do the same with a trip to Pottery Barn, so I agree. "Fine, give me his number and I'll set it up."

Renée hands me his card and replies, "He'll be here tomorrow morning at ten."

"You already made the appointment?"

She smiles, "I didn't think you'd go for it."

I huff, "That's pretty sneaky. What if I wasn't here?"

My oldest sister answers, "I would have been here and gotten started without you. In fact," she adds, "I'm planning on coming anyway. Hope you're good with that."

What can I say? Clearly, I have no say in the matter. Of all my family members, Renée makes the most sense as a helper. She lives in a house nearly as big as this one so she understands what it takes to make it homey.

Muffy says that she and Kevin love living on Mercer St. and I'm delighted to hear it. I miss my house so much that last night I wanted to drive over and crawl into bed with them. I'm pretty sure that would have gone over like a lead balloon so I made myself stay put. Maybe I'll have Andrew start with the master bedroom so I can at least be comfortable in there.

Ginger slips her shoes off and props her feet up on the coffee table. To say her ankles are huge would be an understatement of epic proportion. Her ankles appear to be the size of her thighs. Our mother notices at the same moment I do and gasps, "Ginger, your ankles!"

Gingers sighs, "They're pretty big, huh?"

Renée answers, "Not big, no. More like dangerously huge. What's going on?"

Triplet mama answers, "They started swelling a few days ago. I've been told that's pretty normal though so I'm not worried."

Renée responds, "Ankle swelling is normal, but there's nothing normal about this. You need to see the doctor."

Ginger doesn't believe her until we help her up and show her the reality of her cankles in a full length mirror. "Holy, heck, I think you're right! Who wants to drive me?"

We all want to go so Mom offers, "There's enough room for us all in my mini-van. I'll drive."

You might be wondering why my mom has a mini-van and the answer is actually pretty sweet. When she found out she had four grandkids on the way, she traded in her Acura so she could drive all the babies at the same time. When asked where she thinks she'd be driving four babies at once, she replied, "None of you girls would sleep during the day unless you were in a moving car. I figure I'll just pull up to your houses, pick up the kids and take them for a snooze cruise." Now that, right there, is grandmother of the year. I'm sure Ginger will particularly appreciate the break.

Speaking of Ginger, we all load into the mini-van and head straight over to see Dr. Fermin. Even though my sister doesn't have an appointment, the nurse takes one look at her and ushers her right back to an exam room.

Dr. Fermin rushes in and declares, "Let's take your blood pressure and see what's going on." With the cuff firmly in place we all await the outcome. The doctor, announces, "Okay, then, we're off to the hospital."

I unthinkingly do my Bugs Bunny impersonation and ask, "What's up, doc?"

She announces, "Preeclampsia." She explains, "Which means high blood pressure. If Ginger were a couple weeks farther along in her pregnancy, we'd be taking those babies out today."

We're all stunned. We're speechless. I'm the first to find my voice and ask, "So how are you planning to proceed?"

Dr. Fermin replies, "Hospitalization and bed rest." To Ginger, she adds, "We're going to start giving you some steroid injections to speed up the babies' lung development as well. The nurse is calling the ambulance. I'll meet you all at the hospital." Then she hurries out of the room.

It feels like time stops. None of us jump to action. We all just stand around and stare at each other consumed by fear. Ginger finally asks, "Will someone please call Jonathan?"

Her request pops the bubble on our paralysis and we all start scurrying about. Moments later the paramedics come in and move my sister onto a gurney. As they push her out the door, my mom asks the EMT, "Can I drive to the hospital with her?"

Before they can answer, Ginger pleads, "Please, let her." There's something about a crisis that makes you want your mother above all others. It doesn't matter if you're thirty-seven and about to become a mother yourself. There's nothing as comforting as Mom.

Muffy, Renée and I all pile into Mom's mini-van and call our significant others to inform them what's going on. They all want to come to the hospital but we order them to stay put and await further instruction. For the meantime, our father is the only one we allow.

After an hour, Ginger's blood pressure starts to come down a bit, but the doctor tells her she's seen the last of the outside world until after the triplets are born. This news makes her cry. The thought of being in the hospital for so long is daunting but not as scary as the idea of the babies coming too early.

Dr. Fermin assures us there is a high chance of long term complications if the triplets are born too soon; cerebral palsy, vision and breathing problems being the most worrisome. Although, Ginger's health is the first and foremost important thing, she assures us they will take the babies that day if the situation becomes life threatening for my sister.

We're all a nervous wreck and want to stay by her side but the doc wants us gone. "Ginger will be able to relax more easily if you're not all hovering around her."

Jonathan assures, "I'll call you the moment anything changes."

We only agree to leave once we've worked out a schedule between us. We'll all come every day, just at different times. This arrangement allows Jonathan to keep working so he'll be able to take more time off after the birth.

Chapter 30

Ginger has been in the hospital for four days. She's holding her own but still won't be sprung until after the birth. Meanwhile, we're all thrilled that no one's been born yet.

Renée's friend Andrew is one of the most eccentric gay men I've ever had the pleasure of meeting. He's a dead ringer for Andrew McCarthy in his younger days, which makes him a treat to look at, even though he's a total prima donna. He doesn't seem to want any input from me other than the "feel" I want for the house.

I reply that I want it to feel like it did when the last owners lived here. So he asks me, "What did that *feel* like to you?"

I answer, "It felt warm and welcoming. It was homey and oddly cozy given the dimensions of the place."

The whole time I'm talking, Andrew is shaking his head like I've got it all wrong. "It felt like contemporary meets traditional for an espresso at an outdoor café by the Seine."

I look between him and Renée and demand, "What in the hell does that even mean?"

Andrew clucks his tongue and retorts, "I need visions,

emotions; I need colors! I can't work with pedestrian sentiments like 'warm' and 'cozy.' Give me sensations and locations!"

What I'd like to do is give him a black eye. But I really want to get this meeting over with so I try, "How about traditional meets casual for French fries in Central Park?"

Andrew responds like I've just goosed him. He squeaks and jumps before going silent. He stares straight ahead as though he's in some kind of hypnotic trance. Then he closes his eyes and rotates his head around his shoulders. I look at Renée to see if this is normal or if he needs a medical intervention. She just rolls her eyes as if to say, "Yeah, he's dramatic, just go with it."

After about three minutes, the flamboyant designer pops his peepers open and declares, "I can work with that!" He pronounces, "I'll have designs for you later in the week."

Before he leaves, I take him up to Sophie's room and declare my vision for her space. I sum it up as feminine meets whimsical eating scones while punting on the Thames. If nothing else I'm looking forward to his interpretation of that. Of course I'm really just screwing with him.

Abigail moves in today and I'm oddly excited to see her again. Now that we've hired Andrew to decorate, I won't need her help in that arena so I'm hoping to start her on organizing the kitchen cabinets.

Elliot's been working on his new book nonstop since we've moved in and I'm starting to feel neglected. But I don't want to come off all needy and pathetic by complaining or worse yet, sitting in his office and staring at him while he works. This is part of the reason I'm excited Abbie is moving in before Sophie's born. It'll be nice to have another adult to talk to.

As soon as the doorbell rings, I move as fast as my cumbersome body will let me. I open it to find a wide-eyed nanny on the step. The first thing out of her mouth is, "*This* is where you live?"

I nod my head in response, "We moved in last week."

Abbie shakes her head, opens her mouth, closes it, shakes her head again and manages, "I like the other house better."

"Really?" I ask. That surprises me. I thought I was the only one to find my new home overwhelming.

"Really," she answers. "This," she gestures towards the façade, "is big enough to fit my whole town in Oregon!"

I pull her inside. "I agree, it's a bit much, but Elliot loves it. Actually, I love it too. It's just taking me some time to get used to."

I offer Abbie some tea and cookies and then we sit down to chat in the breakfast nook. I confide, "Elliot grew up in houses like this. His father's an earl."

Abigail looks appalled. "Oh my God, really? I mean, it's just that …well… you know about the royal family, right?"

I answer, "I know of them. I'm not sure what you mean, about them." I prod, "What about them?"

My new employee actually looks like she might be sick before answering, "Oh, nothing."

"What do you mean nothing? What is it that you know about them that I don't?"

The nanny shrugs her shoulders, "Nothing, really." Then she changes the subject by asking, "So where's my room?"

I thought we'd put Abigail out in the pool house. That way

she'd have her own space and we could all adjust to each other without constantly being in each other's path. Elliot thought Abbie should have the connecting room to Sophie's but I'm not so sure. I tell him we can always have her move into the main house if we need to but let's start out my way. So I take her outside and show her her new digs.

Abbie's response is actually giddy excitement. The pool house isn't big, probably under eight hundred square feet, but the nanny loves it. "Wow! My own little house, really?" She walks around taking it all in and exclaims, "I love it!"

I'm glad to see her enthusiasm. What with her initial reaction to our house and horror that Elliot is from such an illustrious line, I thought we might lose her before she even moved in. After expending her excitement at her new space, Abbie nervously asks, "Is Elliot related to the royal family?"

I have to think for a moment before answering, "If so, it's very distantly. He's only eighteenth in line for the throne, so it can't be too close of a relationship."

All color fades from her face and Abbie answers with a question of her own, "He's in line for the throne?"

"Very distantly." I try to assure her.

Again I get the feeling like she wants to bolt. "Abbie, what's going on? Why do you hate the royals so much?"

Her smile is as unconvincing as her answer, "Oh, gee, I don't hate them, really. I don't even know them." There's a story here that I plan on getting to the bottom of but I'm going to have to use some stealth tactics to creep under her radar. In the meantime I lead her back to the kitchen to start operation cabinet organization.

Chapter 31

I'm very excited when I wake up to an unexpected phone call from Pip. She's coming to town early and plans to stay until after Sophie's born. She arrives next week which means she'll be here for several weeks.

Elliot is thrilled and suggests I have Andrew hurry and finish a room for her. Abigail is not so excited. In fact she looks about as close to the opposite of excited as you can get. She's also been treating Elliot a little strangely, like he's not quite human or something.

Elliot says he doesn't notice but I'm not really sure he cares. He's so focused on finishing his book, we could probably walk around here dressed like nuns and he wouldn't be any the wiser.

After breakfast, Abbie asks, "So, what's Elliot's sister like?"

I want to tell her all about Pip but having been warned against sharing her talents with people outside the family, I don't. Instead, I answer, "She's kind of quiet and reserved. She's lovely and unassuming." And she talks to dead people, which of course I don't say.

Abbie has started to cook for us. Last night she made stir fried tofu and veggies in a peanut sauce served on a bed of whole wheat soba noodles. If I saw that particular description on a restaurant menu, there's no way I'd have ordered it. But the truth is it's delicious.

This morning for breakfast she makes purple quinoa with roasted butternut squash and sautéed spinach topped with a fried egg. I would have actually run from this one but oh, my stars, yummy!

I tell our nanny I don't mind her cooking for us once and awhile, but as soon as Sophie arrives, she's off the hook. She just smiles and replies, "We'll see."

When Abbie sees how big the garage is (four cars), she asks if she can use an empty corner for her art space. I see no reason why not and tell her to have at it. She's been collecting castoff items from Andrew's decorating project to use on a piece she's working on. So far she's collected carpet samples, empty boxes, scrap wood from the crates that Elliot's stuff is arriving in from England and fabric from upholstery samples. I have a horrific vision of what's going on out there, but I don't ask to see it so I'm not tempted to offer an opinion.

It turns out there isn't much for our nanny to do now that we have a decorator and a cleaning lady. So she's started taking a shift at the hospital with Ginger. As the former director for the Museum of Modern Art, Ginger loves chatting it up with Abbie. In fact, the new piece she's working on is at Ginger's behest. My sister wants to see what the young artist can create with items she's been instructed to use, instead of things she's inspired to choose. The whole thing makes my brain hurt.

Speaking of Andrew, I can't believe I'm saying this but his initial design for the house is so incredibly beautiful and more "me" than the previous owner's design, that I'm completely amazed. I give him four seemingly unrelated things; 1.) Elliot's style: classic 2.) My style: casual 3.) My favorite food: French fries 4.) The location of Elliot's and my first date: Central Park. He throws all that into the quirky little pot that is his head and whips out perfection! So what if he's a bit over-the-top and a little pretentious, he's made my Christmas card list for life.

Ginger is holding her own, but her blood pressure is beginning to creep up again. Dr. Fermin told her to plan on delivering soon. She's hit the thirty-two week mark so chances of long term complications for the babies are greatly reduced. They will have to spend some time in the Neonatal Intensive Care Unit, but we were expecting that anyway.

My artsy sister and her husband have decided to go with the names of the artists they like best, which God help them, are Freda, Salvador and Moses (as in Grandma, not the one parting the sea.) I'm helpless to stop this. Firstly, because they're not my kids and secondly, Ginger has gone through so much to get them and keep them, the last thing she needs is for some busybody up in her business. However, I will approach the kids, when they reach their teens and offer to take them to have their names legally changed.

I'm officially thirty-one weeks pregnant and as graceful as a drunken giraffe. I can't see my feet anymore. I've recently gotten the dreaded hemorrhoids and I'm as continent as a potty-training toddler. My hands have started to swell so I can no longer wear my wedding set and I have acne. It's like God's saying, "Hey, since you've done your bit by continuing the race, you don't need to be attractive anymore." And I'm not, by anyone's estimation. However, Elliot doesn't seem to be looking too closely because he's as amorous as ever, which is one thing I'm not complaining about.

I can no longer get into the bathtub comfortably because once in, I can't get out. There's got to be an easier way to bring life into the world. Whoever came up with this whole pregnancy thing for humans clearly didn't consult the gender destined to grow aforementioned life. Why can't we be like fish and just lay our eggs and be done with it? Even birds have it better than we do. While I'm sure it's uncomfortable to lay an egg, it's out relatively quick and then all they have to do it sit on it and the daddy birds can help. It's not all up to the mama.

Abbie is keeping Ginger company at the hospital, Elliot is editing and Andrew is Andrewing, so I decide to drive to the mall and start buying baby things for Sophie. My first stop is Cinnabon where I consume my allotted daily calories and then some. While I'm licking the last little bit of icing off my fingers, I hear Fat Bottomed Girls start playing on my phone signaling a new text.

I pull out my Android and see a message from Abbie, sent to my whole family. Ginger is being prepped for her C-section and we're all to meet at the hospital, stat!

I break into a cold sweat. This is it. Holy crap! I'm worried for my sister, worried for the babies and as excited as all get out at the same time. A text from Elliot comes right on the heels of Abbie's. He says he'll pick me up on his way.

I message him back to just meet me there. I appreciate his concern, but why go through all the hassle of having to retrieve my car later? So I heave myself up, stand in line to order another dozen sweet rolls, because we're going to need something to occupy our time while we worry about Ginger, and then hightail it out to my Honda.

I'm the last one to arrive in the maternity waiting room. It looks like a chamber of caged animals. My parents are pacing back and forth, Muffy is twitching like she's had six too many espressos, Kevin's twiddling his thumbs like he's trying to spin imaginary gold and Elliot looks like he's about to be sick. The only calm in the whole storm appears to be Renée and Laurent who are quietly speaking to one another in the corner.

I walk in to a round of, "Meems!" I feel like Norm on that old sit-com, Cheers. My mother approaches me first and declares, "Sit down, honey. Have a rest."

"Mom," I remind her, "I'm okay. I'm not the one about to have her babies." Then I pat my tummy and add, "Sophie's in here for a few more weeks yet."

My dad retrieves the box of Cinnabons from my hands and Elliot approaches me, "How are you holding up?"

I whisper, "I'm scared to death." Then ask, "Why did they decide to take the babies today?"

Abbie overhears my question and answers, "Ginger's blood pressure skyrocketed in a matter of twenty minutes. I've never seen people move so fast in my entire life."

This is not good news. It means there will be additional risk to Ginger's health. Crap. I ask, "How's Jonathan holding up?"

My dad replies, "I've never seen him look so stressed, but he's holding it together for your sister."

Ever the voice of reason, Renée announces, "Come on every one, have a cinnamon roll and relax. Ginger's in great hands and everything is going to be just fine."

Her words work like magic and the room calms down almost immediately. Now all we can do is wait.

Chapter 32

One hour and twelve minutes later, Jonathan stumbles into the waiting room still wearing his scrubs. He looks totally wrung out, yet the smile on his face is the dead giveaway that he's the bearer of good news.

With all eyes glued on him, he announces, "Everyone is doing great!" Once that proclamation is made, he seemingly wilts into an overstuffed chair and starts to cry. "Ginger is just amazing. She was so calm and relaxed through the whole thing." His voice catches and he continues, "And the babies are all doing fine. Their heartbeats are strong, they're pink as can be and I can assure you that three crying infants is quite a sound!"

My mom demands, "How much did they weigh?" Birth weight will play a big part in how long they'll have to stay in the hospital. Statistically, babies weighing less than two pounds are looking at a much longer stay. This also greatly depends on lung development and their ability to feed.

Jonathan informs us that Freda weighed in at four pounds five ounces, Salvador at four pounds nine ounces and Moses (baby three) was four pounds two ounces; all-in-all amazing weights for triplets born at thirty-two weeks.

My dad's eyes are tearing and he's smiling, like the cat that ate the canary. He demands, "When can we see them? When can we see Ginger?"

Jonathan responds, "She's in recovery and will be for about another hour. It'll probably take that long to get the babies all checked out and ready to be seen. So why don't you all head over to the cafeteria for lunch? I'll meet you by the viewing window in the NICU in about an hour."

Not that any of us are actually hungry after devouring our weight in Cinnabons but we all head to the cafeteria to give us something to do while we wait. We're all hopped up on sugar, adrenaline and relief. It's a heady combination.

By the time we meet Jonathan in the NICU, we're a bit calmer, but not much. Jonathan signals for the nurse to open the curtain and we get our first glimpse at the new members of our clan. Words escape me. They're perfect and precious and such a miracle that all I can do is thank God for them. It's hard to believe baby number three (because I'm hard-pressed to call her Moses, yet) looks so strong and healthy after giving us all such cause for worry.

The family won't be allowed in to touch them for a couple of days, although Ginger and Jonathan will spend the majority of their time with them. Jonathan is officially on leave for a month so he and Ginger will both have a great opportunity to bond with their children.

As we're walking through the maternity ward, I realize I still haven't made my appointment for a tour, which all moms delivering there are encouraged to do. I also haven't taken a labor class yet. I'm torn between Lamaze and hypno-birth. The thought of being hypnotized into an easier delivery holds a lot of appeal, but there's the side worry of clucking like a chicken through the whole thing.

Ginger looks positively radiant. She's glowing and bright-eyed and has normal blood pressure once again. The doctors are keeping her in the hospital for a minimum of three days and then if all is well, she'll be released. I don't know how she's going to be able to walk out of there without her kids, but she's proven to be so strong, I'm sure she'll do it with grace.

Renée is the first to hug her and demands to know, "Now that we know you're healthy and on your way to recovery, we need to talk about these names." Leave it to the oldest to address the elephant in the room in such a straight forward fashion.

"What about them?" Ginger asks innocently.

"What are we really supposed to call them? I've been trying to come up with acceptable nicknames but I'm drawing a blank."

Jonathan comes to the rescue, "We're actually planning on having them go by their middle names." He looks at his wife and shares a mischievous smile before adding, "We want them each to have a strong and unique first name, but we don't want them to feel hindered by them until they have a chance to grow into them."

Muffy interrupts, "Well thank God for that! We've all been so traumatized by their first names, we haven't even asked about middle names. What are they?"

Ginger announced, "Freda's is Elaine, Salvador's is Jonathan and Moses' is Maureen, for Mom." She smiles at our mother who grabs her hand for a meaningful squeeze. "So we're going to call them, Ellie, Johnny and Mo."

"Hallelujah!" I don't realize I've said this out loud until every eye in the room turns to me. "What I mean is…"

I stumble wondering how to extricate myself from this obvious faux pas, when Kevin comes to the rescue. "What you mean is, hallelujah!" Everyone laughs and Ginger and Jonathan don't appear to take any offense, so all is well.

The Finnegan mob prepares to leave in order to give Ginger and Jonathan some private time. We promise to come back tomorrow at scheduled intervals so as not to overwhelm them.

I wind up leaving my car in the hospital parking lot and driving home with Elliot. We don't say anything on the way to the parking garage but once we get into the car, he grabs my hand and kisses it. "That's going to be us in a few short weeks."

I haven't the words. I'm so totally flooded by emotion and all for my sister. I can't imagine what it's going to feel like when it is us.

Chapter 33

Pip arrives on the same day Richard calls to say he's coming to Chicago on a business trip. Of course I invite him to stay with us without mentioning that Elliot's sister is here as well. No sense in scaring him off. Although I like to think he manned up enough at Thanksgiving to handle it.

Andrew has finished Pip's room and she declares it so perfect she may never leave, which suits me just fine. I find that I love living in a big house as long as it's full. Bodies in motion have a way of making space feel useful, not indulgent.

Abigail's still making most of our meals and while they're truly delicious, they are entirely outside my scope of normal. Quinoa, kale, kohlrabi and hemp milk are now staples in our refrigerator. Thank goodness Milanos, Triscuits and colored mini marshmallows are in the pantry to balance out all the crazy health food.

Abbie chases me around the house with offerings of 12 raw almonds and goji berries for healthy snacks. She makes sure I have organic frozen blueberries at least once a day and has created a chia seed pudding that rivals my lifelong favorite, tapioca. She's also replaced my Jif peanut butter with the freshly ground stuff from the co-op that would normally stick in my throat for a week. But she adds some honey to it and I find it totally addictive.

I'm starting to realize I've needed a nanny my whole life and I'm worried I won't be able to share her with Sophie. I've gone from being a completely independent and self-sufficient adult to one who has a full staff and may need more. It's like I'm devolving before my very eyes.

Abbie is giving Pip a rather wide berth which I'm sure has to do with her distaste for the aristocracy. Pip doesn't realize it yet because she's just settling in.

Over dinner of butternut squash linguini, fried sage and toasted pine nuts, Abbie is forced to speak to Elliot's sister. "So, Philippa," she starts, "are you in line for the throne, as well?"

Pip chokes on her water, "Good God, I don't think it'll ever come to that."

My nanny eyes her curiously and asks, "You don't want to be the queen?"

Pip laughs, "I'd rather be a mime in a nudist colony."

Abbie spits out her hemp milk in laughter. "Now that's a visual!"

Elliot rolls his eyes and says, "You're very graphic, little sister. Stop it, so I can enjoy my meal."

Pip giggles, "Truthfully, Abbie, can you imagine something as boring as being a royal? All that hand waving and dressing up only to have the press dissect you like you're an insect. No thank you! I'd rather have to put up with the oddities of my own life."

Abbie inquires, "How strange can your life possibly be? I mean, look at you. You look like a royal even if you claim not to be one."

My sister-in-law responds, "Elliot, I'm about to tell Abigail how odd I am. Do you want to leave the room?"

I shoot my husband a look that says, don't you dare move a muscle. Sit still and support your sister.

Elliot smiles indulgently at Pip and replies, "By all means, tell her."

Pip raises her eyebrows in surprise and turns to Abbie, "Your little sister Katie would like you to know, you were always her favorite."

My nanny's fork stops mid-way to her mouth. "Excuse me? What did you just say?"

Pip adds, "She says to tell you she particularly loved turning hay bales into a summer swim pool."

Abbie's eyes start to dart around the table nervously. She eventually manages, "How can you know about that? I haven't even told Mimi anything about Katie."

Philippa smiles and gently takes Abbie's hand. She continues, "She says you blame yourself for her death and that's ridiculous. She knew she wasn't supposed to sneak out of the house and it was her own fault."

Abbie deflates before our very eyes. One moment she's a self-assured young woman bent on suspicion and the next she's transformed into a grieving little girl.

I reach out and touch her arm, "Do you want me and Elliot to leave?"

Abbie shakes her head, "No, you don't have to go." Then

to Pip, she asks, "You can hear Katie?" When Elliot's sister nods, she continues, "Can you ask her if she's happy?"

Philippa responds, "She's very happy. She didn't want to leave form so young but wants you to know she's having a very nice life in the next dimension."

After an emotional hiccup, Abigail asks, "Ask her if it's like the heaven we used to talk about."

Pip answers, "She says it is, only so much more. She's not allowed to give you particulars, but wants you to know your thinking is on the right track."

Abbie asks, "And what about Mom and Dad, are they on track too?"

"She says yes. She wants you to start doing those same things in your own life."

"But how?" Abbie demands. "I don't have my own house or land. How can I do that?"

Pip looks to me and then to Elliot before answering, "She wants you to do them where you are now. Elliot and Mimi will have no objections."

If my attention wasn't captured before, it certainly is now. I inquire, "What won't we have any objection to?" Elliot seems to be as curious as I am.

My sister-in-law explains, "Katie would like Abbie to start a garden and get some chickens."

"Really?" I look to Elliot. "I have no objections, how about you?"

My husband smiles, "I don't see why not. I love eggs and I'm certainly a fan of fresh vegetables." He thinks for a moment and adds, "We haven't hired a gardener yet, what with snow still on the ground, but we can make sure whoever we hire will help you till the soil and do whatever else you need."

Abbie's smile transforms her face. "Thank you very much, Elliot." Then she looks to me, "And Mimi. You've both been incredibly welcoming. Like my very own family."

Pip adds, "Katie would like you to tell your parents that she's okay and she's very sorry for disobeying them by sneaking out."

Abigail nods her head slowly, "I'll do that. And Katie, I love you so much! We all miss you beyond belief."

The table sits in utter silence. Poor Abbie, I want to ask what happened to her sister but it's really none of my business. She'll share it with us when and if she's ready.

Elliot seems truly impressed by his only sibling and catches her eye before announcing, "Just so you know Pip, my days of doubting you are over. That was an incredible thing to witness."

Pip eyes her brother and smiles. "No more telling people I'm mental?"

He shakes his head. "I never said that, exactly. But no, no more reservations, only support from here on out."

Abbie stands up and excuses herself, "I think I'll just go and call home, if you don't mind."

Of course none of us do. This had to be quite a surprise for Abbie, a good surprise, but still a bit of a bombshell.

Chapter 34

Richard arrives while Pip and Abbie are holed up in the pool house going over garden plans. It turns out that Elliot's sister has a bit of a green thumb, herself. So much so, the gardener at the family's country home reports directly to her.

I'm delighted to see my friend. He's as handsome and sweet as ever and he's brought me twelve onion bagels baked fresh that morning, sealing his welcome. I pop a couple in the toaster and get him a cup of coffee. "How was your flight?"

"Intriguing, actually. A woman was ushered off the plane for accosting the lead singer of her favorite band."

"Really? How'd she do that?"

He laughs, "He was seated in first class and while she was walking through to the coach cabin, she spotted him and threw herself onto his lap. When the stewardesses tried to extricate her, she grabbed his shirt and wound up ripping it right down the middle. Then she screamed that she wanted to have his baby right there."

"Wow, I always get the boring flights." I smile. "Richard, I have something to tell you."

My friend interrupts, "Mimi, first let me speak. Please." He implores. I nod my head and he continues, "About your sister-in-law."

Oh boy, I try to stop him before he can continue, "Richard…"

But as I start talking, Pip walks into the room. The energy that flies between her and my friend is positively electrifying. Seriously, if you put a kettle of water between them, it would boil in an instant.

Richard is the first to find his voice, "Philippa." It's said with such feeling that tingles rush up my arms. It's a bit of accusation mixed with surprise and perhaps a touch of longing? I know that seems an odd one but there you are. It's almost like Richard Bingham has missed Elliot's sister.

Pip looks from Richard to me, then back to Richard before responding, "Richard. What a surprise to see you here."

He defends himself by declaring, "I'm in Chicago on business. What are you doing here?"

Pip responds, "I don't need an excuse. Mimi and Elliot are my family."

Just as I'm about to intervene and smooth things over, I feel a particularly strong Braxton Hicks contraction and let out a moan. I grab the underside of my giant stomach and breathe slowly through it.

Richard is obviously alarmed and demands, "Mimi, are you alright? Should I call for an ambulance? Where's Elliot?"

In contrast, Pip inquires, "Another Braxton Hicks?"

I nod my head in confirmation. Pip turns to Richard and clarifies, "She's having practice contractions. They're very normal, just her body's way of getting ready for the actual birth."

My friend appears visibly relieved and declares, "Thank goodness! There's more to this baby thing than a man realizes, isn't there?"

If only he knew the extent of it. But I'm not going to be the one to share how ugly it gets. Let him discover when his own offspring is on the way. I don't want to scare him off parenthood.

Once the contraction is over I decide to quit messing around and shoot for complete candor, "Pip, please join us." With a glance to Richard, Pip slowly walks over and sits down next to me. Then I demand, "What's going on with you two, anyway?"

Richard's reaction is to get prickly and I feel him about to withdrawal so I forge ahead. "Look Richard, I have no idea what Pip's message was to you because she won't tell me." Pip nods her head in confirmation. "So why don't you tell me here and now, so I can help smooth things out between you?"

His eyes dart between the two of us like he's trying to convince himself we aren't in cahoots with each other. I'm still not sure what his male mind has decided when he sighs deeply and replies, "Philippa has had word from my father. My father whom I did not have a very close relationship with in life."

"And?" I prod. "What did your dad have to say?"

Richard clears his throat, "Apparently, he seems to think it's time I get married."

I nod my head and shrug my shoulders simultaneously. "Yeah, well so do you. You told me in New York that you wanted to settle down and have a family. What's so upsetting about that?"

My friend glances to my sister-in-law and answers, "My father," he quantifies, "if you believe this nonsense, seems to think Philippa is the woman for the job."

Wait, what? Wow! I don't know what I expected but it wasn't this. I look at my sister-in-law with sympathy and manage, "Holy, cow, Pip. That must have been a pretty hard message to deliver."

She nods her head in response. "Certainly harder than most. But you know what would have happened if I declined."

I do know what would have happened; she'd have broken out like a teenager until she delivered the message. And what with her and Richard living on different continents, I can see it was less painful to just get it over with. I've been rendered speechless, which is no small fete.

Richard continues, "So you can see how unexpected it was for me to have a strange woman approach and announce herself as my future mate."

Pip interrupts, "Wait a second, Richard. I did not say I agreed with this nor did I throw myself at you. I passed on the message. That's all I'm supposed to do."

He ignores her and speaks straight to me, "And being that I had entrusted you to find my future spouse, I'm sure you will agree this was a bit off-putting."

I actually do see that. But Richard is only viewing this from his perspective. "Richard," I start, "do you believe there are people out there who can actually communicate with the dead?"

He's quiet for a moment before answering, "Yes. I believe there are a chosen few who have that ability."

I continue, "And you saw Pip at Thanksgiving, right? You saw how the homeless at the soup kitchen lined up to hear what she had to say?"

He nods his head so I plow forth. "Do you believe she had real messages for them?"

My friend slowly begins to nod his head. "I think she very well may have."

"So," I demand, "why do you think she lied to you?"

Richard responds, "A wealthy single man at a wedding is a bit of a target, don't you think?"

Pip can't stay quiet a moment longer, "Oh for Christ's sake, Richard, I venture to guess I'm probably worth at least twice what you are!"

He defends himself, "How was I supposed to know that? Some strange woman approaches me at a wedding reception and announces, "Your dead father thinks you should marry me." That's not normal behavior, Philippa."

Pip fumes, "First of all, you arrogant creature, I didn't say it like that. I've learned to deliver these messages with more decorum. And secondly, of course it's not normal. But what would you have me do? I've apparently been chosen to be this other worldly beast of burden and I don't seem to have an out."

I can see an intervention is needed. "What else did Richard's father say, Pip?"

She gasps, "You know I can't tell you that, Mimi. Ask Richard."

Richard allows, "Go ahead and tell her. She already knows the worst of it."

So Pip says, "He apologized to Richard for not being a more present parent and asked his forgiveness. He said that he was proud of him and only wants the best for him."

"Richard," I declare, "that's lovely!"

Pip continues, "He also told Richard he wishes him a wonderful life full of children he can dote on."

I turn to my friend and demand, "Richard Bingham, what's your problem? That's positively beautiful!"

Richard responds, "Yes, but it all goes back to a peculiar woman declaring herself at a wedding, don't you see?"

"No, I do not." I look at Pip, "Pip, do you even want to marry Richard?"

Elliot's sister looks aghast. "Good Lord, no! Why on earth would I want to marry a man who doesn't even believe me? I would much rather go it alone. Plus," she adds, "it's not my way to ask random persons to be my husband. I certainly don't know this man well enough to have any idea if I want to marry him."

I look at Richard, "There you have it. She doesn't even want to marry you. So can you just get off your high horse and let this go?"

Richard looks about as comfortable as a chicken in a nugget factory. He finally responds, "Philippa, you have my apologies. I forgive you."

"Forgive me? Mister Bingham, I have done nothing that requires your forgiveness. But just to show you that I'm the bigger person, I forgive you for your narrow minded, pig-headed behavior." Then she gets up and storms out of the room.

That went well.

Chapter 35

Ginger is released from the hospital after three days and just as expected it's positively brutal for her to leave her babies behind. Dr. Fermin recommends she make the most of her nights and get caught up on her rest because when Ellie, Johnny and Mo are sent home, she'll need a solid foundation of sleep.

Ginger and Jonathan spend most of their days at the hospital holding, feeding and bonding with the triplets. If all continues to progress as planned, they might be released in as early as three weeks.

Elliot and I stop by to see them every few days and they've already changed so much from the day they were born. They've gone from three little furry monkeys to looking a lot more like real babies. Ginger says it's because she's expressing breast milk around the clock for them. Six hours a day she's hooked up to a double pump like a dairy cow.

I'm looking forward to breast feeding Sophie but the thought of trying to produce enough milk for three is totally daunting. My sister says she eats like a Clydesdale in order to keep going but doesn't know if she'll be able to continue to the same degree once the kids come home.

Richard stayed for three days and he and Pip avoided each other for the most part. At family dinners, they spoke occasionally. Things like, please pass the cashew butter and garbanzo bean cutlets. Not much beyond that.

When Richard left, he promised to come as soon as Sophie was born. I told him that Pip would still be here and suggested he spend some time trying to get to know her. I promised that she's really a lovely person and not at all after his precious money. He's agreed to think about it.

I've started having a very hard time sleeping at night and have discovered the joys of late night programming. The show that's grabbed my attention above all others is an alarmingly entertaining one called *Doomsday Preppers*. I watch episode after episode and am beyond surprised at the degree and variety of people planning for the end of the world.

There's one couple in the middle of Detroit who've purchase forty-seven dead bolts so when the end comes, they can protect their basement full of mac and cheese and potato chips. Apparently they've decided to go out in a blaze of high sodium comfort foods, not that I blame them.

The strangest person by far, is the forty-something retired archeologist cum yogi that lives in Hawaii. When "the event," whether it be an electromagnetic pulse, domestic terrorism or WWIII hits, he's heading straight for the cove where he's hidden his canoe under palm fronds. Once there, he's going to paddle himself to a deserted side of the island and start climbing to the top. He has no plans to take any supplies with him as he's sure the island gods will care for him. When asked what he'll do for fresh drinking water, he responds he'll drink his own urine until he finds a source. He finds it tastes remarkably like chamomile tea, his favorite.

I find the "bug out" people the oddest as a whole. I mean, I guess if you lived in a city like New York and another 911 hits, bugging out would have its appeal. But a lot of these folks seem to be ditching a comfortable home in civilization for a completely rustic setup because they're expecting man to exterminate themselves and they want to be well out of the way.

One family in Texas is so sure the poles are going to shift, as in the North Pole will become the South Pole, that they've completely rigged out an old school bus to transfer their crew of nineteen to their top secret survival camp, which is somehow not going to be devastated when the rest of the world collapses. Near as I can figure, unless their bug out location is the moon and their bus is a rocket, if polar shifting occurs, they're going to be as susceptible as the rest of us to those consequences, as long as they're still on earth that is.

But needless to say, I'm delighted to take my mind off of impending motherhood and my ever decreasing bladder size by watching the antics of these folks. At the same time, I worry for their stress levels. It can't be a very relaxing existence when you're constantly expecting Armageddon.

Abbie is making great strides in her plans for our garden. She says she doesn't really know what grows well in Illinois but according to her research all the basics should do very well. She's planning on starting with corn, green beans, tomatoes, potatoes and strawberries. Once the trees bud, she's going to see what fruit trees are on the grounds so she can add to them if necessary. Necessary for what, I don't know but she's enjoying her plans so much, I'm not going to stop her.

Elliot and I have talked and we've decided to offer Abbie's services to Ginger and Johnathon for three weeks once they take the babies home. This should get her back to us in time for Sophie. Abbie's all for the idea and even suggested that she sleep over at their house to help them adjust to the nighttime schedule.

Andrew is nearly done decorating and I am in awe of his considerable talents. There is no way I could have come close to making the rooms look so comfortably lived in and homey while still radiating elegance. And yes, just so you know, I can imagine eating French fries in each and every one of them.

Sophie's room though, is by far my favorite. It's a soft, sumptuous and simply perfect nest for my daughter. I can't wait to bring her home and show it to her.

Speaking of bringing her home, I've finally started to shop for her. I've bought layettes and diapers and teething rings and every single item in the Target baby aisle. Abbie refused to let me buy any edibles because we are apparently going to be making all her food with things that we grow, organically. I love that our nanny has already taken such an interest in the welfare of our daughter. It makes me feel warm and fuzzy knowing we're creating such a nurturing environment for her.

Chapter 36

I believe I've previously mentioned my susceptible nature, yes? As in, if I see a commercial for a particularly appealing peach pie, I suddenly start to crave it and can't continue on with my day until I drive to the store and purchase an identical pie.

Well, today's craving is for candy. Not just any candy though, it's for the truffles from Vosges-Haut Chocolat downtown. I'm talking to Muffy on the phone about the baby shower that she and Renée are throwing for me and Ginger. She thinks it would be a nice idea to purchase an assortment of truffles to put in these little baby carriages she bought at the flower mart.

Of course I think it's a lovely idea as well and immediately begin to obsess over truffles. If I knew I had six months to live or had a tip about a devastating asteroid about to hit the planet, I would bug out to Vosges. I would pitch a tent on the corner of Rush and West Grand for easy access.

For breakfast I would dine solely on their assorted bacon chocolates, for lunch I would open myself up to a truffle buffet and for dinner it would be caramel toffee and bonbons.

There's no hope for it, I have to drive downtown and get truffles. I feel almost panicky in my need for them.

It takes me a grand total of thirty-five minutes from the onset of my craving to find myself in my idea of paradise on earth. My intention is to get two truffles and eat them slowly so as not to overdo. Ah, that road to hell and those good intentions, huh?

First thing I do though is to relieve myself. It's been thirty-seven minutes since my last potty and with Sophie doing the Macarena on my bladder, I can't hold it much longer. Once my mission is complete a lovely French woman asks if she can be of service.

"Yes," I tell her. "I'd like to buy a couple truffles."

"Do you know which kind you would like?" she asks, accommodatingly.

"I'm not sure," I respond therefor sealing my fate of listening to the equivalent of confection porn.

"Let me tell you what we have." And like Vanna White she glides along the case but instead of flipping letters, she gestures toward champagne truffles, crunchy hazelnut truffles, caramel and coffee truffles. She uses adjectives like silky, creamy and heaven on the tongue. On and on she goes until I can't contain myself.

I finally shout out, "I'll take one of each!" This is how my modest intentions turned into the most hideously sad display of self-indulgence. No, I am not going to eat all forty-eight truffles in one sitting, but neither am I going to let anyone else know about them. I'm plotting to put them in my underwear drawer and take one bite every time a craving comes upon me.

I decide to allow myself one on the way home. Instead I eat four. I plan to have one more before dinner, but I have six. The only thing to finally stop this truffle binging is the fact that Sophie is so hopped up on sugar she can't stop jiggling about. For the next three hours of kicks, turns and flips I feel like the worst mother in the world.

In order to try to atone for my sins, I eat an extra-large kale and spinach salad with dinner. FYI, kale and chocolate is a disgusting combination. I wind up drinking a large glass of soda water to calm my stomach but the resulting burps are enough to gag a rhinoceros.

Chapter 37

"Mimi, Darling, it's time to wake up." An insistent hand pulls at my arm.

I respond with a, "Lemme sleep." And roll over to cuddle my maternity pillow, the one with the fuzzy white pillow case that feels like I'm snuggling up to a mink colony.

"Sweetheart, you don't want to be late for your ultrasound." The crisp British voice of my husband persists.

Those words do the trick. This morning I'm going to get to see Sophie for the last time before she's born. I love to look at her on the monitor, watching as she wiggles her tiny toes and flashes all her little baby gang signs with her hands. I find that as long as I do my yoga breathing, I'm virtually panic-free about her potential claustrophobic situation.

Elliot rubs my back. "I'll get breakfast started. What do you want?"

I order two fried eggs, two turkey sausage links and one piece of sprouted wheat toast with the blackberry and kiwi jam that Abbie made last week.

As my hubby prepares my meal, I reflect on how his

relationship with our nanny has blossomed. Abbie no longer treats him like a criminal and he in turn has greatly enjoyed her enthusiasm about the garden. We're operating like a real family and it's delightful.

I'm currently thirty-eight weeks pregnant. The last month has gone very smoothly. The baby shower was lovely and I only stole three peoples' truffle favors. I justify this thievery because I'm the mother-to-be and the party was half thrown in my honor, so the truffles were really all mine anyway, right? I don't buy it either but it's all I've got.

Abbie spends her days at Ginger and Jonathan's house helping with the triplets. They declined her offer to stay at night. Ginger figures that the sooner they learn to handle it, the better. I'm all, Billy, don't be a hero, but she appears to be doing quite well. She does take a two hour nap every day while Abbie's there, to recoup.

I've totally neglected to sign up for birthing classes. Why, you ask? I mean now that I have a nanny, a cleaning person and a decorator; it can't be that I'm too busy, right? The truth is I'm totally freaked out about how Sophie is getting out of me that I've chosen the path of denial. I've even suggested we go all old-school and knock me out for the birth. Dr. Fermin isn't a fan of the idea but assures me that even if I don't have the classes, the baby will still find her way out. And that, right there, is what worries me.

In the doctor's office, Elliot suggests, "Why don't you just get the epidural and then you won't feel a thing?"

I look at him like he's proposed I run through the doctor's office naked while spraying cans of whipped cream at everyone

I pass. "Elliot, you do know what an epidural is, don't you?"

"Of course, darling. It's a little needle in your spine transferring numbing medicine."

To which I roll my eyes and sigh, "That's right. It's a needle in my spine." Then I throw him a very Italian gesture and repeat, "A needle in my spine! What's wrong with that phrase?"

He ventures, "I'm going out on a limb here but I'm going to guess the needle in your spine part?"

"Winner, winner, chicken dinner!" I touch my nose with the finger on one hand and point to him with the other.

He's saved from further trying to reason with me by Dr. Fermin's arrival. "How are Sophie's parents doing?"

I respond, "Sophie's mother is fat, tired, incontinent and excited." Then I add, "Sophie's father is insane. He's talking needles in my spine again."

My OB laughs, "Well, Mimi, we're going to have to have that talk pretty soon. You're running out of time to make a decision." Then she squeezes the warm gel on my stomach and continues, "But for now, let's make sure little Miss Fielding is in the right direction."

I stare up at the monitor and look at my sweet angel. I can actually see the hair on her head and it looks like she's giving me a thumbs up gesture.

Dr. Fermin announces, "It looks like an epidural!"

"What?" I demand. "Why does it look like an epidural?"

She replies, "Your daughter is breech and it appears like she's digging her heels in."

Elliot worries, "Does that mean a C-section?"

The doc answers, "Most probably. I could schedule Mimi for an attempted turning, but it's a bit late for that." She explains, "The bigger the baby, the harder it is to turn them and a good percentage of our attempts wind up with an emergency C-section, anyway. I suggest we just schedule the procedure and avoid possible complications."

Two things. One, I'm kind of excited because this means I don't have to pass an entire human being through my hoo ha and truthfully, that's had me seriously freaking out. Number two, now I get a needle in my spine and have to lie there wide awake while they cut me like a ripe melon. I cannot believe these are my only two options for delivering this baby. What kind of an archaic world do we live in?

I feel myself begin to hyperventilate and Elliot hands me the barf bag I carry in my purse for moments like this. I breathe into it and eventually catch my breath. I finally manage, "When are we going to do this thing?"

Dr. Fermin types into her computer and answers, "Let's plan it two days before your delivery date. There's no guarantee you won't go into labor before then but there's a pretty good chance you won't."

"Okay," I manage. Good thing I didn't bother with a birthing class. "What time?"

"You're going to need to be at the hospital by six. Don't have any food or water after midnight the night before and by 7:30 or so, you'll be holding your daughter."

Relief, excitement and nerves boil in me and begin to leak out of my eyes. Elliot holds my hand and stares at me like I'm the most miraculous thing in the world. And you know what?

I feel like the most miraculous thing in the world. I grew a whole person inside of me! I can't think of one thing that's a bigger deal than that.

Chapter 38

Ginger assures me that her C-section was a breeze. "Seriously, Meems, I've had more painful facials. As long as you keep up on your pain killers for a couple of days, you'll be fine."

Up until this point, I've been so focused on the needle in the spine portion of the program, I hadn't even thought about the pain following delivery. I demand, "What about the epidural?"

She tries to assure me, "They numb the area before even inserting it. You barely feel a thing."

"You better be right about that or I'm coming for you." I'm only half joking.

"Scouts honor," she replies. "You'll do great!"

"Well, now that that's over. How about we take the kids out for lunch?" Because the babies are still considered preemies, they're not actually allowed out in public. So Ginger and I go to lunch via the drive thru at Burger City. The babies sleep through the whole thing but my sister gets an outing, such as it is.

She declares, "I'd love to! I'm burning so many calories

producing milk; I can't seem to eat enough." And right there is nature's reward for putting you through all the pregnancy/delivery hell. I'm totally looking forward to my binge fest during the nursing months. I seem to eat all the time now, but I can't consume a lot at one time because there's precious little room in there.

When I pull up to Ginger's house, Abbie helps her bring the babies out and buckles them into her mini-van. My car isn't big enough for three infant car seats. On the way to Burger City, my sister declares, "I'm fucked."

"Excuse me, what?" Ginger is the least likely of the sisters to resort to vulgarity so this proclamation is more than shocking. "What are we talking here, literally or figuratively?"

Ginger looks at me wild-eyed. "Never literally, again. Seriously, Johnathan has had his fun. He's cut off forever."

"Does he know that?"

"Who cares what he knows? The asshole went back to work! Can you believe that?"

I try to reason with her, "But honey, he's been off for more than a month. Someone has to make the money."

Ginger yells, "Then I'll make the money! God dammit, I made almost as much as he did. Why do I have to be the parent?"

I reason, "Because you volunteered when you guys had the discussion about who was going to stay home?"

Ginger slams on the breaks at a stop sign. "Well, I didn't know what I was getting into. I plead ignorance and now that I'm not ignorant I want out."

This has me a little worried for my sister. I guess, "Were you up a lot last night?"

"Every blessed half hour on the hour. As soon as I closed my eyes and began to drift off to sleep, another one of them woke up demanding to be fed. My God, they never stop eating!"

I ask, "Why don't you supplement with formula? That would give you a break."

My sister sighs, "I might have to. I was just hoping to be able to do this on my own for at least the first few months." Then she looks at me, all panicked and adds, "Renée was right. This is flipping hard work."

I almost feel guilty for only having one baby inside me. I try, "Why don't we drop you for a pedicure and you can eat your lunch there?" I offer, "I'll drive the babies around while you get a little pampering."

My sister readily agrees. So, while she's getting her nails done, I park under a tree to eat my burger and turn on my secret new radio obsession, *The Preppy Prepper*. Her stage name is Blaire Morgan and she's a self-professed Doomsday Goddess. She claims the government is not actually run by the people we elect but by a shadow group that remains so far in the depths that we'll never know who they are. It's all a bit overboard on the conspiracy theory, if you ask me, but she does make some interesting points.

On today's episode, she's outlined thirty-eight ways to use the pin of her kilt for survival. The obvious ones include using it to poke an attacker's eyes out and to open cans, but did you know you can use a kilt pin to build a fire, signal for help and cut meat? This woman is a genius, a scary genius, but still totally brilliant. She's almost convinced me to buy a kilt pin for my purse.

On yesterday's episode, she walked us through skinning an animal and tanning its hide. Because apparently, when the shit hits the fan we'll be making our own deer skin moccasins and fur coats.

My favorite show by far was the one on how to make vermin stew, which is essentially the same as road kill casserole with more water. All you have to do is collect as many rodents or small wild animals that you can find, skin them and then boil them whole until the meat falls off their bones. Yum. Throw in as many weeds and herbs and wild berries that you can find to season it. Cook it down until it's a nice stew-like thickness and eat up! She even explained how to remove a skunk's stink gland without rupturing it. That's in case a skunk is the only meat you can find for dinner. She didn't cover how you're supposed to kill it without setting it off though.

Blaire hails from Texas and talks with a Southern twang. She sounds like Miss America meets Hulk Hogan. Some of her diatribe is very feminine and ladylike but then she goes all ninja on you. She claims to have been the president of her sorority in college and is the wife of a local oil tycoon. Her real name isn't really Blaire Morgan. She's keeping her real name under wraps so the government doesn't take her out for sharing "the truth."

As soon as I'm done eating I drive the babies around for another hour to give their mama a break. When I pull up to the salon to pick her up, I can see her sitting in a massage chair fast asleep. I decide to let her catch up a little and listen while Blaire teaches me how to make a noose with common household items.

Chapter 39

Elliot's parents have decided to come a week before the C-section is scheduled. Hurray! That means they'll be here tomorrow and I haven't begun to prepare for them, not that there's much for me to prepare. My "staff" seems to have everything in order.

Andrew has gone so far above and beyond in the guest room, where the earl and countess will be sleeping, that I'm surprised he hasn't installed butt massagers in their bed. Although, who knows, maybe he has.

The color palette he went with is nothing short of sumptuous. Golds, creams and hunter green are the main hues with some burgundy to accent. The drapes are a rich velvet over impossibly filmy sheers and the curtain pulls look like something Henry the Eighth might have used to tie up a misbehaving wife. I'm hoping they find their room so much to their liking they spend the majority of their visit there.

Abbie is about as excited to meet Elliot's parents as she was to meet Pip, but I've assured her that since she's come to love both my husband and his sister, I'm positive she'll do great with their parents. I don't actually think that at all. Victoria and the earl are pretty much as royal as you get without having to kiss a ring, but I don't want to panic the nanny.

Now that she's back with us instead of at Ginger's, Abbie has asked to stay in charge of all the meals until Sophie's born. I'm all for it, but I have no idea what Elliot's parents are going to make of her beet Wellington.

Richard is coming the day before the birth, so we're going to be a pretty full house. It's actually very nice to have the space to effortlessly house so many, and I find that I love having people around. I'm hoping he and Pip will play nice and might actually form a friendship. They are both such wonderful people, it would be amazing if they actually wound up together. Although, I'd settle for them being civil.

Elliot has been playing phone tag with Beatrice for a few months. At first I thought it was because she and Clive were in the throes of new love and totally wrapped up in each other, but now I wonder if she isn't avoiding us during our happy time. It's occurred to me that Beatrice will likely never have children of her own, even if she gets rid of the cancer. I'm worried that our pregnancy has been hard on her, reminding her of something that probably isn't in her future.

Elliot's ex is such an unsuspected friend for me. I used to think of her as my rival for his lordship and that caused some pretty nasty feelings, but when she learned Elliot and I were in love, she came forward with the truth that her feelings for him didn't extend beyond friendship, releasing him to marry me. Her reward was Clive. I wish the two of them a wonderfully long and happy life together. I vow once Sophie comes out,

I'm going to call her myself and invite her to visit. No, scratch that, I'm going to beg her to visit.

Miss Sophie is camping on my sciatic nerve and I'm in utter agony most of the time. My lower back, butt and left leg are constantly hurting. The only time I get some relief is when I'm laying down, but being so hugely pregnant, I'm only allowed to lie on my side, preferably the left side. I can't wait to roll over on my stomach, sleep flat on my back, or in the fetal position, if I choose. I've always loved a variety of sleeping positions and am finding my limited choice very frustrating.

My latest pregnancy symptom, and thank God it only started last week, is snoring. I'm not talking soft little purrs either. I'm talking raucously loud hog snorts. The first time I did it and woke myself up, I thought it was Elliot, so I hit him and told him to roll over. The second time, I realized it was me and not my husband. Horror doesn't begin to describe how I felt.

Also, I'm just plain not sleeping anymore. I'm lucky to settle in and close my eyes for forty minutes before I have to go to the bathroom. Once I get back into bed and resettle, the pattern continues. Dr. Fermin suggests I take a Tylenol P.M. to help get into a deeper sleep cycle. With the thought that once there, I won't be so aware of my need to go to the bathroom.

I've given up caffeine and alcohol for this pregnancy so I reason a little sleeping aid won't hurt. I'm nothing near rested, but its cut down my nighttime potty runs from ten to six.

Most of the time, when I'm lying in bed, not sleeping, I dwell on what a wuss I am. I'm seriously not sure I can ever be pregnant again. This is the most uncomfortable I've ever been in my entire life and that includes the time a tree fell on me in church camp and broke my arm. How my mother did this four times is beyond me. Ginger, doing it with triplets, makes her eligible for sainthood in my eyes.

Then I think about how if I was giving birth to Sophie a hundred years ago, I might have very well died while they tried to remove this big breech baby from my insides. Died! That's the thought that usually guarantees no hope of rest.

Elliot seems to love my great big giant self more than ever and he's always touching me. I find this extremely sweet and annoying at the same time. I'm thrilled he loves me and our baby. I'm delighted he's still attracted to me even though I look like Shamu's not-so-distant cousin, but seriously, I've got enough going on here, hands off.

Have you seen those cast moldings woman have done of their pregnant bellies? You know, so they can immortalize the moment for life? Yeah, well I received a gift certificate for one of those at my shower. Renée gave it to me and told me I could have it bronzed, painted or even tiled so I can turn it into a planter. She regrets not having gotten them done when she was pregnant with Finn and Camille, so she's torturing me with it.

That's what I'm off to do right now. I'm not particularly excited, but I don't see how I can get out of it either. Renée's driving me so I'm trying to focus on how nice it is to have a sister day with my oldest sibling and not obsess over some strange person covering me in plaster coated bandages.

When we pull up to Castoffs, Renée exclaims, "Aren't you excited?"

I try to produce a euphoric response, but can only manage, "Help me get out of the car. I'm stuck."

We have to walk through a beaded curtain to get inside the place and the décor is a cross between I Dream of Jeannie's bottle and an opium den. It's way too groovy for me. I'm about to tell Renée I've had second thoughts and suggest she get her money back when a tall robust African American lady walks in. She introduces herself as Madam Lala.

Renée takes her hand like she's meeting the Pope and gushes, "Madam Lala, I love your work! You've cast so many of my friends that I just had to bring my sister in."

Madam Lala smiles hugely and looks at me. With a pure flat Chicago accent she declares, "I cannot wait to immortalize this beautiful woman! Come in, come in!" Well now I'm stuck. She's a perfectly nice lady and I would be insulting her if I demanded Renée's money back.

Madam Lala shows us a wide selection of casts that can be done. Some women have gone as far as molding their entire bodies, front first and then the back. This, she explains, is usually when they are planning to bronze the whole thing as a statue.

The look of horror on my face suggests this is not what I'm going for, although Renée is remarkably jazzed by the thought. "Oh Meems, I think you should do it! Have your whole body cast. Elliot will love it!"

Not even trying to hide my revulsion, I demand, "Where in the hell will I put a bronze statue of this hugeness in my house?"

Madam Lala, in all her wisdom suggests, "Why not put it in the garden?"

I stare at her with my mouth hanging wide open and demand, "For the whole world to see?"

She responds, "They don't have to know it's you. They will most likely just assume it's a beautiful piece of artwork."

My sister feels the need to add, "And that's exactly what it will be!" Then it turns ugly and she begs, "Oh please, Mimi, do it for me!"

The only thing that saves me from this impending nightmare is that Madam Lala adds, "Of course you'll have to hold your bladder for two hours." She explains, "It takes a lot longer to cast a whole body."

I grab onto that out like the lifeline it is and explain, "Too bad. I go every half hour. Guess I'll just have to do something less dramatic." And hide it in my closet when it's done, I don't add.

The next hour is spent posing me in the proper position and slapping plaster coated strips across my naked flesh. This crosses the border of unpleasant and lands smack in the territory of torturous for me, but it's not the worst part. The worst part is sitting still for forty minutes while the cast dries. I conjure imaginary itches that I can't scratch and just knowing I can't go to the bathroom is enough to drive me insane. Then there's my sciatic nerve which decides to hate the pose fifteen minutes after it's too late to change it.

Madam Lala keeps the cast while it cures and will send it off for the next step, once I decide what that is. I just want to get home and shower.

Upon walking through the front door, Abbie hands me a kale and kiwi smoothie. I don't even balk at it. I know it's going to taste highly questionable, but it's good for Sophie so I down it on my way to the bathroom.

Chapter 40

The first thing the countess says to me after not laying eyes on me for months is, "Mimi, you're huge!"

I want to reply, "And you're a bitch." But I don't. Instead I greet, "Victoria, how nice to see you. We're so glad to have you here."

Conversely, the earl's smile is so big it looks like it's about to swallow his face. He's completely lost it because instead of shaking my hand or nodding his head in royal acknowledgment, he wraps me in a near bear hug and exclaims, "You look beautiful, Mimi!"

Elliot and Philippa greet their parents as well and then we all retire to the library. I offer everyone tea and Elliot fetches it. I've been a bit clumsy during this last part of my pregnancy and neither of us wants to see me face plant with the tea service.

Abbie is following him when he comes back. She's carrying a tray of scones and cookies she's created for the occasion and she looks like she's about to hurl.

I introduce, "Victoria, Archibald, this is Abigail, our

nanny." I hurry to add, "Although we've come to think of her as our friend and member of the family."

The countess offers a smile that doesn't quite reach her eyes and says, "How nice."

Elliot hurries to contribute, "Abbie is a great cook. In fact, she made the scones and cookies."

"She makes most of our meals. She's really quite extraordinary." I know it might sound like we're overselling her, but Elliot and I both want to put Abbie at ease.

Pip pipes in with, "She's also the most remarkable gardener! She's hard at work on a plan for a garden she's going to put in here."

"My goodness," the countess clucks, "do you walk on water, too, Abigail?" I think she's trying to be funny, without success.

Abbie is positively mute in response. I can see Elliot's parents are everything she feared they'd be, pretentious, officious and very snooty.

I manage, "Thanks so much, Abbie. What time do you want us ready for dinner?"

Our nanny tries to smile, and suggests, "How about six o'clock in the dining room?"

We eat all of our meals in the breakfast nook attached to the kitchen, but Abbie thinks Elliot's parents will prefer a more formal setting. I'm sure she's right.

While Elliot shows our guests to their room, to rest up from their trip, I head to the kitchen to check the menu for dinner, ala Cora Crowley, The Countess of Grantham. As far as countess's go, Cora's way more my speed. Yes, she's rather grand but she's delightful and loving and she cares about her staff. Victoria should really watch Downton Abbey so she can see how it's done.

I find Abbie at the sink scrubbing potatoes like she's trying to skin them alive. She's grumbling, "Fricking creepy lizards, makes my skin crawl."

"Lizards?" I inquire. Which causes the nanny to startle and let out a blood curdling scream.

"Mimi!" she gasps. "I didn't hear you coming."

I laugh, "You were too busy giving that potato what for." Then ask, "What lizards are making your skin crawl?"

She looks around all shifty eyed and responds, "What do you mean, lizards? I said buzzards."

"Okaaaaaay, what buzzards?"

Abbie's face turns as red as my hair and replies, "Oh, nothing. Just something I saw on TV last night."

I adore our nanny and think she's an amazing young person. She's been an invaluable member of our little tribe and I'm sure she'll be remarkable with Sophie. But there's something a little off about her when it comes to the British aristocracy. Normally this wouldn't affect me at all but I've married into this highbrow can of mixed nuts and I'd like to figure out what's setting her off.

Alas, I know today won't be the day, so I ask, "What's for dinner?"

"I'm starting out with a vichyssoise and then serving a beet and pistachio salad. The entrée is white bean stuffed portobellos."

The drool forming in my mouth is positively Pavlovian.

"Bravo!" I clap. "That is a meal guaranteed to impress! What's for dessert?"

She answers, "I made a coconut milk ice cream that I'm serving with brandied cherries."

In awe, I inquire, "Why didn't you become a chef? You're certainly good enough in the kitchen."

The nanny looks disgusted. "I would hate cooking in a restaurant!"

"Why?" I demand. "I bet you'd have diners lined up out the door."

"I'd stop loving to cook if I had to make the same meal over and over. No thank you. I prefer being creative and designing new stuff every day."

The world's loss is my gain. I offer, "Abbie, I know Elliot's parents are a lot to take on at first, believe me, I know. They're just different from us. I promise they'll warm up as they get to know you."

She looks like she'd rather crawl into bed with a boa constrictor than get to know Victoria and Archibald. Then she answers, "I don't think they want to get to know me. In their eyes, I'm the help, and truly, that's fine by me."

I smile half-heartedly. "I do know what you mean. I don't think they even tried to tolerate me until they found out I was pregnant and even then it took some time."

"Yes, well, you're breeding one of them. That sort of makes you important."

Chapter 41

When we're all seated for dinner, Abbie and Pip bring in the soup. The nanny dishes it up while Elliot's sister serves. Victoria takes a tentative bite and announces, "My goodness, I don't think I've had better!"

I glance at Abbie and send her an encouraging look. She merely shrugs her shoulders as if to say, whatever.

Archibald is next and he concurs, "Delicious!" Then to Abigail, he winks and inquires, "I don't suppose you'd like to come work for us?"

Our young helper, would in fact, probably rather eat her own feet, but has the grace to smile and answer, "I'll have to decline. After all, I'm here to help with Sophie."

That starts a round of excited chatter about their future grandchild. Victoria asks, "Are you nervous about the C-section, Mimi?"

"Terrified." I answer. "I know they're considered very commonplace but I can't get over the idea of the epidural."

The countess concurs, "It was much more civilized when they put you to sleep and only woke you once your child was born."

"Is that how you delivered us?" Pip inquired.

"How I wish," the countess responds. "They no longer offered that service when Elliot was born. Instead, they strapped my wrists down and screamed at me through the whole thing. It was simply dreadful."

"Strapped your wrists down? That sounds barbaric!" I exclaim.

Archibald chuckles and adds, "It might have had something to do with Victoria's threats to rip their heads off if they didn't remove the baby immediately."

I can't help myself and smile at the thought. I can't imagine Elliot's mom with so much as a hair out of place, yet alone delivering a baby and making threats like a common thug. I would have actually paid good money to see that.

The countess contributes, "In my defense, Archibald, Elliot was over nine pounds. If there ever was a time to threaten violence, that was it."

I say a little prayer of thanks for my C-section and confess, "It's just the whole needle in the spine thing that's throwing me."

Victoria, very uncharacteristically reaches over to grab my hand and offers, "Mimi, believe me, it's a gift. It will be over in a moment's time and you can bring my first grandchild into the world in comfort. I couldn't wish for anything better for you." I believe her. It's like we just had a real moment.

I look around the table and realize that Abbie isn't sitting with us, so I inquire as to her whereabouts.

Pip replies, "She said she'd prefer to eat in the kitchen tonight. I tried to persuade her but she was rather insistent."

Knowing how she feels about our guests, I decide to let it go for tonight when Elliot declares, "That's ridiculous! I'll go fetch her." As Elliot leaves the table he collects the empty soup bowls and clears them into the kitchen.

I hear an exchange of words, although I can't quite make out what's being said. The next thing I know my husband and the nanny are carrying in the next course. Once all the dishes are served, Abbie sits down in the only remaining seat, right next to the countess. She looks like she's on death row.

Victoria turns to her new dinner partner and announces, "I just love how democratic you Americans are!"

Pip shoots her mom a dark look, "Mother, Abbie is our friend."

The countess plays dumb, "Of course she is. But that's exactly what I mean." She adds, "In England, it wouldn't occur to us to befriend the staff."

Before anyone can think of a response, the earl pipes in with, "I think it's rather refreshing. My best friend growing up was our housekeeper's son and I have to say, I missed him dreadfully when his mother left our service."

I want to yell, "Go Archie!" for his moment of realness.

The countess, fully unaware that she's offended Abbie, asks her husband, "Did you ever try to look him up, dear?"

Her husband replies, "Yes, actually, I did. We met at a pub for tea one day, but by then it had been twenty years since we'd seen one another." He confides, "It was all a bit awkward."

No one knows what to say after that so we eat our salad course in virtual silence. Finally, Victoria breaks the silence by asking, "Where do you hail from, Abigail?"

Our nanny inhales a pistachio and starts to choke. After several coughs, she gains her composure and replies, "I'm from Oregon, Your High…, rather Vic… I mean, Your Ladyship."

My mother-in-law responds, "Please, call me Victoria." She looks around the table and adds, "After all, when in Rome." Then she asks, "And did you mother teach you how to cook like this?"

Abbie grimaces, "Actually, no, I grew up with eight younger siblings. Cooking was my contribution to the family effort."

I ask, "Were you always this good?"

She laughs, "Not unless you consider peanut butter and gravy sandwiches good."

"How in the world did you come up with that revolting combination?" my husband inquires.

"Well," Abbie answers, "I didn't want to cook so I figured if I made horrible stuff they would figure something else out. Of course with nine kids and a small farm to care for there wasn't any time. So they just kept eating what I made. Sometime after mushroom and banana pancakes I decided to make the most of it and experimented with combinations that actually sounded good."

The earl contributes, "Well cheers to you, my dear. You've totally won my heart."

Good old Archie. I'm starting to think he's the warm fuzzy one in the couple.

Chapter 42

The rest of the week flies by with uncharacteristic speed. My family kicks in to entertain Elliot's parents and it's April 26th before I know it. Richard arrives today, which means tomorrow is Sophie's birthday.

I've packed my hospital bag at least six times hoping I haven't forgotten anything. Elliot assures me he'll bring me anything I've neglected to include, but it's not so much about the bag as it is about feeling in charge of the situation, which I simply am not.

Elliot's taken his family out to lunch, so they're gone when Richard arrives. My dashing friend shows up on my doorstep with two dozen long-stemmed pink roses and a box of truffles from La Maison Du Chocolat in New York. I hug him as best as my giant belly will allow and drag him into the house.

"Richard, I've missed you!" I declare.

He smiles at me lovingly and replies, "I've missed you too, Mimi." Then he adds, "But being that you chose Elliot over me, I've finally decided to start dating."

"Really?" I ask. Why I'm surprised by this I don't know. I

mean Richard is a very attractive and eligible bachelor so it makes sense he'd be dating. "Any luck?"

He shakes his head in disgust, "Not a bit. It's a jungle out there. Every woman I meet sees dollar signs before she even bothers to see me. I'm so tired of the jaded socialites and shallow gold diggers, I could spit." He shakes his head, "I don't know where to look to find someone real."

I suggest, "I think you need someone with more money than you."

My friend laughs, "That's going to be a hard find. But I assure you, all the ladies of independent means I've encountered, are a real bore. They don't get excited about anything."

So I try, "You need a woman of independent means who's a bit eccentric."

Obtusely, Elliot replies, "I'm looking, but I'm seriously getting a bit a despondent over the whole thing."

I go for less obvious, "Maybe you need a matchmaker from the great beyond." Then I drop the hammer, "Perhaps your father has an idea."

Richard chuckles, "Perhaps he does."

Wait, what? "Richard, are you thinking about giving Pip a chance?"

He shrugs his shoulders, "Why not? She's really quite beautiful once you get over the whole shock of her talking to the dead." He continues, "As you mentioned, she's a woman of independent means, so she's not after me for my money. And truthfully, I haven't given her a chance. So I figure, why not?"

Wow and wow. "Richard," I start, "you're going to have to be pretty smooth about getting to know Pip. To say that you've put her off would be a great understatement. You've been downright rude to her."

Richard nods his head, "I have. And I'm very sorry about that. But I think the best way to proceed is to just move forward and make no mention of our uncomfortable history."

"Well good luck to you, Richard Bingham. I'm looking forward to watching the show." And just then my water breaks. Amniotic fluid comes gushing out of me soaking our new sofa and dribbling onto the carpet.

Richard seems completely unaware of the drama that's occurring until I yell, "Oh hell, I think my water just broke!"

Richard jumps up and demands, "Let's go!"

I counter, "I can't leave without my bag. Go get it, will you? It's in my closet." My friend runs up the stairs and is back in remarkable time.

He ushers me out to his rental car and hands me his phone. "Call your husband and family and let them know we're on our way to the hospital."

I'm about to do just that when I'm hit with what I can only assume is a contraction. This baby puts all those piddling little Braxton Hicks cramps to shame. I groan in agony and try to focus on breathing when it moves around to my back. That's when I let out a blood curdling scream, almost sending Richard off the road.

He pulls his car into the ambulance bay and starts laying on the horn. Two nurses rush out to find out what all the commotion is about. Richard explains that my water broke and I am in a great deal of pain.

One nurse rolls her eyes and says, "Labor's painful." To Richard she demands, "Get your car out of here and meet us inside."

They wheel me into the waiting room when I'm hit with another agonizing cramp. "Holy shit, this hurts!"

The on call doctor comes over and asks how long I've been in labor. I reply, "Maybe ten minutes. It started right after my water broke."

He suggests, "Let's take you back and see how far you're dilated."

I respond, "But I'm scheduled for a C-section tomorrow. I can't deliver Sophie vaginally, she's breach!"

That kicks him into gear. He asks the name of my doctor and gets the nurse to page her. Then he calls the O.R. to schedule a room. By the time he checks my cervix I'm already 5 cm dilated. He declares, "Your baby appears to be in quite a hurry. Is your husband with you?"

"No!" I yell. "Crap, he's having lunch with his parents. My friend brought me in."

At that moment Richard slams through the door and exclaims, "Everyone's on their way!"

Chapter 43

The anesthesiologist is a very young looking Asian man. Actually he looks more like a boy of twelve or thirteen. In the midst of another contraction I scream, "Look here, Doogie Howser, I want a doctor who knows what he's doing. No way are you getting near me with that epidural."

Dr. Lou smiles calmly and responds, "Mrs. Fielding, I assure you, I've been doing epidurals for ages."

I snipe, "What, on the pigs in anatomy class? Get away from me and get me a real doctor, someone who's old enough to shave."

"Unfortunately, the only other anesthesiologist on call right now is eighty-seven and he just fell asleep in his soup in the doctors' lounge." I can't tell if he's toying with me or if he means it. Crap. Then he adds, "Would you rather have a doctor with good eyes and no hand tremors or should I go wake him?"

"Gah! Fine, go ahead but if you paralyze me, I'm going to sue you for every chopstick you've got!" I'm normally WAY more pc than this but I'm terrified and in pain. It's a combination that brings out the worst in me.

Dr. Lou opens the back of my gown and rubs a cold wet cotton ball on my lower back. He says, "I'm just cleaning the area before I numb you with a small shot under the skin. It's going to prick a little, but it's not the epidural."

I feel the prick and then I start to feel hot, tingly and finally numb. Blessedly numb. I take a deep breath and command, "Just give me notice before you jab that needle into my spine. And I want to know how many you've done before mine. This is information I'll need for the lawsuit."

"I've done two before you."

"What? Don't touch me! Get the old doctor with tremors. Do you hear me? You are not to touch me!"

Then he laughs out loud and replies, "This is my three hundredth and eighty-seventh epidural and it's already in."

"Really, it's in?" I burst into uncontrollable tears of relief. "Okay, I probably won't be suing then, as long as you didn't paralyze me."

At that point Elliot storms through the door looking wild-eyed and panicked. "Mimi, darling, are you okay?"

I reach out to him. "I'm fine, Elliot. I'm just fine." Then I point to Dr. Lou and announce, "This child just gave me my epidural and he did a pretty good job."

Dr. Lou shakes Elliot's hand and announces, "I'm thirty-four but your wife has been flattering me for the last several minutes." Then he says, "Good luck to you and congratulations. I'll see you both in the O.R."

Elliot grabs my hand in his. "Thank God Richard was there to drive you to the hospital! Are you sure you're okay? I was worried when I heard you shout."

I'm about to assure him again when a nurse comes in followed by Renée. "I'm just here to shave you for surgery."

"What do you mean, shave me? I'm having a C-section."

"That's right," she confirms, "but the doctor likes to have you shaved anyway."

Well, this is embarrassing. I look to Elliot and beg, "Can you please give us some privacy?"

The nurse intervenes, "You don't need to leave the room. I'll just draw the curtain." She proceeds to turn on the loudest, most archaic, sounding beard trimmer in the universe. Seriously, this is no pleasant little mild hum. It sounds like she's firing up a chain saw. I'm mortified.

I swear she's shaving for at least ten minutes when Renée yells out, "My God, are you shearing a sheep in there? What's taking so long?"

The nurse laughs, "I think we could use a new shaver."

I promise to send her a case of them if she'll just hurry up and get it over with already.

I'm feeling so confident that nothing can go wrong after the epidural that I let a student nurse put in my IV. Note to self, they're students because they don't know what the hell they're doing. I'm going to be black and blue for a week.

Meanwhile, Elliot dons his disposable surgical outfit and we're both given fashionable blue shower caps to keep our hair out of the sterile operating room. We manage a quick moment alone and my husband even pulls out his phone so we can do a pre-baby selfie. Of course, had this happened tomorrow, as planned, we would have had a slew of pictures to document the moment.

Elliot kisses me gently on the lips and declares, "We're about to become parents, you and I." Then he rests his head on my forehead and adds, "I love you Mimi Fielding, with my whole heart."

My first impression of the O.R. is that it's white and looks nothing like the operating rooms on soap operas or medical dramas. It looks more like a conference room. Just get rid of the gurney and tray full of surgical cutlery (look away!), and insert a large table with chairs and you'd be all set for a corporate takeover.

Dr. Fermin rushes in, still tying the back of her blue scrubs. "Hello, Fieldings! Looks like your little girl wanted to pick her own birthday, huh?"

I try to laugh, "Looks that way."

Then Dr. Lou puts a mask over my nose and explains, "We're just going to give you a little oxygen."

Before I can put my thoughts together to ask another question, the whole surgical team becomes engrossed in birthing my child. The doctor explains, "You're going to feel some pressure but you shouldn't feel any pain."

And true to her word, that's exactly what I feel, pushing and pulling sensations but no pain. Yay, the epidural is working!

I close my eyes and let them do their bit until I hear the words, "And here she comes! Well hello, look at what a big beautiful baby you are!" Then Dr. Fermin holds her up for us to see. She's covered in a white coating called vernix which I understand is to protect her skin from constant contact with the amniotic fluid. Isn't the human body amazing?

I can't see her as well as Elliot because I'm lying flat on my back, so I demand, "How many fingers and toes does she have?"

My husband doesn't answer right away. I don't know why it's taking him so long to count to ten so I repeat, "Elliot, how many fingers and toes does she have?"

He replies, "I don't know, I'm still counting."

His answer floods me with panic. "Are there more than ten?" I'm picturing nineteen fingers on one hand and three on the other. A similar horror about her feet grips me. I demand, "Elliot, answer my question, now!"

He looks at me with tears running down his eyes, which either means she's hideously deformed, or he's so full of emotion he's having a hard time seeing to count. I know it's the latter when he finally answers, "Five fingers on each hand and five toes on each foot." As an afterthought, he adds, "Two feet and two hands."

During all this, the doc cuts the umbilical cord and Sophie lets out her first scream of displeasure at being pulled out of her cozily warm environment. That's another thing I didn't know about operating rooms, they're freezing cold.

Then I hear Dr. Fermin laugh, "Good job, Miss Sophie." Then to us she explains, "She just piddled all over me. Looks like things are working."

The nurse takes Sophie over to be weighed and I hear her exclaim, "You're a big girl like your mommy; nine point two pounds!" First of all, what the hell does that mean, big girl like your mommy? And secondly, who cares, my baby is here and she's healthy!

The same nurse, casting aspersions about my size, brings Sophie over to me, all rolled up in a newborn hospital blanket, ala baby burrito, and plops her next to my head where I get my first real look at her.

You know how some women will tell you the second they saw their newborn, they recognized him/her like they've know them all their lives? So that's not what I'm feeling at all. I look at my little Sophie and think, huh, look at you. I thought you'd look different. I pictured her looking like a mini-me. I had brown hair as a small child and Sophie's is quite strawberry blond like Elliot. My skin is a bit darker and she's as pale as a porcelain tea cup. Then she pops her eyes open and they are cerulean blue, not baby blue, destined to change color in a few months. They're a light clear icy blue that seem to hold the secrets of the universe in them. Holy, cow, I'm a mom.

The nurse removes my daughter from the side of my head and instructs Elliot, "Okay, Dad, you come with me." Then to me she announces, "Your husband is coming with me to the nursery to clean up your daughter and make sure we get all the right wrist bands on her. He'll meet you in recovery."

Elliot stops to kiss me firmly on the mouth, dripping tears on me and whispers, "Thank you. Thank you for our daughter. I'll see you soon."

Doctor Fermin starts a monologue about what she's doing and how long it will take, but I find my thoughts drifting off. My life has just changed. I, Mimi Finnegan Fielding, am a mother. I know to the depths of my soul this is the biggest thing I will ever do. I've created life, I've birthed it and now I'm responsible for it. I am so overwhelmed I can barely breathe.

Chapter 44

True to plan, Elliot meets me in the recovery room, followed by a nurse carrying Sophie. The nurse hands the baby to Elliot and then approaches me. "The first order of business is to get that surgical gown off you."

She manhandles me until I'm totally naked to the waist. Then she takes Sophie from Elliot's arms, unwraps her from her blanket and drops an equally naked miss right on top of me. "Skin to skin contact is the most important part of bonding." To Elliot, she adds, "This goes for you too, Dad. Babies don't see very well for a while, so they have to get the smell of you to bond with you."

Sophie's noodling her face right into my chest and the nurse announces, "She wants to nurse. It's the first instinct to kick in." Then she arranges her so that her tiny mouth is on my breast and Sophie begins to suckle. This is a positively unreal moment. As if it all weren't miraculous enough, I'm creating food for my child. I totally want to high five our creator for coming up with this ingenious engineering.

After a half-hour of bonding, Dr. Fermin walks in and

greets, "Nice work, Mimi! Let's take you up to your room and get you settled." Once there, the parade of family members starts.

The room is rather small, but it's private, so I'm not complaining. My parents come in first. With superhuman roadrunner speed, my mom has Sophie in her arms and starts cooing at her. My dad comes right to my bedside and sits down. He praises, "Good job, honey. I knew you'd do great." He takes my hand and squeezes it. "I couldn't be any prouder of you, Meems. You're going to be a wonderful mom!"

I'm so overcome with respect for my parents at this moment. They did this four times. I can't imagine being responsible for four lives. It's a hugely overwhelming thought. Then I think of my sister who just gave birth to three. Holy crap! I had no real concept of how she must be feeling until now. The thought of three Sophie's is positively awe inspiring and a bit nauseating.

My dad takes his turn holding his newest granddaughter, before my mom announces it's time they let the baby's other grandparents meet her. They promise to come back as soon as the excitement winds down a bit.

I'm not sure how I expect Elliot's parents to act when they first see Sophie, but if push came to shove and I had to speculate, I'm sure I would expect them to be very dignified in their delight. You know, something like, "My goodness, look at you. Good job, Mimi." and perhaps a mini tiara for Sophie, thrown in as a gesture of goodwill. What happens is nothing like that.

Victoria comes first and she's initially drawn to Sophie,

much like my mom was, but she doesn't pick her up. Instead, she gently kisses her finger and touches my daughter's cheek. Then she just stares at her. By the time she looks at me, she's full on bawling. Her shoulders heave with emotion and she doesn't even try to wipe the tears from her eyes. Then she walks over to my bedside and throws herself in my arms. Still sobbing, she manages, "Thank you, Mimi. Thank you for all you've done for my son and thank you for my grandbaby! You are an amazing woman!"

If I weren't already lying down, you'd have to pick me up off the floor because I'd have fallen in a dead faint upon hearing those words. I'm not sure how to respond. I'm afraid Victoria is going to be embarrassed by her outpouring of emotion, once she realizes what she's done, so I don't want to get too mushy with her. Although, not to enjoy this moment would be a shame because there's no guarantee she'll ever like me this much again.

I tentatively hug her back and respond, "This is quite the thing, huh?" Then I clarify, "Motherhood, I mean."

She's doesn't lessen her grip even one iota when she responds, "Yes, yes it is."

The earl finally breaks it up and announces, "Move over, Victoria. I need to give Mimi a hug of my own." Then he proceeds to nearly squeeze the stuffing out of me before standing up and pulling a small box out of his jacket pocket. He hands it to me and says, "A token of our appreciation."

With a look to my husband, I hesitantly take the box and open it. Inside is a gorgeous round cut yellow diamond in a very old and intricate gold setting. The earl announces, "This ring has been worn by the lady who's birthed the Fielding heir since 1720. It's been Victoria's since Elliot was born and now it's yours to care for until your first grandchild is born."

I'm overcome with the importance of this moment to Elliot's parents. They are fully welcoming me into the fold and have entrusted me with the care of a precious family heirloom. This is quite a momentous event.

I thank them both sincerely and try to imagine a similar scenario in my family. I get an image of my mother handing Renée my great, great grandmother's silver salad tongs explaining, "These have been in our family since 1920. They've tossed salads for generations and now they belong to you." Seriously, I think those tongs are the closest thing my family has to something of heirloom quality.

After Elliot's parents leave, Renée and Laurent come in. Renée smacks kisses all over Sophie's face and declares, "No biggie, right? I knew you could do it!"

They only stay a couple of minutes before Ginger and Johnathan arrive. Ginger stares longingly at Sophie and sighs, "Look at that. There's only one of her." Then to me, she adds, "You're going to love her so much."

Muffy and Kevin are stuck at The Buff Muff and can't get away until later, so Richard and Pip come in next. Richard picks up Sophie and holds her close to his heart. With a kiss on the top of her head, he hands her to Pip and approaches Elliot. With his hand out, he offers, "Congratulations, Elliot, you have a beautiful family."

Elliot takes his hand and an unspoken declaration of peace passes between them. My sweet English husband replies, "I wish the same for you, Richard." Then his eyes dart to his sister and back to Richard, in a silent endorsement of whatever may come.

After everyone is gone, I nurse Sophie again and then hand her off to her daddy while I take a nap. It's amazing how tired I am considering I've just been laying around all morning.

Chapter 45

Sleeping without having to get up to go to the bathroom is the most amazingly wonderful thing in the world. I was catheterized for the surgery and am happy to learn it will stay in place until sometime tomorrow. If I'd had the option, I would have had one put in around my sixth month of pregnancy.

Sometime during my nap, I start to sweat like a marathon runner in the throes of her twenty-second mile. I'm positively drenched. I understand from Renée that I should embrace this with great joy as it means the pregnancy poundage is starting to release itself. The nurse comes in twice to change my bedding before nighttime.

After a very full first day of motherhood, I'm ready to hit the hay when Muffy and Kevin finally arrive. My sister flops down into a chair and exclaims, "I'm so sorry we're late. We have a tournament going on at The Buff Muff and neither one of us could get away."

Kevin asks, "How're you feeling, Meems?"

I reply to them both, "No worries, at least you're here now, and I'm feeling completely and utterly exhausted. Throw in a dash of nerves, a pinch of accomplishment and a gallon of sheer excitement." Then I wink, "That's my recipe for the most intoxicating cocktail on the planet."

Muffy demands, "Where's my niece?"

"She's in the nursery. I was just getting ready to go to sleep. Let me ring the nurse for her."

A moment after I push the button, Trista, the night nurse peeks her head in. I ask for Sophie and she goes to retrieve her.

Kevin asks, "Where's Elliot?"

"I told him to go ahead and sleep at home. I just want to pass out and the nursery is taking care of the baby. I figure he's going to need as much rest as he can get before we take her home."

Before the nurse can bring Sophie back in the room, I fall sound asleep. I don't wake up again until they give her to me to feed at 4 a.m. They have to change my sheets again and then I fall back into the arms of sweet slumber until Elliot arrives at 8.

My husband greets me with an achingly tender kiss and a takeout order from The Cracked Egg. "Belgium waffles, a farmer's omelet and pigs in the blanket," he announces. I dig in before he can even take his coat off.

In between mouthfuls of heavenly nourishment, I answer his many questions. I slept wonderfully, I'm still tired but I'm more excited than anything else and yes, I think our baby is the prettiest and most perfect in the whole world.

Our families spread out their visits during the day so there's constant company, though it's a much more relaxed pace than yesterday. Abbie is with us much of the day doing her own bonding with Sophie. Our nanny appears to love our daughter on sight and I'm delighted by what a natural she is with her.

Flowers are delivered every hour until the hospital room looks like a green house. My work sends a bouquet, Elliot's publisher sends one, there are more from various family and friends and at 4 p.m. we receive a very royal bunch from the Queen of England. Elliot offers to take some of them home so there's still enough room for my bed.

While he's gone, the doctor checks my vitals and removes the catheter. She informs me that I'll be in for two more nights before she okays me to go home. Then she helps me out of the bed and into the bathroom for the first time since yesterday morning.

My body doesn't quite feel like my own. My legs are rubbery from the epidural and inactivity, I feel about a million times lighter and my stomach has no sensation at all. When I touch it, I don't feel a thing. Doctor Fermin informs me that's because she cut a bunch of nerves when she made the incision. She assures me as they grow together I will return to normal.

I manage to use the bathroom and get back into bed before Sophie is brought in to nurse. I love to hold her and smell her and snuggle with her. It's amazing I lived all these years without her. How did I do that? Time seems to have restarted itself with her birth and already it's hard to imagine I was ever happy before her.

Abbie goes home at five to put dinner on for Elliot's family, and for the first time all day, I'm alone with my baby. I stare at her fingers, kiss her toes and rub her back. What a perfect little being she is. I wonder what life has in store for her as the lyrics of that old Doris Day song, Que Sera Sera, run through my head. It's then I realize I have no control over what Sophie's future holds and I feel a shot of fear run through run me.

I hum to my sweet child and vow that I will give her everything in my power. I will dedicate my life to her. I will nurture her, comfort her, teach her and beat up anyone who hurts her. I know at this moment that I won't go back to work until she's ready for school. Even then, I might just wait by the door and stare at it until she comes home to me.

Chapter 46

At three o'clock in the morning I wake in a blind panic. Where's Sophie? I start hitting the nurse's call button like my child's life depends on it. When my daughter is finally brought to me, I grab her like I'm rescuing her from a sinking ship. What is going on?

I try to calm myself enough to discern the root of my terror. Was it a bad dream, I wonder? Yet, I don't even remember dreaming. Have I suddenly become psychic and am reacting to a real threat to my child? This is highly unlikely as I've never shown any propensity for having more than the requisite five senses.

What in all that's holy is happening to me then? The anxiety is not lessening. I wind up spending the entire night sitting up in bed holding my baby, wrapped in fear that something malevolent is lurking. By the time Elliot gets here, I'm beyond exhausted. I don't explain what's going on inside of me because truthfully, I have no idea what it is. I just command him to hold Sophie and not to put her down until I wake up.

Three hours later, I open my eyes to find neither husband nor baby are in the room. The panic returns like a flip of the switch. I throw off my sheets, swing my legs over the side of the bed and tentatively try to stand. I must be behind on my pain killers because my incision stabs like I've just been attacked by a pack of wild dogs.

I very gingerly begin my first real exercise since giving birth. I walk out the door of my room and take off down the hall. A few people pass me, nurses, doctors and random visitors. Everyone smiles pleasantly like I'm not in the middle of the worst nightmare of my life. I can't find my baby!

I must look normal enough because nobody offers to help me. I'm about to scream when I spy Elliot about ten doors down coming toward me. He's alone.

I yell out, "Where's Sophie?"

My husband picks up his pace and greets, "Good morning sweetheart, how did you sleep?"

I don't answer. Instead I demand, "Where's Sophie?"

Even Elliot doesn't seem to be aware of how upset I am because he simply responds, "The nurse took her for a hearing test."

"Why?" I demand. "Is something wrong with her hearing? Are you sure it was a nurse? Did you check her ID?"

My sweet husband is beginning to clue in that all is not well with me. "Mimi," he starts, "are you okay?"

"No!" I screech. "I'm not. I need to see my baby and make sure she's okay." Then I add, "Now Elliot, go find her!" He clearly doesn't know what to do. I see that he wants to help me but the only way he can do that is to bring me my child.

He finally seems to fathom my command and instructs, "Go back to your room and I'll find the baby." I nod my head like he's explaining quantum fusion to me. The words eventually soak in and I begin to return from whence I came.

I want to rip my head open and pull out this new interloper, fear. It's a real thing, not just some fleeting sensation. This bitch appears to be digging in like an inoperable tumor.

Once I get back to my room, I use the bathroom and then start pacing until Elliot walks in with our daughter. I demand, "Hand her to me."

As soon as she's safely in my arms, my breathing starts to calm. Elliot helps me into bed and I nurse Sophie. It's like I've just been given a shot of Valium. I immediately start to calm down, but I'm still not the person I was when I went to bed last night. That blissfully ignorant woman is nowhere to be seen and I miss her.

Elliot finally asks, "Mimi, what's going on?"

I look at him wild-eyed and confess, "I don't know. I woke up in the middle of the night full of terror that something bad was about to happen to the baby. I couldn't sleep all night. By the time you got here I was so tired I could barely keep my eyes open. When I woke up and couldn't find you, it was like the middle of the night all over again. Elliot," I say, "something's happening to me and I hate how it feels."

Completely missing the degree of my distress, he tries to sooth, "You're a mother now, darling. Things are bound to feel different."

I let him think his words are profound and helpful but

they're not. I'm afraid if I try to convey the level of how crazy I feel, he won't understand and will be afraid to leave Sophie with me, and Sophie is the only thing I can focus on.

I ask, "Would you mind going out and getting me a hot chocolate?" I want a hot chocolate about as much as I want an enema, but I need to get rid of him so I can talk to a nurse and find out what's going on with me.

My clueless husband kisses me on the forehead and replies, "I'd be happy to, darling."

As soon as he leaves I ring for the nurse. When she arrives, she introduces herself as Carol and I explain, "Carol, I'm feeling a little crazy here."

She laughs, "Well, why wouldn't you? You've just given birth and your hormones are all over the place." She assures, "It's normal, honey."

"Carol," I begin, "I don't just feel a little off. I feel completely nuts, like I want to rip my brain out through my nose. What can we do about that?"

Again, missing the degree of my distress, the middle aged hospital worker replies, "Honey, it's just the baby blues. They don't last long, so you just have to hang in there with it. You'll be fine in a couple of weeks."

Calling what I'm experiencing, something as benign sounding as "the baby blues," is the equivalent of comparing Godzilla to a cute little monkey. This is no piddling little thing like feeling a tad weepy. This is a real monster and I have no idea what to do about it.

When the doctor arrives later in the morning, I send Elliot on another fool's errand, this time for graham crackers and cool whip. I approach her a little more intensely than I did the nurse. "Dr. Fermin," I start. "I feel completely insane. I woke up in the middle of the night in a panic that something was wrong with Sophie and I can't seem to shake that worry."

She smiles at me and responds, "Being a parent is a whole new world, Mimi. You're bound to experience a plethora of new emotions."

I explain, "I feel like I have a fear demon in my head. I'm anxious, panicky and very, very afraid." I clearly state, "This cannot be a normal reaction to motherhood."

My doctor replies, "Everyone feels something different. Look," she explains, "you're almost thirty-six years old. Two days ago you were filled with all of these wonderful pregnancy hormones that were approximately the equivalent of what your levels were when you were sixteen. In the course of twenty minutes, you gave birth and those hormones started to revert to those of a woman in her late thirties."

I want to point out that I'm most definitely in my mid-thirties, not my late thirties, but I realize in her eyes they're similar enough, so I hold my tongue.

She continues, "Most woman experience some level of postpartum, even if they aren't aware of it. It's bound to be elevated in your case. If you don't feel better in a few weeks, let me know and we'll figure something out."

"A few weeks?" I demand. I want to rip my head off now. "How in the world am I going to handle feeling like this for a few weeks?"

She smiles, "With the help of your husband and family.

You can do this, Mimi. You're a strong woman."

The hell she says. I cannot do this, but sadly there doesn't seem to be an alternative.

Chapter 47

When Elliot comes back with my snack, the one I have no intention of eating, I ask him to call everyone and ask them not to come to the hospital today. He seems a bit surprised but concedes to my wishes readily enough.

I'm constantly thirsty. I know it's because I'm nursing and my body craves fluids, but I'm having the hardest time eating or drinking anything. I find the only way I can consume water is to close my eyes and take slow sips. The liquid can't be too cold or I feel panicky, it can't be hot or I feel panicky. It's like the three little bears, on crack, playing it out in my head. Everything has to be just so or I can't handle it.

I start to feel a little calmer with no visitors. Elliot doesn't leave my side all day and he holds Sophie when she's not in my arms. It's just the three of us in our sterile hospital bubble. I'm lured into the false hope the anxiety is decreasing. Maybe this is just a fast moving thing and my hormone levels are almost balanced again, and maybe I'm about to sprout wings and fly.

The nurse comes in and suggests I take a shower. This sounds like a lovely idea. I've been sweating like a pig for two days and my hair feels like a bucket of grease has been dropped on it. Suddenly, I want to get clean more than I want to draw breath. She helps me out of bed and into the bathroom before leaving me to my business.

The water feels heavenly spraying down on my scalp. I lather myself like I'm trying to wash away raw sewage. That's when it hits. I become dizzy, so I open my eyes to catch my balance and realize the walls of the tiny shower stall are closing in on me. It's like I'm being sucked through a straw. My heart starts racing and I can't catch my breath. I try to call out to Elliot to help me but I can't get enough air in my lungs to make a sound.

I wind up sitting on the toilet, soaking wet, and covered in suds for a good five minutes before I can talk myself into returning to the shower to rinse off. Even with the curtain open, it is the singularly hardest thing I've ever done. That includes the ten mile marathon I ran in high school and staying up all night to cram for tests in college. I would have much rather gone for an excruciating uphill run, barefoot in the snow with a boulder on my back or spent eight agonizing hours immersed in German verb conjugation, than go back into the minuscule capsule of a shower for even a minute.

By the time I'm finally clean and cross the threshold of my room, I'm in tears. I sob to my husband, "Elliot, I've started to feel claustrophobic." I hiccup and shake as my shoulders convulse, "The walls were closing in on me. I , I , I ..." but I can't catch my breath to go on.

He stands up, puts Sophie in her bassinet and welcomes me into his loving embrace. I let him hold me until I process he's no longer holding the baby and I scream, "Elliot, pick up Sophie! Remember our deal?" I remind him, "If I'm not holding her, you are. Got it?"

His lovely lordship has no idea what's going on with me and looks a bit frightened by my latest outburst. I would love to console him and tell him not to worry, that I'll get over whatever's happening, but the thing is; I'm not sure I will.

Yet, I don't want him to think I'm insane and worry about Sophie's safety with me, so I try to put his mind at ease and relay, "Dr. Fermin says this is all normal and falls under the scope of a postpartum reaction to rebalancing hormones." I call bullshit on that nonsense but it seems to make Elliot feel better.

The only time I don't want to smack my head into the wall in hopes of killing the fear monster is when I'm nursing my baby. I'm sure my body is producing some lovely chemical that works as a tranquilizer. I only wish someone would bottle it so I could supplement whatever I'm making, because it doesn't seem to be quite enough.

Elliot stays in the hospital with me that night so I can sleep. We keep Sophie in the room with us. Just knowing he and the baby are right there seems to quell my anxiety enough for me to surrender to unconsciousness. Elliot brings my daughter to me when she wants to nurse and then changes her diaper and puts her back into her bassinet.

The next morning, Dr. Fermin comes to make sure that I've had a bowel movement. Pooping seems to be the holy grail of surgery. Once your body can perform that basic function, you're well on your way to recovery.

Sophie will visit the doctor in four days to make sure all is well. My first appointment won't be for six weeks. My doctor instructs me to call her in three weeks to let her know how my anxiety is. I was thinking a daily check-in would be better, but I reluctantly agree to her schedule.

Elliot loads the flowers, gifts and bags into the car while I sit and feed the baby. It's 11 a.m. by the time he comes for us and I don't want to leave. This tiny little nothing of a hospital room feels like my new home. I've bonded with it. It's the only residence my daughter's ever known. I burst into tears like I'm being forcibly removed from my childhood home. I feel like a total lunatic.

Once we get Sophie all buckled into her infant car seat, I get into the passenger's side next to Elliot. Before he can pull out, I stop him. "I'm going to sit in the back with the baby."

As soon as I get out of the car, I start to scan the parking garage like I expect suicide ninjas to attack. I hurriedly climb into the back and yell, "Lock the doors and step on it!"

There's nothing you're thinking that hasn't already crossed my mind. I'm eighty-seven percent sure no one has hired ninjas to come after us. I fully know how idiotic my thoughts are, but there's nothing I can do to stop them. It's like someone else has moved into my brain and they're forcing these ridiculous feelings.

Elliot has forewarned his family, Richard, and Abbie to make themselves scarce when we get home. I do not want to see anyone. I take Sophie straight up to my room and shut the door. I crawl into bed and lay her next to me before falling into a deep sleep. When I wake up I'm not even sure who I am, yet alone where I am, although my first instinct is to reach out for my baby.

Elliot comes in and asks if I want to eat. I don't, but I know I need to in order to keep my milk production up, so I ask him to bring me what everyone else is having. He arrives a short while later with a goat cheese and fennel salad and a steaming bowl of lentil soup. It looks and smells wonderful but still manages to have the appeal of a bowl full of raw slugs.

The Englishman sits next to me on the bed while I pick at it. "Mimi," he says, "I know you're having a rough time. I want you to know I'm here for you. Anything you need or want, just tell me."

I fear I need a padded room and want the fear monster to die, but I know he can't help me with those, so I merely thank him.

He asks, "Everyone would like to come in and welcome you home. Is that okay?"

I shake my head, "No. No one comes in." Then I throw him a bone, "Maybe tomorrow."

I can imagine my husband trying to explain my behavior to our families, and I know how I must sound to them, but the reality is so much worse that I can't seem to care.

Chapter 48

Abbie knocks on the door the next morning and asks to be let in. I don't want to let her, but I reason she's probably not going to kill us, so I respond, "You can come in, but only for a minute."

She peaks her head around the corner before walking over to the bed. She sits down next to me and declares, "Mimi, you need some exercise."

I shake my head. "Can't. The doctor says not for two weeks."

She responds, "You can't actually work out for two weeks but you have to get out of bed and walk." She promises, "It's the only thing that's going to help fight the demons in your head."

I look up at her in surprise, "What do you know about the demons in my head?"

She answers, "My mom had horrible postpartum depression with her last baby. It was bad, Mimi. I know you're terrified and I know you don't feel like yourself. I'm telling you, you've got to get out of this bed and start moving." She continues, "Your body will produce some righteous chemicals as a reaction and those are what's going to get you through this."

She's so sure of herself and so forceful in her belief that I trust her. I believe her enough to have her get Sophie's stroller ready, because God knows I'm not leaving my baby behind. I quickly get dressed in some yoga pants and a heavy sweater and venture out of my cave.

The house feels bigger than I remember and I worry I won't feel secure ever again. Without drawing any attention to myself, I bundle Sophie into her stroller and walk out the front door. At first, I just stroll around the circumference of the fountain. I do this about twenty times before venturing down the length of the driveway. I manage that about ten times before I start to feel a little better. Twenty more laps around the drive and I feel nearly as normal as I did before the baby was born.

When I finally go inside, I'm ready to see people. Victoria is the first person I run into. She stays at a distance and doesn't crowd me, just greets, "Mimi, welcome home. How's Sophie?"

I reply, "She's fine and thank you. I'm glad to be home." Not. But our relationship is already weird enough. I don't want to add fuel to her fire.

She smiles and declares, "Maybe we'll see you at supper."

I make a noncommittal sound and walk by her on my way up the stairs. By the time I get back to my room, I realize I don't feel as anxious as I expected to, talking to someone other than my husband. Maybe I really will join them.

I make three more trips outside to walk off the looming

crazies. I worry about the most insane array of things. I'm constantly scanning the grounds to make sure there are no snipers hiding behind shrubbery. The same goes for the trees. I keep looking up to prepare myself for a drop attack.

I remember the woman from the support group who incessantly worried about terrorist attacks and I decide to adopt her fear as my own. I believe I've already mentioned how susceptible I am to suggestion. So I now scan the horizon for low flying airplanes, and God help me, missiles.

I know you're thinking, Mimi you need to go back to that support group. You have to let them help you get through this. Yeah, well that's not going to happen. If I go back, I'll hear fifty things that haven't occurred to me to panic over and I will, once the idea is introduced. No outside commiserating for me. I've got to do this on my own, in the relative safety of my home.

Abbie's made my favorite, beet Wellington with garlic potatoes and a peach crisp with vanilla ice cream to tempt me. I find after two hours of walking and copious breast feeding, I've worked up quite an appetite.

Everyone seems happy to see me when I walk into the dining room with Sophie snugged in her baby carrier next to me. Richard is the first to speak, "Welcome home, Mimi! How are you feeling?"

Pip, who's sitting in the seat next to him, smacks him in the arm and reprimands, "Richard! You know how she's feeling. Shhh."

The earl hurries to add his own sentiment, "We're so happy the birth went well. Good job, Mimi!"

After a few more "go Mimi" moments I decide to address the elephant in the room. "Look everyone. I know Elliot's told you I'm not myself. And I'm sure Abbie's mentioned something about postpartum issues. They're both right." I explain, "I can't explain what's going on in my head, but it's not pretty. I'm anxious, fearful and claustrophobic. I won't let anyone but Elliot hold the baby and I may not be around much. Thanks to Abbie, and her edict that I walk, I'll probably be in the driveway for a good portion of my days until this passes."

Pip interrupts, "Your grandma Sissy says the same thing happened to her. She promises you'll be okay, just take it one moment at a time."

Richard turns to Elliot's sister, "Philippa, what a lovely sentiment. I'm sure Mimi is thrilled to hear from her grandmother."

Pip snaps, "Are you being sarcastic, Richard? Because I don't think this is the time or place."

"Quite the contrary," my friend responds. "I think your gift is wonderful and people are lucky to have you share it with them."

My sister-in-law doesn't look convinced. "Except when my message is directed to you, is that it?"

"Not at all," Richard rejoins, "I'm very happy to receive all messages that come your way for me. Do you have another by chance?"

"Not at this time," she looks skeptical, "but I'll keep you posted."

Abbie and Elliot bring in the dinner plates and the nanny

joins us. She announces, "Mimi, you need to eat a lot of protein to keep your blood sugar up. It'll really help with the postpartum, so I'll be supplementing your food throughout the day."

I smile, "Thank you, Abbie. I'm not sure what we would have done without you these last couple of months."

Elliot contributes, "You may not be allowed to touch the baby, but we're delighted to have you on as our cook and house organizer."

The nanny replies, "Don't worry. Mimi's going to do great and she'll eventually let me help with Sophie." When pigs fly. This is my baby and unless you helped make her, hands off. But I don't say that out loud.

I enjoy everyone's company but I'm more than ready to retire to the solitude of my room when dinner's over. Elliot accompanies me and carries the baby.

When the door is closed, he asks, "How are you feeling?"

"Very, very tired. I think I'll just crawl into bed and go to sleep."

Elliot kisses me on the forehead and replies, "You do that, darling. I'll go back down and play host. Just call out if you need anything."

The first thing I do when my husband leaves is to check all the windows to make sure they're locked. Then I address the bathroom, closets and under the bed. Once I'm assured there are no boogey men about, I change into my nightgown and crawl into bed to nurse Sophie.

Sophie is only four days old and already I can't remember what life was like without her. What did I do with my time when there wasn't a baby to care for? What did I think about when not constantly gripped by fear? I vaguely remember my old life but it no longer seems like it was mine. It's more like I'm experiencing someone else's memories.

Chapter 49

Sophie wakes at three a.m. and seems bent of being up for a while. She doesn't want to nurse; she just wants to be held. So I carry her downstairs to the den. This way I can turn on the light without disturbing Elliot.

After thirty minutes of playing 'Where are Sophie's Toes?' she's ready to eat. I get situated on the soft brown leather sofa, cover us with a cashmere throw and settle in. I haven't watched television since the baby was born and decide to see if there's an old movie playing. I'm a huge devotee of old romantic comedies. Anything with Rock Hudson, Cary Grant, Tony Randal or Doris Day totally floats my boat.

I'm in luck! *Lover Come Back* is on TCM, with Doris, Rock *and* Tony! I've only seen it about twenty times, but can't wait to experience the hijinks all over again, as it's one of my favorites. Just as the Universal logo shows up on the screen, I'm overcome with a new emotion, nostalgia. Not nostalgia as though I'm reminiscing about a good time in my own life. I wasn't even alive when this film was made. I'm flooded with a deep melancholy that this amazing era has come and gone. It's no more and never will be again. My heart hurts so badly, it feels like it's going to stop working.

This new symptom of my insanity leaves me breathless at the thought that two of these three actors are dead, not even on the planet, and the other is an old lady barely clinging to life. Oh my God, oh my God, oh my God, a surge of grief rushes through me and I'm about to climb the walls. I try to force myself to watch the show and pass through the moment but it's no good. Every time Doris shows up in a snappy new outfit, I want to cry. How can I ache so much for a time I never experienced to begin with?

Sophie is sound asleep and I don't want to wake her by dragging her up and down the driveway in the cold. Not to mention, there are so many untold dangers lying in wait in the dark, I could never keep us safe. So I do the next logical thing. I situate her in the center of the room and start walking laps around the den. This isn't quite as crazy as it would have been in my little yellow house on Mercer St. Our den now, is as big as my whole downstairs used to be. Still, I know it's plenty nuts, but throw me a bone, huh?

As the days unfold, I adopt the strange schedule of all new mothers. I sleep when I can and am often up for a good portion of the night. I talk to my family and allow them to visit in small groups. I let no one hold the baby.

I find I'm unable to talk to Ginger for very long, which is weird. You'd think I'd be craving her company more than anyone else's, as she's in the same new motherhood boat I'm in. It's just I'm afraid I'll start to panic for her much like I did for Sophie when she was still in utero. I can't even think of my sister for too long without feeling itchy. I have no idea how she's handling the rigors of new motherhood. If I were her, I'd have to be institutionalized. The jury is still out whether or not there's a padded room with my name on it.

Sophie's first doctor appointment comes and goes and she's thriving. My visit isn't for weeks and I can't wait. I need fixing and I need it now.

Richard stays for a week and if you can believe it, decides to commute back to our house on the weekends to continue his pursuit of Pip. Elliot's parents appear to have moved in and I don't even suggest to my husband that he tell them to leave. They pretty much leave me alone and take care of themselves so I figure, no harm, no foul.

Abbie and Pip spend their days stringing off the areas in the yard they envision for the gardens. It used to be just one garden, but they've gotten creative and want to plant several smaller ones with interwoven paths. They're calling it a permaculture paradise. As long as they leave me and the baby alone, I'm good with it.

The nanny continues to cook all of our meals as well, which truthfully, is a godsend. We'd be eating a lot of Cheerios and frozen pizza if it was up to me. I join the family for dinner every night, but other than that, see very little of them.

Now that I can no longer watch old movies or old television shows (same reaction to those as I have to the movies) I've have to discover new forms of entertainment. It turns out laugh tracks cause me extreme anxiety, so sit-coms are out. News programs are definitely a no-no because of all the dreary tidings they bring. I try to watch a variety of talent shows but find myself in a state of terror for the contestants. That's when I land on my new addiction, alien programming. Apparently there's such a profession as 'ancient astronaut theorist,' and they are full of ideas on how our planet became populated.

If you believe what they're preaching, earth was settled by various ET colonies. Our brothers from other worlds landed here and bred with the 1.0 version of man in order to form a slave population to do their bidding. Early man supplied the physical form that could sustain life on this planet and the aliens contributed the grey matter which allowed us to evolve into semi-intelligent beings.

If you grew up Christian, like I did, these theorists even credibly explain away biblical miracles as being of otherworldly origin. For instance, manna from heaven is the food the aliens brought to keep Moses and his followers alive when they were banished to the desert for forty years. These theorists even speculate they've found the remnants of a manna machine, which I muse is really just an ancient bread machine. Chariots in the sky, Jesus's ascension and Jacob's ladder are all references to spaceships beaming up, Star Trek style.

One of the theorists, who likes to wear his hair in creative ways, ponders why humans are so willing to believe in miracles of old, and are so set in this historic thinking, they're unwilling to listen to a plausible explanation. He asks, "How can man be so eager to accept something unexplained on the basis of faith and not be willing to hear possible elucidation?"

Another ancient astronaut theorist, who claims to have

been brought up in the church wonders, "Why would a God as powerful and great as ours stop creating at humans? If He could form vast colonies of galaxies and dimensions, why would He pick earth, the equivalent of a speck of dust on sheep, and call it quits?"

I get so worked up over this whole thing, I decide to call Father Brennan. I share I've been having a hard time since Sophie was born and ask him to please stop by the house when he has time. Today is that day. I've asked Abbie to come and get me when he arrives, which is at two p.m. sharp.

Father Brennan has been my family priest since I was a kid. He's got to be nearly seventy, so I'm thinking my questions are going to shock him to the core. After all, he grew up before Steven Spielberg introduced us to the possibility of close encounters of any kind, yet alone the third kind.

Abbie has made us madeleines and Red Zinger tea and she serves us in the library. "Father Brennan," I greet, "thank you for coming!"

He stands up to hug me and replies, "Thank you for inviting me. I assume I'm here to talk about Sophie's baptism."

"Um, no, not really," I explain. "I haven't begun to think about that yet." I confess, "I'd really like to talk about aliens."

Father Brennan sits down and asks, "What would you like to know?"

I start, "I'd like to know what you think of aliens. Do you believe they exist?"

He smiles, "Well, Mimi, I'll level with you. I do." Of course this is not the response I anticipated. I expect him to refute the prospect and call my faith into question for even suggesting the possibility of life on other planets.

I ask, "Is this your opinion or the church's opinion or both?"

He replies with a question of his own, "Did you know the Vatican owns the second largest telescope in the world?"

I did not know that and I say as much. "What does the Vatican need with a telescope?"

"The church doesn't believe religion and science are separate entities. In order to appreciate the world that was created for us, we need to understand it. We look to the heavens to learn and we look to the heavens for further appreciation of God."

I'm floored by his response and ask, "So the church believes in aliens?"

Father Brennan confirms, "One of the Vatican's astronomers wrote an article for the Vatican newspaper called, ***The Alien is My Brother***. I've committed to memory the following quote because it so beautifully addresses human speculation of other worldly beings." He quotes, "'*As there is a multiplicity of creatures on earth, so there may be other beings, intelligent, created by God. This does not conflict with our faith, because we cannot put limits on the creative freedom of God.*'" He explains, "If I tell you there is no such thing as extraterrestrials, then I'm taking it upon myself to speak for God and that's not my job. My job is to share the love of God, the word of God, but not to speak for Him. That is His job alone. And He does it in a myriad of ways." Taking a sip of his tea, he adds, "If only man were paying closer attention."

I venture, "Do you believe these beings are visiting earth

and trying to make contact with us?"

He answers, "I believe if it is in their power to do so, they would be crazy not to establish communication. I'm sure they're just as curious about us as we are about them."

If I didn't think I was stark raving nuts before, I do now. "Father Brennan, if they're here, do you believe they're here to help us?"

My priest goes quiet while he contemplates his answer. "I believe," he eventually states, "that we would be very foolish indeed, to accept all extraterrestrial life as benevolent. Mankind certainly runs the gamut of intention. I think we would be well advised to believe the same of life created in other worlds."

Well crap, now I not only have to worry about suicide ninjas, terrorists, old movies and enclosed spaces; I have to worry about mean spirited aliens invading our planet. I want to press rewind on my life and go back to a time when I didn't think about any of this.

Chapter 50

Over the next week, I totally focus my anxiety on the presence of aliens on our planet. I add more programming to the 'ancient alien theorist' brigade and now have more questions than ever.

For instance, I've been very comfortable not knowing how the pyramids, Stonehenge and other ancient marvels were built. I've just accepted them as a fait accompli, until the alien theorists got ahold of me. Now I'm left wondering if these awesome structures weren't built as communication towers by the beings that fashioned them. You know, ET phone home?

How could pyramids have been erected all over our planet before intercontinental travel and communications were even possible? Some chief in Mexico and a King of the Nile wake up on the same day and think, "I know, let's start building an impossibly huge, triangular-shaped edifice that won't even be finished in our lifetimes. You know, just for kicks."

Without technical knowhow, how did our early ancestors even fathom such a thing? If you believe the theorists, which I'm starting to do, it was made possible by civilizations from other worlds that had the technology, and who guided said construction.

If you triangulate the pyramids in Egypt with the ones in Mexico and Indonesia, they point directly to the star system Pleaides, which some claim is the cradle of all life in the cosmos. They are supposedly the humanoid type beings that seeded our planet.

I make another call to Father Brennan about this because the concept seriously rocks my religious foundation. My priest encourages me to remember the bible was written by humans, at a time when they didn't understand technology. He assures me we have to interpret the stories not as absolute truth, because our knowledge is so much greater than theirs was, but more metaphorically.

He encourages me not to place so much emphasis on how we were created but what we are going to do with our creation. "Remember, Mimi," he says, "even if God used another one of His creations to start ours, we are still of His design."

By watching these shows I learn more bizarre information. Ancient spaceship shaped earrings are still housed in the museum in Machu Picchu. If you look closely at some of the paintings from the old masters, you can spy UFOs in the background. Sculpture and glyphs dating back to 10,000 B.C. clearly depict other worldly phenomenon. Then there are the Nazca lines in Peru and disappearances of whole cultures like the Anasazi, in North America. Oh my aching head! Why does all of this come into my life now, when every day is a challenge to get through?

Tonight, I'm up with Sophie at three a.m., as per her

norm, and I flip on a new alien program. This one is dedicated solely to exploring the origin of man through an alien-human assumption. They discuss how RH negative blood types are considered an indicator of extraterrestrial ancestry. My mom's AB negative. Super! What in the hell does that make me?

I really perk up when they broach the subject of the royal family. As you know, my husband has some genetic ties there, so this directly affects me, or rather Sophie, who shares her father's blood. Apparently, there's a species of beings that lives under the earth's surface in an intricate underground cave system spanning the globe. They are known as the reptilians, and are hypothesized to be the offspring of an ancient civilization that was forced to move underground because of a catastrophic atmospheric phenomenon, like the eruption of a mega volcano which would have resulted in ice age like conditions above the surface.

The more I hear about the reptilians, the more I want to pour bleach in my ears and scrub the images out of my brain. They are supposedly a malevolent society bent on world domination. They began creeping out of their holes around the time royal families started to pop up in history. It's theorized all royal families, including American "royalty" like the Vanderbilt's, Rockerfellers and Kennedys are of reptilian lineage.

I know this all sounds totally absurd and I'm sure if I had working use of my faculties, I'd disregard it as lunacy. But I'm not currently sane and even my family priest seems to be of a mind to believe some of this alien nonsense.

That's when it hits me. This is what's been freaking Abbie

out! She has revulsion for all things royal and was even mumbling about creepy reptiles when Elliot's parents arrived. Holy crap! I do the only thing I can think of and that is to grab the baby and go bang on the pool house door.

Yes, it's four in the morning and no, I haven't considered how rude it is to wake the nanny because I'm obsessing over my husband's potential connection to malicious under lords. I just do it.

Abbie opens the door looking dead tired and worried. "Mimi, what's going on? Is everyone okay?"

I push my way in and lock the deadbolt behind me. "Abbie, do you think the royal family are reptilians?" After all, why not just sound completely ridiculous from the get go? I don't know how you'd ease into a conversation like this other than just going for it.

Abbie gasps and looks around like she's searching for a hidden camera, before pulling me over to the sofa and demanding. "Have you seen something? You know, they supposedly shape-shift when they get tired or angry. They can morph into lizards before your eyes!"

I did not know that and if my creep tank wasn't already filled to capacity, this information would have certainly done the trick. "Why in the world do you think all this?"

My young friend responds, "My roommate in college." She further explains, "Kathy is very quiet and introverted. I've never known a saner person." Then she explains, "She's had contact with aliens since she was a small child and they told her."

"What? What do mean she's had contact? Did they abduct her?"

Abbie answers, "Hers wasn't typical gray-style abduction." She's referencing the creepy little gray aliens that steal people out of their beds and perform experiments on them. OMG, talk about being too freaked out to ever sleep again. "She used to have visitations from entities she called the Light Beings. They claim to be one of only two alien races who wish good things for our planet."

"Wait, what? How many different kinds of ETs are here?" I look around for a paper sack to breathe into.

"Hundreds have visited but thirty-eight have taken up residency."

"WHAT? They're living here?"

My fellow conspirator explains, "Not only are they living here but some of them are working with our governments."

I place my nose on Sophie's head and inhale her innocent baby smell. It works to calm me. "What in the world are they doing with our governments?"

She answers, "They're giving us information on technology in exchange for permission to do things they want to do, like kidnap people and experiment on them."

"Abbie, that's just ridiculous! How can you believe something like that? Our government is in place to take care of people, not farm us out to ET's for nefarious purposes."

She shrugs her shoulders, "What if the government wasn't given a choice? What if the ET's had the power to just take over our planet if we didn't agree to their terms? At least with the government working with them, we have some idea of what they're capable of. The real question is, if they're more advanced than we are, and we need to assume they are if they've been able to travel to us, then how would we have stopped them?"

I can't even begin to absorb this horror, so I ask, "What about the reptilians? What does your friend say about them?" I still haven't decided whether or not to believe what Abbie says about her friend is the truth. I mean, it's one thing to think your husband might be a giant lizard set on planetary domination, it's quite another to accept this nonsense about thirty-eight different kinds of other worldly creatures walking amongst us, right?

The nanny responds, "According to her, our planet is about to be undeniably introduced to the presence of aliens. They've been planning their unveiling for several years. Once that happens, an escalated bid for planetary control will take place. As in, the powers that be will fight it out with each other. At that time, the reptilians will step up and make a play for ownership of earth."

"Abbie, this sounds like a bad movie. There is no way something this absurd is going to happen."

"Why?" she asks. "Why won't it? Incredible things have existed on this planet long before man did. If you can believe in something as fantastic as dinosaurs, why can't you believe in this?"

I stammer, "Because we have proof dinosaurs existed!"

"But what if we hadn't found their bones yet? People would think you were crazy to think giant lizards once inhabited the earth." She's got a point. She continues, "What happens when the mothership lands in front of the White House for the entire world to see? You'll have your proof. What will you believe then?"

I feel like I've just stepped through the looking glass. If even a fraction of what we're talking about is true, my whole life has changed forever, just when I have another person to protect and care for. I am so screwed.

Chapter 51

The next morning, Abbie and I don't make any mention of my nocturnal visit, but we do exchange knowing looks. I stare at my husband with suspicious eyes. Over coffee at the kitchen table, I ask, "Elliot, have you ever been underground?"

"You mean like in a mining shaft or something?"

Interesting, maybe mining shafts are the entrance to his other world. So I answer, "Sure, like a mining shaft?"

He responds, "I never have. Truthfully, I would be afraid of a collapse."

Is he saying this to throw me off his trail, or is it true? Of course he probably doesn't know I'm suspicious, yet, but I have to be careful, I don't know the extent of his powers. So I ask, "What do you think of lizards?"

He looks up from his magazine and asks, "In what regard? As in would I like one for a pet, a belt, dinner?"

"Any of the above," I answer.

The Englishman answers, "None of them. I can't see cuddling up with one on the couch. I guess I'd eat one if I was starving and that's all there was, but I'm not going to go out of my way to cook one for dinner, and I prefer leather belts to reptile belts."

I don't feel any better after hearing his answers. After all, maybe reptiles don't like to cuddle and that's why he wouldn't want to snuggle up with one, although he does cuddle with me, which could be a result of him trying to hide his true self or it could be that he has enough human DNA that he actually likes to cuddle. Ah, my head! I have got to stop thinking like this.

So I change the subject, "Do you have any other ideas for a middle name for Sophie?" As easy as it was for us to find her first name, it's been equally hard to settle on a middle name.

"How about Prudence? I've always loved that name and then there's the Beatles song, Dear Prudence. Good song."

Elliot's Englishness is showing. He comes up with names like Prudence, Theodora and Imogen and I'm thinking things like Marie, Elizabeth and Ann. Although Elizabeth is now off the table on the chance the queen is really the ruler of the lizard people as well as the English monarch.

Before we can get into a good heated debate about middle names Elliot's cell phone rings. He looks at me and declares, "It's Beatrice."

He answers, "Beatrice, how are you?" Clearly it isn't his old flame because he changes that to, "Clive, good to hear from you." Elliot gets up from the table to pour himself another cup of coffee while he talks. I get caught up in my own thoughts and don't listen to anything he's saying. After all, I've the weight of the intergalactic world on my shoulders.

When my husband hangs up, he's in tears. I demand,

"Elliot, what's going on? Is Beatrice okay?"

Elliot sits next to me at the table. "That was Clive."

"Oh, Elliot, please tell me the chemo's working. I *need* to know it's working." I can't take any more unsettling news right now. I don't think my brain can handle it.

Elliot shakes his head sadly and whispers, "Beatrice died last night in her sleep."

I'm totally confused, "What do you mean she died? She was having chemo, she's getting better!"

Tears flow freely down my husband's face. "Apparently they found out two months ago the treatment wasn't doing anything and Beatrice decided to stop. She wanted to spend her last days with Clive, without throwing up all the time." Then he sobs, "They didn't tell us because they didn't want to burden us with news we could do nothing about." Then he adds, "Especially when we were so excited about our little girl coming into the world."

Oh my God, oh my God, oh my God! I get up, hand Elliot the baby and start pacing. I don't know what to do with myself. I feel like I need to scream. I need to DO something and there's nothing I can do. I release a gut wrenching moan and crumple to the ground. I cannot believe how incredibly unfair life is. I'm so devastated and confused, I feel like I'm going to go out of my mind.

Elliot calls for Abbie and hands her Sophie. I'm so distraught I don't even care that someone other than my child's parents are holding her. My husband gathers me in his arms and embraces me. Our tears flow freely and neither of us makes any move to get up off the kitchen floor.

I finally find my voice and manage, "Her middle name will be Beatrice. Sophie Beatrice Fielding." Then I choke on my breath and become completely unglued.

Chapter 52

There's no way in this world I can go to Beatrice's funeral. Sophie is too young to fly and I can't stand to be away from her longer than it takes for a quick shower. Elliot and I decide he will go and his parents volunteer to accompany him. Pip, Abbie and I will stay home and hold down the fort. I keep waiting for a panic attack to hit at the thought of Elliot being gone, but thank God, it never does.

My husband and his parents depart this morning. Elliot plans to be there for four days. I know he wants to stay longer to take care of some business in London, but he's worried about leaving me for too long. I don't encourage him to dally, either. I'm equally concerned about how I'm going to hold it together while he's an ocean away.

Both Pip and Abbie stay pretty close and check up on me often. I fritter away the time by holding the baby, nursing the baby, watching her sleep and perusing Amazon. I'm afraid to watch television for fear some new information will come my way that I can't handle. So I start to plan what I'll need when the aliens take over. Yes, I know how that sounds, but better to be safe than sorry, right?

I decide The Preppy Prepper is right. You can never be too prepared. Where I was once contented to just listen to her on the radio, that's no longer the case. I order all six of her books from *Deadly Kilt* to *The Preppy Pink Pantry*. The Preppy Prepper never shares what she's prepping for, but she's going to be ready for anything, which makes me think, I need a gun.

Don't go freaking out on me here. I'm as big a fan of gun control laws as anyone. I certainly don't think I need a missile launcher. In truth, I might, but I concede it would not be prudent for that to be legal. So if I ever require one, I'll just have to purchase it on the black market. I scour the Internet for local gun sales and find what I'm looking for. I discover it will take three days to perform a background check so I start the process.

I decide on a Glock 37 because the salesperson uses adjectives like, big-bore technology, large caliber and packed performance. All those descriptions sound like something I'll need if I'm called on to protect my family from alien invaders.

While I'm waiting for my background check to clear, I start to think about how society is going to spiral downhill when everyone learns we're not alone on the third rock from the sun. I figure no one will bother going to work anymore, so food is going to be in short supply, which is how I come to order $18,000 worth of staples from Beprepared.com. I get everything from freeze dried milk, eggs, butter and prepared meals to chem-splash protective suits in case of a bio-emergency. I'm not even sure when one of those suits would come in handy, but they're under fifteen bucks each, so I get ten.

I order gas masks and water cleaning pellets, Mylar blankets and burn ointments. All in all, I'm prepping for my whole family, Elliot's family (if we decide they aren't aliens themselves), Abbie and Richard. I'm going to need more guns; one isn't going to do the trick.

I decide to trust Abbie to watch Sophie while she naps so I can check out the basement situation. I didn't even go down there before we bought the house. I realize this makes no sense, but I'm really squeamish when it comes to subterranean anything, hence the added wig factor about the reptilians.

Abbie has instructions to not leave Sophie's side for anything. She's not to read a book or look out the window. She's to stare intently at my daughter to make sure she keeps breathing. If she needs to use the bathroom, she's to call me on my cell phone and I will come up from the basement to take over.

With these important directives given, I gather an armload of cleaning supplies and head down under to see what waits. I know the basement is unfinished and I'm expecting the worst, so I'm nicely surprised to find it's relatively clean. There are no earthen floors which greatly reduces my fear that someone buried bodies underneath. There are no manacles attached to cement walls and there aren't any spider webs. All-in-all, it looks like it will make the perfect storage area once my prepping supplies start to arrive.

The basement is sectioned off into a variety of rooms. If we ever decide we need an extra five thousand feet of living space, I don't think it would take too much to make it habitable. I decide to store my supplies in the room directly under the living room. It's far enough away from the stairs that I'm pretty sure no one will ever stumble across it unless they're looking for it.

While I'm mapping out storage, I decide to go onto Costco.com and order a gun safe for the additional weaponry I'll be buying. I wonder if hand grenades can be purchased on the open market. I make a note to Google that. Also, I'm going to need to stock up on bullets, lots and lots of bullets and maybe a spear thrower. Note to self: look up poison darts and how to acquire them.

Abbie does a fine job of watching Sophie. When I climb back up from the depths, I find her right where I left her, intently watching my child. This trial does a lot for instilling confidence that I might be able to let our nanny help care for our child, someday.

My family has done their best staying away, as per my request, but I know they're chomping at the bit to come over and check on us, especially with Elliot and his parents away. So when the doorbell rings later in the afternoon, I place bets with myself on who it is. My guess is my mom or Renée. Ginger is overwhelmed caring for the triplets and a trip out means at least an hour of preparation, and Muffy spends all her time at The Buff Muff with Kevin these days.

So imagine my surprise when I peek through the peephole to find Richard at my threshold. I swing the door wide open and greet, "Richard! What are you doing here?"

My sweet friend kisses my cheek and replies, "I'm here for my weekend wooing of your sister-in-law. Did you forget?"

With impending planetary demise on the forefront of my

mind, I had forgotten. In fact the last time I saw Richard, I was only mildly insane compared to what I am now. Who would have thought I'd be missing the days right after Sophie was born. I thought they were so horrible, and then the aliens hit.

I invite Richard in and offer to make him a cup of tea. Once he's settled, I tell him about Beatrice. He's very sorry to hear the news and offers, "She was a lovely woman. It's so sad when someone that young passes."

We sit quietly for a moment, both lost in our thoughts, when Pip walks in. "Richard, what are you doing here?"

He stands to greet her and replies, "I plan on visiting over the weekends to spend more time with everyone." His eyes twinkle when he looks at her.

Pip stutters, "Well then, I'll just leave you alone."

My dashing friend responds, "Certainly you're part of everyone, aren't you? Why don't you sit down and join us?"

My sister-in-law isn't sure how to handle his invitation. After all, Richard has gone out of his way to avoid her until now. You can see she's not sure of his motives. She finally concedes, "I guess I could stand a cup of tea."

Richard only sits down again once Pip is settled. He asks her, "How is the lovely Miss Sophie doing?"

Pip glances at me before answering, "One would assume she's fine. But no one really ever sees her."

"Mimi," Richard begins, "are you still hiding your baby away from everyone?"

I respond, "As you can see clearly, she's right here." I point to the cloth wrap that I wear as a harness. It keeps Sophie attached to me whenever I'm not nursing her or when she's not in bed sleeping. I add, "She is *mine*, Richard. I have no contractual obligations to let any of you hold her."

He exchanges a look with Pip before asking, "What does your doctor say about your behavior?"

I defend, "She's says it's completely normal and that every woman responds differently to postpartum." I don't explain that I'm due for my checkup soon, where I will beg her to fix me. That's none of his business.

I do realize my behavior has been a cause of great concern for those who love me. I appreciate they're worried, but I do not want their input. They have absolutely no idea what I'm going through or how hard I struggle to appear somewhat normal. I'm not going to let any of them in on it, either. My greatest fear is they'll discover how unhinged I am and take Sophie away from me.

After a couple more moments of chit chat, I excuse myself on the grounds of needing a nap. Although instead of heading to my bedroom, I go directly to Elliot's office and start researching crossbows.

Chapter 53

Dr. Fermin assures me postpartum eventually leaves, but if it's as bad as I'm telling her, and heaven knows I'm not sharing everything, I have to prepare myself that it may last as long as a year. There is no way on God's green earth I can feel like this for an entire year without peeling my skin off one layer at a time.

She says I have two options; one is to take medication, which will get into my breast milk and the other is to start actively working out in hopes of flooding my body with natural endorphins to help get me through.

I certainly don't want to quit nursing my child and I most definitely don't want to taint her milk, so I decide to hire a trainer to come to the house. I can't go to the gym because I'm not going to leave the baby in anyone else's care. If the trainer comes to me, I reason, I can have Abbie keep an eye on Sophie wherever I'm working out.

Muffy recommends her friend Alba for the job. I don't waste any time and call her immediately explaining my predicament. She offers to come over later in the afternoon for a consultation.

As soon as I walk through the front door, I'm accosted by an angry Pip, who demands to know why Richard is really visiting. She announces, "Everyone knows *you* don't want to see anyone, so really, what's the point of him being here?"

"Pip," I explain, "he's here to see you. He's decided to listen to his father and see if you wouldn't be the perfect wife for him, after all."

"What?" she demands. "That's ridiculous! Why would he do that?"

"Are you telling me you don't believe your messages are real?"

"Of course I do. I mean I know they're real." She laments, "It's just, why has he decided to believe me now?"

I respond, "You've given him some pretty convincing displays of your abilities." Then I ask, "Are you attracted to him? You know, he's pretty hot."

My sister-in-law blushes, "I would have said yes if it wasn't for all the nonsense he put me through. Now, I find him more annoying than attractive."

I advise, "Let it go, Pip. You're bound to have more fun with Richard if you don't get caught up in your irritation. And who knows, maybe he's the one for you. Wouldn't it be nice to be with a man that believes in your gift for change?"

She looks like she's really considering what I'm saying when Sophie lets out a cry of distress. I pick her up out of her carrier and snuggle her. "And," I add, "you might even open yourself up to motherhood. What do you think of that?"

Philippa laughs, "I would love to be a mother someday. Although truth be told," she eyes me closely and adds, "I'm starting to think there might be more to it than I previously thought."

I let out a sarcastic snort and roll my eyes. "You think? God knows, I don't make it look easy, but believe me when I tell you, it's the best thing I've ever done." Of course I don't mention my postpartum suspicions that she and her family are aliens bent on world domination. That might really scare her off if it turns out she's as human as the rest of us.

I ask, "Where's Abbie?"

"Out in the garage working on her latest sculpture. Any idea what she's making?"

"None," I reply. "I like modern art about as much as I'd like to vacation on a mosquito farm. It's just not my cup of tea."

Pip says, "Abbie and I have been having a lot of fun planning the garden. She's really a great girl." She asks, "Did you know she grew up on an organic farm?"

I nod my head, "From what I understand her parents are still living there." Then I ask, "Any idea how Abbie's sister Katie died?"

She responds, "No. All I got was the message from her, nothing else."

At that moment Richard trots down the stairs looking as handsome as ever. I'd really like some time on my own to further research available weapons, so I suggest, "Richard, would you and Pip mind running into town to get me a couple things?"

Richard looks delighted by the prospect, but my sister-in-law doesn't.

She interrupts, "Why don't you go Richard? There's something I need to take care of here."

"Nonsense," I declare. "It will do you both the world of good to get out for a while." I don't add that it will do me a world of good to be left alone.

My dapper friend offers Pip his arm, "Madam, what do you say? We could find a nice place for lunch while we're in town."

Pip sighs, "Fine, let's go." Her heart doesn't seem to be in it, but now that Richard has decided to work his magic on her, I don't think it will take much for her to get on board.

As soon as they're gone, I run around the house making sure all the windows are locked. Once that's done, I check to see that all the appliances in the kitchen are off. I quickly do fifty jumping jacks and jog in place for five minutes before I start licking light switches and stepping over cracks so I don't inadvertently break my mother's back.

By the time Alba arrives I'm feeling crazy again. I explain what's going on and she assures me I'm not her first postpartum mental case. She suggests we focus on exercises that won't create as much lactic acid because babies have shown a dislike for it. They'll often stop nursing if their milk provider works out too strenuously.

For that reason, she's going to be focusing on walking, stretching and yoga. She tells me to drink at least a gallon of water a day, not only to keep my milk production up but to make sure any residual lactic acid is diluted.

I like Alba. She's in her mid-thirties, she's fit without being intimidating and she looks and sounds sane. I hope some of that will rub off on me. She earns extra points when she doesn't ask to see or touch the baby. What's up with strangers and their unseemly penchant to put their hands on your child? The next one to pull that shit is going to get a piece of my mind. Either that or I'm going to spit on them. We'll just have to see which way the winds blowing.

Elliot calls this afternoon to tell me the funeral was excruciating. Clive is understandably devastated, but he's nearly catatonic, as well. He barely spoke to anyone and Elliot says he doesn't even seem fully aware that Beatrice is dead. He kept talking about her in the present tense and even told Elliot he was still planning to take her away that summer.

I cannot even conceive what he's going through. Imagine meeting the love of your life and losing her a mere six months later. Life is bitterly unfair and I find I have to get off the phone and do my yoga breathing before I start to rip my hair out.

I eat dinner in my room that night. I find the news about Clive so distressing that I'm choking on my panic again. I suggest Abbie serve Pip and Richard and then make herself scarce. I let her in on the plan to get them together. Apparently, spectacular postpartum and grief isn't enough to kill the matchmaker in me.

Chapter 54

At 6:52 this morning, the doorbell rings. First of all, we live at the end of a very long driveway secured by a code locked gate, in a rather unpopulated area. I can't imagine it's the paper boy. Secondly, it's not even business hours for anyone other than the milkman, who went extinct sometime in the nineteen sixties. Who the heck is it then?

It's the Counterterrorism Squad from the State Department. No, I'm not kidding. Apparently, all my mad Googling about weapons and survivalist gear, coupled with my rather large purchase at BePrepared.com has set up some red flags with the big boys in Washington.

I count six burly looking men in khaki pants and denim shirts, striving way too hard to look casual. There are three large black SUVs in my circular driveway. The man standing in front introduces himself as Special Agent Frick. He flashes a badge and asks to be let in.

Due to my new sense of paranoia, I'm not about to let these men into my home without some assurances they are who they say they are. After all, I know from *Ancient Aliens* that large black SUVs are one of the tools of the men in black. OMG, what if these men are aliens? What if they're here to warn me about my concerns over the reptilians? Holy crap, what if Elliot knows them and they're part of his real life as an under lord of the earth?

I start to get a little dizzy and Special Agent Frick, if that's really his name, and his cohorts push their way into my foyer. They ask if they can look around, but they've already started doing just that. One of the goons demands, "Do you have a pressure cooker?"

What the hell kind of question is that? "Um, no." I respond. "I've just ordered a pressure canner though." I figure with all the produce we're going to be growing; I'm going to put some of it up for my emergency stores.

Another man, probably Special Agent Frack, demands, "What other kind of cooking machines do you have?"

I tentatively answer, "We have a slow cooker and a rice machine."

"That you use to make bombs, right?"

God, if I didn't feel crazy before, I certainly do now. I respond, "My nanny uses them to make dal mikhani and purple quinoa." I start looking around for a place to run, but I realize they've effectively surrounded me. There's no way to extricate myself from this group while insuring Sophie's safety. My daughter is in her carrier next to the couch and if I make a run for it, they'll be on her before I can get to her.

Another in the group demands, "Are those ingredients for your bombs?"

What? I stammer, "They're ingredients for dinner. Dal

makhani is a vegetarian Indian dish and quinoa is kind of like rice, but better for you."

They demand to know all kinds of things like where I'm from, what my parents' names are and why I need ten chem-splash suits. I answer that I'm from Pipsy, my parents are the Finnegans on Vance Lane and I don't know why I purchased the chem suits. I just thought they looked kind of cool. I explain that I just had a baby and I'm having a really hard time with postpartum. I'm overwhelmed with responsibility for this new life.

Special Agent Frick breaks rank and says, "Aw, crap, lady, I'm sorry. My wife had a time of it, too. How old is your baby?"

I tell him and he asks to see her. I break out in a cold sweat in response. Does he want to see her so he can grab her and take her hostage? Is he going to drag her into the bowels of the earth and cook her for dinner?

The next thing I know I'm lying flat on the ground regaining consciousness. All six of the government men are surrounding me. One of them announces that they just met the nanny and laid eyes on the baby and as soon as they're sure I'm okay, they'll leave.

I jump to my feet, sway a little and exclaim, "I'm just fine! You can go now."

Agent Frick responds, "I understand your husband is Elliot Fielding." Abbie must have told them. I nod my head in response.

Another of the goons says, "We must not have his new address updated in our system. If we had, we wouldn't have had to bother you."

Wait, what? Elliot's in their system. This makes me think he must be in cahoots with whatever nefarious plot they're cooking up.

Special Agent Frick explains, "Authors are always Googling the most bizarre stuff. I assume your husband is working on a new book."

I nod my head again and before I can say, Bob's your uncle, they're gone. Holy freaking hell, I'm not sure I'll ever recover from this. But I do say a prayer of thanks for Elliot and his unorthodox career. It might have just kept me out of prison.

I have to tell Abbie about my prepping. There's no other way to explain the visit from the Counter Terrorism Squad than by just coming clean.

I learn Abbie's family has been doing their version of prepping ever since she was a baby. They used to live "normally," but with the more children they had, they felt a greater burden to prepare in case anything went wrong. Their first concern was with so many mouths to feed, they had to be able to grow their own food. The only way to do that was to give up some of life's creature comforts and buy land. They live on ten acres, eight miles from the nearest town.

Abbie says they raise their own meat, from cows to chickens and pigs, and they supply a minimum of 80% of all of their other dietary needs. They have bees that provide pure, raw honey and beeswax that they use to make candles. They make all of their own soap and skincare supplies and they even tap their own maple trees for syrup. I'm astounded by their degree of sustainability.

I ask, "Are you the only vegetarian in your family?"

Our nanny responds, "I'm not a vegetarian."

"What do you mean, you're not a vegetarian? Everything you've ever fed us is vegetarian."

"No it's not. I use meat broths all the time."

I wonder, "Why don't you use meat then?"

She answers, "After growing up on a farm where we slaughter our own, I've just overdosed on the whole reality of it. I can't be in on meat preparation anymore. It wigs me out." She adds, "But I love a nice steak and I go to Burger City all the time for lunch."

Will wonders never cease? I thought Abbie was some diehard moral vegetarian but she's really just a woos. It makes her seem so much more human.

The nanny asks what kind of prepping supplies I've been purchasing and I show her the list. She makes some great suggestions, like freeze dried garden seeds. She says she plans on harvesting seeds from our garden this year for next year but it never hurts to have extras on hand. She also thinks I should get some basics like extra toilet paper and cleaning supplies. Those aren't necessary for survival but they sure will make the transition easier. She also recommends a generator. She is so full of information that I decide to take her to the basement to show her the setup I envision.

We decide to purchase as many items in person as we can, so as not to be on another receiving visit from the State Department. This is how we wind up at Costco buying 28 cases of toilet paper. That's all we can fit in Elliot's SUV with both of us and Sophie's car seat. On our next trip, we haul home two generators that are both battery and propane operable. After that, we hit Burger City for lunch and then wind up at Home Depot where we buy 24 empty propane tanks. Abbie will be responsible for filling them, a few at a time, and storing them in one of the sheds on the property.

Once we get home, we go on Diapers.com and order enough diapers, in all sizes, to get four infants straight through potty training. I'm exhausted, but the more we spend and the more we prepare, the calmer I get. Now, I think I may actual be able to survive this postpartum if only I can get confirmation that my husband and his family aren't in fact the devils I'm preparing for.

Chapter 55

Lizard or not, I'm so thrilled to see Elliot when he walks through the front door, I launch myself into his arms. He holds me for several moments before demanding to hold Sophie. He's followed by his parents, who both seem inordinately happy to be back at our house. They both hug me with heartfelt emotion and I find I'm equally glad to see them.

Abbie brings tea and scones into the library for everyone and the countess totally shocks me when she embraces the nanny in greeting. When she sits down, she sighs, "Life is just so precious. I can't believe poor Beatrice is gone."

I want to know how everything went but at the same time I don't want to know because I'm not sure I can handle the inevitable panic it will bring. Instead I ask, "How was your flight?"

They all confirm it went well. The earl inquires, "And what did you do to keep yourselves busy while we were gone?"

I share a conspiratorially glance with Abbie and reply, "Not much. Richard was in town for the weekend, we worked on the garden plan a bit and other than that, just pretty much took it easy." Liar, liar, pants of fire! But there's no way I'm going to confess a visit from the Counter Terrorism Department and $24,000 in prepping expenditures. They would never understand.

Elliot's parents excuse themselves, claiming they'd like to rest for a while. Pip and Abbie go back to work on their Territorial Seed order. Apparently Territorial is where Abbie's parents get their seeds and she swears they're the best. This leaves me alone with my husband and baby.

Elliot asks, "How are you really doing, darling? What did the doctor say?"

So I fill him in on hiring a trainer and assure him that I think I'm going to be able to handle the postpartum as long as I remember to exercise like a fiend and practice my yoga breathing. "It's just so much harder than I ever thought it would be." I elaborate, "I thought we'd just bring our baby home and live happily-ever-after. I didn't expect all this other crap."

My husband holds me in his arms and decides, "We *are* going to live happily-ever-after. This is just one little bump in the road."

For a moment I believe him. After all, I don't really want to think he's a giant lizard bent on world domination. I don't want to think our government is conspiring with ETs to keep their evil agenda hidden from mankind and I certainly don't want to be prepping for the end of the world as we know it. Maybe I really will wake up one day to find my hormones balanced and have my head back to normal. God, what an intoxicating thought.

I've decided it's time to start letting my family come over again. So I've invited them all to dinner tonight. I figure if I get overwhelmed, I'll just take the baby upstairs and hide from them.

I told Abbie to just order Chinese takeout for everyone to make things easier and put out some paper plates so she doesn't have a horrible clean up. I don't want her feeling like she's our cook when in fact she's our nanny, although she's become so much more now that I've taken her into my confidence. She's my partner in crime. She's my teacher.

My parents are the first to arrive and my mom bursts into tears when she sees me. "Oh Meems, I've been so worried! Are you doing okay now? Do you feel more normal?"

I answer that I'm doing a tiny bit better and I expect with my new workout routine I should be feeling better soon.

Renée and Laurent arrive next. They left Camille and Finn at home with a sitter to help keep the noise down. Renée shares, "Camille cannot wait to meet her new cousin. She's madder than a hatter at me for not letting her come, so I had to promise to bring her over next week."

Ginger and Jonathan appear next, with all three babies in tow. They both look positively exhausted and I know it's a Herculean show of support that they came. As soon as they're through the door, various family members help to unbundle the babies and hold them.

Muffy and Kevin arrive with 24 of the most gorgeous cupcakes I've ever seen, which is a good thing because I hadn't planned anything for dessert. I find myself practicing my yoga breathing as the house fills with bodies. While everyone moves into the kitchen to load up their plates, I grab my coat and do twenty quick laps around the driveway.

I get through dinner better than I expected I would. Having gone from a nearly empty home to one filled to the gills can overwhelm anyone, let alone a certifiable head case. My mom is going to come back every day for as long as I let her stay. She understands this might only be for ten minutes and she's okay with that.

Ginger assures me she's doing okay and by unspoken agreement, neither of us shares too much of what we're going through. I just pray she's having an easier time of it than I am, which would be truly amazing, because she's doing it with three times the babies.

Over cupcakes, Kevin and Muffy pop open a few bottles of champagne and announce their engagement. I react by bursting into tears and screaming, "Oh my God, oh my God, oh my God, I'm so happy for you!" Then I grab them both and dance around the kitchen.

Muffy and I became a lot closer in the weeks she stayed with me during her divorce. Until that point, we were probably the least close in our quartet of sisterhood and I'm so glad I had the opportunity to get to know her better. I feel very close to her now and plan on keeping that up.

Kevin and I lost contact after high school and only reformed our friendship last year. We bonded through Weight Watchers, at a time when we were both at our most vulnerable. He's proven to be the truest and dearest friend I have outside of blood relations. Having him in the family is the best thing I can imagine. Okay fine, being sane is the best thing I can imagine, but having Kevin for a brother runs a close second.

They've decided to aim for a summer wedding and as it's a second for both, they're opting to keep it pretty small. Muffy declares, "We both had big first weddings so we want this one to be relaxed and intimate."

Kevin adds, "We're going to throw the mother of all cookouts about a week after though, and ask everyone to come celebrate with us."

While I have no idea what the summer will hold for me, I can only hope I'll be back to normal. But until then I need to setup my crossbow training course in the basement. I just got an email that it will be arriving tomorrow, along with all of my emergency supplies.

Chapter 56

I have no idea how to get Elliot, his parents and Pip out of the house so they aren't around to witness the epic UPS delivery. I decide to call Renée and see if she'll invite them over at three o'clock for tea. I'm banking on the fact that their British DNA will make it nearly impossible to resist a proper tea.

Renée agrees when I falsely confess that I absolutely can't stand having them home for another moment. I site postpartum related crazies and plead with her to help a sister out.

Elliot needs my assurance that I'll be fine while they're away and I give it. I even encourage, "I'm sure I'll be feeling much better after a training session with Alba." Yet another lie.

I wave them all off at 2:50 knowing full well our UPS delivery is always at three. Like clockwork, the phone rings at exactly three with the UPS man looking to be buzzed in. He's brought the extra big super-sized truck and I tremble as I speculate how much of it's mine.

The first words out of his mouth are, "Hello, Mrs. Fielding! You have quite a load here. Where do you want me to put everything?"

I ask if he'd mind wheeling it through the house to the basement door. When he asks if my husband is around to help me carry it down, I answer, "No, he's away on business. My nanny and I will haul everything down ourselves."

It turns out we're Jeff's last stop of the day. I'm guessing he must have been a Boy Scout because he offers to help us carry the load to the basement. I weigh the sincerity of his offer against the chance that he's an evil doer and decide to trust him.

On his one hundred and twenty-third trip down the basement stairs, or maybe it was his four hundred and second, I gave up counting at forty, he asks, "You must be prepping for one hell of a winter!"

Holy crap, I can't have him thinking I'm a prepper! Then he'd know where to come when the shit hits the fan and God knows how many people he'd bring with him. So I laugh, loud and hard and I'm hoping convincingly, when I respond, "Oh heaven's, no! We're collecting for a food drive at our church." Note to self, make a nice donation to the soup kitchen to atone for a fib of this proportion.

He nods his head and asks, "What's the flame thrower for?"

"Just a little summer BBQ we're having. We thought we'd offer some competitive events."

"Ah," he responds, "that must be why you ordered crossbows."

"Exactly!" I reply. "We have some really athletic friends."

The gun safe weighs too much for us to carry down the stairs, so we help Jeff tilt it over and slide it down. It lands with a twelve hundred pound thud, but no harm is done. I have Jeff haul everything into my secret prepping room and then Abbie rewards him with two dozen of her famous chocolate chip chia and pine nut cookies. I add a hundred dollar bill to the mix and we bid Jeff a good day.

Ho-lee crap did I order a ton of stuff! It's 4:45 by the time Jeff leaves and I feel like I've been bench pressing a house. The good news is that mentally speaking I don't feel too bad. All this physical labor has left me feeling pretty level-headed.

The bad news is I'm going to have to figure out how to organize all this stuff without drawing attention to myself. Thankfully, I have Abbie to help.

By the time Elliot and his parents get home, I've showered and am fast asleep on our bed. Elliot kisses me and whispers, "Hey lazy bones, did you sleep the afternoon away?"

If he only knew. I smile and answer, "Guess I just needed to catch up."

My husband sits down next to me and says, "I just go the strangest email from the State Department. They wanted to apologize for disturbing you the other day. What's that all about?"

I'm flush with panic but manage to reply, "They said you were Googling some weird stuff on the computer and wanted to make sure no one was trying to make a bomb." I force out a nervous giggle.

Elliot responds, "That's strange. My new book has nothing to do with terrorism, bomb making or anything like that. You know what else is strange?"

I can't imagine so I make noncommittal noise in reply. "Every time I go online, I'm flooded with ads for prepping websites and gas masks. That's never happened before."

I feel bad for what I'm about to do, but there's no getting around it. "I told Abbie she could use the computer in the office while you were away. I'll talk with her and see what she's looking up."

The Englishman shakes his head, "No need. She's probably just researching something to do with gardening, and we've been tagged."

I don't know when the last time Elliot gardened, but gas masks and freeze dried potatoes aren't usually part of the drill. Of course I don't point this out to him.

Chapter 57

In addition to chickens, I want goats. Abbie has promised that if we get goats, she'll make fresh goat cheese and even show me how to spin their wool into yarn. I wonder if I should get a loom. Maybe I'll learn how to knit first and see where that leads. It's like I'm channeling Ma Ingalls from Little House on the Prairie. I won't stop until I'm shoeing horses and re-sodding the roof.

It's the beginning of May, so it's time to get the garden going. Abbie found someone to dig out the beds and till the soil. She also has 500 pounds of assorted seasoned animal manure arriving that will be mixed into the soil. The good news is that it's seasoned so it doesn't stink, but still, it's a lot of poop.

The yard is full of men and machines tearing up our landscaping and I couldn't be more excited. I am, however, not out there witnessing everything firsthand on the chance the gardeners will try to kidnap Sophie and smuggle her across the border. I'm aware Illinois doesn't border another country, but I hear some weird stuff happens in Indiana.

I'm still horribly paranoid, as you can tell. The exercise helps with the panic but the paranoia seems to have taken up permanent residence. Every day is a challenge. Happily, I'm getting more sleep, a ton of exercise and every new thing we do to prep seems to calm me. I long for the Mimi I once was. Faults and all, her life was way simpler than mine.

Richard is in town and he, Pip and the nanny are out directing the workers. My friend and sister-in-law have finally formed a friendship. They laugh together easily and seek each other out. Just yesterday I caught them kissing in the pantry. If things continue on, we may just have another wedding on the calendar.

While the household is in an uproar with all the yardwork going on, I decide to hole up in my bedroom and catch up on some reading. I've just received five new prepping books in the mail and I'm eager to start them.

I've never given preppers the time of day, until recently. Seriously, there's been enough filling my head without inventing end of the world scenarios. But now that I'm a mom, heck, I have to be prepared for any eventuality because I have a child to protect. Why did no one ever tell me what a huge responsibility this is? It's not like I would have rethought motherhood, but I most certainly would have enjoyed my pre-parenting days a little more.

Television shows and the media do their best to make preppers look totally nuts because it's good for ratings. I site the guy who enjoys a refreshing glass of his own urine, comparing it to chamomile tea and the family in Idaho who's building a bug-out dwelling out of potatoes.

However, the books I'm reading are filled with real life horrors that actually happened in the past. The Black Death, or plague as it was more commonly referred to, killed two hundred million people in three years! That's two thirds of the U.S. population, today. To help you wrap your head around that, imagine your entire family gathered at a reunion and remove two out of three of them, and then multiple that by the entire freaking country. It took Europe an estimated hundred and fifty years to rebound from the devastation.

I know you're saying, Mimi, that was almost seven hundred years ago. The plague isn't even relevant today. Fine, how about the flu epidemic of 1918? It killed an estimated fifty to one hundred million people in a year. If that isn't horrific enough, the healthier you were when you got it, the more deadly it was, as it did more damage to healthy immune systems.

If you're one of those people who refuse to believe in the possibility of a pandemic, let me site the 1815 eruption of Mount Tambora in Indonesia. There's no vaccine for a volcano. If it's going to blow, it's going to blow. And while there are no volcanos in Illinois, thank God, the Mount Tambora explosion blew ash twenty-eight miles into the air, blocking out the sun for the entire world. It essentially caused the same reaction as a nuclear winter, and is often referred to as the year with no summer.

No summer, means no food production, which of course leads us to famine. In case you're one of those people who don't think famines are alive and well, let me point you to North Korea, circa 1995 (I was alive for this one!), where an estimated three million people died of starvation.

Scientists claim the Yellowstone Caldera is long overdue for an eruption, and when it blows, it'll make the 1815 Indonesian one look like a burp. We're talking the immediate onset of another ice age. There's absolutely nothing I can do to save us from that.

Along with volcanos, I'm helpless if an asteroid hits the planet. In 1902 something exploded in the air five miles above Siberia and the impact to the outlying area was one thousand times greater than the bomb that hit Hiroshima. It took out eight hundred square miles of land. Scientists hypothesize it was an asteroid that exploded. There's really shit all I can do if something like that happens again. I just hope I don't know it's coming ahead of time and it takes us quickly.

As I'm new to the prepping game, I have to figure out what exactly I'm prepping for. I've picked famine, alien invasion (although I'm still sketchy on how to fully prepare for that one. Note to self: order more bullets), and an EMP strike.

An electro-magnetic pulse is moderately less scary to me than an alien invasion, but only because we know the outcome. In a matter of a second, we would be thrown back a hundred and fifty years in technology. There would be no electricity, all batteries would become obsolete, no phones, no water and no sanitation. As a result, there would be no supermarkets to buy food or clothing stores and really no way to get to them, even if they did exist, other than by bike or foot.

I take a break from Robert R. Forstchen's, scariest book of all time, *One Second After*, to hop on the Internet and buy some bicycles. I settle on eight adult bikes and five to get Sophie through her childhood. I add a couple horns, pretty baskets and handlebar tassels, because there's no sense in not enjoying the end of the world, right?

I make a quick call to a local well-drilling company before I go back to my research. After all, water is the most important thing for survival. I decide to research rain barrels and cisterns next.

By the time the garden crew comes in for a break, I have a wicked headache, but I've accomplished a lot of prepping. I take a moment to thank God I have the resources to do all this. I have no idea how everyone else is going to survive the coming apocalypse.

Chapter 58

Victoria invites me out for lunch today. I'm loath to go, but I can't really come up with an excuse not to. She's been so great about giving me space and not asking to hold the baby, I feel like I owe it to her to throw her a bone. So I make a tiny effort with myself and forgo my normal yoga pants and hoody for a skirt and nice top. When I get a gander at my toes, I opt for closed toed shoes so as not to horrify her by my lack of personal grooming. There is simply no time for pedicures and the like when one is prepping for the end of days.

It's seventy-five degrees, so we decide to eat at a restaurant with outdoor seating. Sophie's snoozing in her car seat, so I just tuck her under the table to keep her safe. I order crab cakes, a salad and an iced tea. Once the waiter's gone, I have no idea what to say, so I just sit quietly and wait for the countess to speak.

Finally, Victoria offers, "Mimi, I know you're having a hard time with postpartum." I don't confirm or deny. I mean, heck, it's painfully clear I'm taking to it as gracefully as an elephant to a tight rope. She continues, "I wanted to share with you that I had a pretty rough time, as well."

Now she's got my attention. In case you haven't heard, misery loves company. "Really?" I ask. "What were your symptoms?"

She smiles painfully, "I was afraid of everything. I was frightened to take the children out of the house and I was frightened to keep them at home. I was afraid we'd get into a traffic accident, an airplane crash or even get run over by a horse. You name it. I lived in fear of danger and as far as I was concerned, danger was everywhere."

Wowza! I didn't see this coming. It turns out my mother-in-law is something of a soul sister. I ask, "What did you do to stop being afraid?"

"Well," she responds, "the first thing I did was take karate lessons."

I could more easily see her joining the circus. I ask, "How long did you take them?"

She answers, "Three years. It took me that long to earn my black belt." She adds, "My hands are registered weapons."

Note to self, do not piss off Victoria. If you'd asked me yesterday, I would have sworn that in a knock down drag out bitch fight, I could have taken her. Not anymore.

She continues, "Then I took race car driving lessons, thinking that I could mitigate some of the dangers on the road with better reflexes. After that, I learned how to fly an airplane."

Oh my God, this woman *is* as nuts as I am! Although clearly, now I need to take karate, learn how to drive a race car and fly a plane because now I can add her worries to my own.

She pauses for a moment before saying, "I tell you all this in hopes that you'll share your journey with me, so I can help you."

I'm so completely overwhelmed by her declaration and honesty that I do what any hormonally challenged insane person would do. I burst into tears. The countess hands me a tissue. "We're not so different, you and I, just two women trying to do the best for our families."

I sob, "Thank you for sharing this with me, Victoria. I truly appreciate it. It's just, I'm afraid you'll think I'm totally crazy if I tell you what's worrying me."

She laughs, "Mimi, I'm a sixty-six year old woman with a black belt in karate, I still race cars and just in case I'm flying on a plane and the whole crew drops dead, I can safely land a 747. I don't think it's possible for you to be crazier than that."

Now she's done it, gauntlet dropped. It's a matter of honor that I tell her the truth, so I start with, "Really? Do you by chance think your husband is a reptilian alien bent on world domination?"

That takes her by surprise, let me tell you. She begins to open her mouth to respond, but closes it. This happens a few more times before she finally manages, "No, actually, I don't."

I'm immediately horrified I told her that. I mean, what will I do if she tells Elliot? He might divorce me on grounds of insanity and get custody of Sophie. I want to take it back but I don't think there's any possibility of shoving that cat back into the bag.

She finally manages, "Why do you think that, exactly?"

So I tell her all about *Ancient Aliens* and the weird stuff I've read online about the royal family. You know how they're really lizards that rule all the important families of the world.

Victoria asks, "Would you mind showing me this program? I'd be curious to hear more."

I demand, "You mean you aren't ready to have me locked me up over this?"

She shrugs her shoulders, "Not particularly. I can assure you, though, if Elliot and therefore Archibald, really are lizards, I've had no indication of it. And I venture they aren't a part of some evil agenda, if they are."

"That's just the thing. I know they're both perfectly lovely men, so it makes the betrayal so much worse if there's something else going on." I continue, "They apparently shape-shift into lizards when their emotions run high. Have you ever seen that?" I ask.

"No, not that I recall," she replies. "I'm pretty sure I would have remembered that." Then she gets an idea, "I know! Let's ask Pip. She's got those otherworldly connections; maybe they can answer some of these questions."

That's actually not such a bad idea. I believe in Pip's gift and maybe my grandma Sissy or someone else would come through with some helpful advice. I agree to give it a shot. Then for some unearthly reason, I add, "That's not all I'm worried about though."

"What else?" she asks matter-of-factly.

I answer, "I've become a bit of a prepper since Sophie was born." I don't dare make eye contact until I hear her reply.

"You know," she starts, "I think preppers are given a bad rap. Ungodly disasters have happened since the beginning of time. People who don't think something bad can happen to them have their heads so far up their own arses, they sure aren't smelling roses."

I haven't a clue how to respond. I think Victoria has just become my biggest supporter and it couldn't be more unexpected. I've just accused her son and husband (and probably daughter) of being reptiles, I've expressed something pretty outrageous thoughts and I've never even let her hold her granddaughter. I can't imagine I would be as gracious in her shoes.

All I can think to say is, "Victoria, you are one class act, you know that?"

She reaches across the table, takes my hand, and squeezes it. "You too, Mimi, you too."

Chapter 59

Victoria and I have a date to meet in the library at nine to watch *Ancient Aliens*. I'm bringing the popcorn and she's bringing a bottle of wine. I haven't been drinking since nursing Sophie but I produce so much milk, I'll just do a pump and dump. I think some alcohol might be in order when introducing my mother-in-law to the alien world.

I'm going to start her out with the grays. They're so common, it'll ease her into the weirder stuff, you know like reptiles. We cover the taller grays who are supposedly the more intelligent. Apparently, they're the rulers of the shorter grays that do the actual abductions and experiments. The shorter ones are often referred to as space monkeys, not by the more appropriate, space vermin, which is what I would have named them.

My mother-in-law seems to be rolling with it. She even offers, "I read Whitley Strieber's book, *Communion*, when it first came out. I don't think I slept well for six months."

I ask, "What do you think? Do you believe they're real?"

She doesn't even consider her answer before replying, "Of

course I do! There are simply too many cases that support one another for it to be some kind of mass hoax."

"So," I venture, "if you believe in one kind of alien, then do you think it's possible to believe in other kinds?"

"Mimi, that's like asking, if you believe in one kind of animal, is it possible to believe in another? Of course I do. It would be a pretty boring cosmos if it was just us and the grays, don't you think?"

I do, which is why I'm ready to introduce her to the reptilians. I switch shows to the more daring, *They're Here*, and surf through the menu until I find the episode, *Reptiles, The Real Lords of the Earth*. Victoria already seems intrigued just by the title.

The show starts out with an interview of a woman who claims to be one of the reptilians. She's just found out because she accidentally shape-shifted in front of her husband and now he's afraid of her. The woman's parents both died when she was relatively young so she can't ask them what's happening. Just let me say, I think I would have found a less public way to inquire, but whatever floats your boat.

The thing is, while this chick sounds totally off her rocker, she's very believable. She's soft spoken and timid. She seems truly traumatized by this unexplained thing happening to her. She even shows photos where it appears the camera has captured her mid shift. I know, you're thinking that can be explained by a trick of the light, but in twenty pictures spanning ten years? When asked why she didn't question the photos sooner, she answers, "I just thought I had some weird angles, but when my husband screamed bloody murder looking straight at me, it made me look at the pictures differently." Then she bursts into very credible tears.

Victoria observes, "If she's one of those reptilians, she's clearly not in on any evil plans. She doesn't even know what's happening to her."

I nod my head. "You're saying if Archibald, Elliot and Pip are aliens, they might not even know it."

She nods her head. "Mimi, what if we're all aliens, would that be so weird?"

"Yes, Victoria," I answer, "that would be very weird." Then I tell her what Father Brennan said and how he believes in aliens, too.

She answers, "There you go. If a man of God, and if what you're saying is true, even the Vatican supports this belief, then why not?"

I tell her how it's hypothesized that people with negative RH factors have alien DNA and that my mom has a negative RH factor. She exclaims, "There you go, you're an alien, too! You're not in on any devilish plans to overthrow the world, are you?"

I shake my head and she continues, "So let's just say we're all aliens. That doesn't mean we aren't all ruled by the same God, right? It just means He got creative when designing all the worlds."

I ask, "Victoria, do you think there *are* evil aliens out there?"

She answers. "There are certainly evil people, why would aliens be any different?"

I haven't the foggiest idea. Instead I ask, "How do I protect my family from them?"

She shakes her head. "I haven't a clue."

So I tell her about the weapons I've been buying. I figure she hasn't judged me yet, so why not just throw it all out there? She thinks for a moment before saying, "We need to find someone to train us how to use those weapons."

"We? Are you planning on getting in on this?"

"Of course I am. If some other worldly creatures think they're going to mess with my family, they've got another thing coming."

I ask, "What if they're smarter and more powerful than us?" I tremble just asking that question.

"Then we don't go down without a fight." She exclaims, "And we take some of those bastards with us!"

Chapter 60

Okay, so now that I have Victoria fully on board with camp crazy, I don't feel so nuts. I think all I had to do was share my fear with someone and have them confirm I'm not destined for a padded room. Yes, Elliot might be part lizard, but so what? He's a lovely man and as long as no shape-shifting occurs, I've decided to be okay with it, so much so I've decided to call off bringing Pip into it. There's no point in worrying her and outside validation of this theory might cause me more stress than living in ignorant bliss.

Richard is coming back to town tonight and I've noticed Philippa has gotten her hair done, put on some extra makeup and even seems to be wearing a new dress. I corner her in the kitchen and say, "So, Pip, looks like things are going well between you and Richard."

She smiles, "We've been enjoying spending time together, that's all."

"Oh really?" I laugh, "Was he giving you the kiss of life in the pantry on his last visit?"

My sister-in-law giggles, "You could call it that."

I cheer, "Go Pip! I'm so glad you finally have a good man in your life and I'm extra glad it's Richard. He's a wonderful person."

Her grin threatens to take over her whole face. "He *is* wonderful. You know what's really nice?" I shake my head. "This stupid gift of mine finally seems to have brought something for me. It's about time, don't you think?"

I agree, "Damn straight, I do. What time does Richard get here?"

Pip answers, "He'll be here at five. Mimi," she says, "I hope you don't mind but Richard's asked me to go away with him for the weekend. He thought we could spend a couple of nights downtown."

I let out a yelp of delight and exclaim, "That's fabulous!" Then add, "I think it's best not to be under the same roof with your entire family when you take your relationship to the next level."

Her eyes twinkle. "I couldn't agree with you more. I'm not sure I could really enjoy myself with my parents in the next room."

When Richard arrives, Pip is up in her room getting her overnight bag. I welcome my friend and tease, "Good job, Richard. I'm proud of you finally getting your act together and listening to your father."

Richard smiles, "You know, Mimi, this is the first time since I lost you to Elliot, that I'm glad I did. I think Philippa is my perfect match. She's beautiful, she doesn't want me for my money and she's just as quirky as you." He gives me a sweet hug and offers, "I think you might just be welcoming me into the family if things keep going this well."

"Oh Richard, I couldn't be happier. You both deserve the very best and I think you've found it."

In the last year of my life, I've met, married and become a parent with the man of my dreams. Richard and Pip are together, my sister Muffy and my friend Kevin have found a second chance with each other and Ginger and the triplets are doing great. All domestic concerns are in great harmony.

That aside, I'm a very different person than I used to be. I'm a mother. I'm so totally in love with my child that I've gone crazy as a result. I'm responsible for her care, her health and her whole life. I feel that pressure with every fiber of my being.

I pray the paranoia will leave. I pray I'll be more peaceful accepting whatever will be, will be. But I know one thing; I'm never going to think bad things will only happen to the other guy. Look at Beatrice. She deserved to have lived a long and happy life with Clive. She didn't get what she deserved.

I can't keep cancer from my child's door and I can't keep aliens from attacking our planet. I can't keep volcanos from erupting or EMP's from throwing us back into the dark ages. What I can do is prepare for as many eventualities as possible, which of course includes taking weaponry training with Victoria every Thursday and Saturday with a retired Navy SEAL. Other than that, I'm going to put my faith in God that my family will live the best life we can and we will rejoice every day.

I'm also going to pray Elliot doesn't have reason to go into the basement until I have a chance to explain.

The End

About the Author

While attending the University of Illinois, in Chicago, Whitney Dineen, began a career as a plus-size model. After modeling in New York City, she and her husband, Jimmy, moved to Los Angeles. In addition to modeling, Whitney spent the California years supplying some of Hollywood's biggest stars with her delicious cookies and candies. Whitney and her husband currently live in the beautiful Pacific Northwest where they spend their time raising their daughters, free-range chickens and organic vegetables.

Whitney loves to hear from her readers. You can contact her via her website www.WhitneyDineen.com, where you can sign up for her newsletter. If you've enjoyed *Mimi Plus Two*, check the following excerpt from Whitney's award-winning romantic comedy, *She Sins at Midnight*. As always, Whitney is very grateful to all her readers who take the time to leave a review.

She Sins at Midnight

Lila Montgomery sat at her desk dreaming about the two things that always brought her thoughts into sharper focus. Namely, piping hot carbs and soft melting fat. She drooled at the thought of grilled cheese on white bread, so perfectly gooey that the first bite would immediately transport her back to the innocent days of childhood. Back to a time before she gave a fig if the button on her size 12 skinny white jeans gave way and inadvertently took someone's eye out. Of course, she wasn't currently in her white jeans, so there was no imminent risk of rendering an unsuspecting co-worker blind.

Absently, Lila petted the sleeve of her ever-so-stylish and sleek Armani suit. She always paired the elegant ensemble with the same white silk blouse. The neckline plunged so low it looked like her girls were trying to escape. That particular outfit was worn when she was feeling "that time of the monthish," or in a word, bloated. Even though the suit cost an entire pay check, it was more than worth it as it covered a multitude of sins. And, as Lila knew only too well, sins should always be covered, kept in the closet, or safely locked in one's attic.

The day she bought the blouse, Lila eyed her cleavage and laughingly declared, "With everyone's eyes trained on 'Team Montgomery,' my big butt and poochy tummy are the last things that this skinny crazed town will notice."

Her friend Cynthia laughed, "Lila Montgomery, you're gorgeous! I say good for you that you're not a carrot stick away from certain death."

Lila raised an eyebrow, "Says the size 2 woman in front of me."

Cynthia interrupted, "Who is nearly 9 inches shorter than you are."

Lila's statuesque build of 5'9" and a size 12 would be coveted by the majority of women in the country. But in La La Land it was deemed overweight, especially if you worked in "The Industry." They (those alien creatures in the film business who held American women's self-esteem in their grubby little hands) considered anything above a size 4 an emergency candidate for gastric bypass. If one more metrosexual Hollywood type told Lila what a pretty face she had, she was going to smile graciously and kick the back-handed compliment giver right in the balls. Why didn't these men understand that "you have such a pretty face" isn't a compliment? Just because they don't speak the rest of the thought out loud, (too bad about the rest of you...) doesn't mean that it goes unheard.

Lila moved to Los Angeles right after college in hopes of becoming the next Scarlett Johansson. Getting the assistant's job at The Amalgamated Artists Agency was her first step in accomplishing that dream. Amalgamated, or the Triple A, as it was referred to by Hollywood insiders, was **THE** talent agency in Tinseltown. Lila's plan was to get her foot in the door of the posh establishment, casually announce that she graduated at the top of her class as a theater major, then POW, steal all of Scarlett's work.

That outcome didn't occur for a variety of reasons, the first being that even at her skinniest, Lila was ordered to lose ten pounds, stat! In Hollywood's rather miniscule attention span for young starlets (and as she was twenty-two at the time) she was clearly running out of time. After all, thousands of brand spanking new eighteen year olds got off the bus everyday with the same hopes and dreams of stardom.

Sadly, the task of losing an unnecessary ten pounds was an impossibility as Lila's love affair with the taboo carbs and seductive fats had already manifested in all its glory. Not to mention, she was told this back when a size 6 was deemed respectable. Now that the goal was to achieve a size 0 or 2, she realized she'd have to be dead for eighteen months before she had decomposed to the current standard of fashion. Letting out a depressed laugh, she imagined that her first movie review would read, "Freshly dug up for the role, Lila Montgomery wows them as the heroine of Night of the Living Dead XXII!"

The second, more dominant reason that stardom wasn't in her future, was that Lila had a deep-seated aversion of trading sexual favors for career advancement. She was aware that not all successful actresses got their start between the sheets (take Meryll Streep for instance) but from what she witnessed first-hand at The Triple A, quite a lot did. The sad truth was that when you weighed the odds of being discovered by virtue of your talent against your willingness to put out, there really was no contest. Putting out was the way to go.

Lila sat at her desk and contemplated the outcome of her almost thirty-three years on the planet. She thought about all the time she had spent tottering around her childhood home in high heels, swathed in feather boas pretending to be either Diana Spencer or Jessica Rabbit, sort of Princess-Pin-Up, if you will. When those dreams faded, her next ambition was to write the great American novel; an historical epoch along the lines of North and South. Yet every time she sat at her computer, some inner vixen took over and began creating volumes of racy fantasies instead of historical intrigue. The fantasies happily filled the gap in her social life, but did nothing for her dreams of becoming a celebrated novelist.

Consequently, the serious historical events that she had set out to portray always turned into alarming bodice ripping incidents. The gallant young officer, who urgently set out to deliver a top secret message, was inevitably delayed by a lush bosomed young thing bent on seduction. What was a red-blooded young man to do?

At first, Lila fought against her tendency to write trash. After all, she wanted to be nominated for a Pulitzer one day. She wanted respect. But after years of struggling to compose a serious narrative, she gave up and let her alter ego (alarmingly named Jasmine Sheath) have her way. Now, Lila, a.k.a. Jasmine, spent all of her free time at her computer orchestrating de-flowerings, seductions and all sorts of bawdy goings on.

As her mind continued to wander, Lila's eyes fixated on the

two letters sitting on her desk. One filled her with a pure rush of pride and excitement. The other filled her with dread. She set aside the envelope full of happy tidings knowing full well she could never share its contents with anyone. In fact, she thought the news was so private that she had best lock it in her desk drawer for safe keeping.

Once that task was accomplished, she picked up the other envelope and let out an audible sigh. In her hands was that bit of correspondence, that depending on what you had accomplished in your life, you either anticipated like Christmas morning or dreaded like a bad case a poison ivy on your private parts. It was the invitation to her fifteen year high school class reunion. It cordially invited the graduate and his/her spouse to the gala affair that was being held at The North Hills Country Club, the very same establishment where half her classmates were already second or third generation members.

Lila didn't begrudge them their memberships to the club, having spent much of her early days treading those same hallowed grounds. In fact, had she never left Bentley, she would probably be teeing off with the Ladies Junior Golf League every Wednesday morning while her offspring learned to doggy paddle in the kiddie pool. What Lila did envy were their spouses and children. She longed for similar domestic bliss. After all, she had worked at least as hard as they had and what did she have to show for it? A twenty-two hundred dollar a month rent payment on an apartment that she didn't own and a five year old Mitsubishi, no husband, no babies, not even a pet.

Three decades had come and gone and Lila finally realized that what she really wanted was the life she grew up with. She didn't need an academy award. She didn't even need a Pulitzer. She just wanted to have someone to love and someone who would love her back. Was that too much to ask?

She Sins at Midnight is available now!

Made in the USA
San Bernardino, CA
01 May 2016

Mimi Finnegan is back and funnier than ever!

Mimi has it all. She's marrying the love of her life, about to have his baby and is moving into the house of her dreams. Things couldn't be better! Until her wedding, that is, when everyone toasts to her perfect life.

Not one to tempt the fates, Mimi is sure her loved ones are jinxing her future happiness. Enter pregnancy drama, aristocratic in-laws and catastrophic postpartum depression. Mimi's journey is hilarious, heart-warming and borderline insane. Hormonal hell leaves her questioning her husband's origins, prepping for the end of the world and wondering if her sanity will ever retur

This book is for every woman who understands that love, laughter and tears are the very foundation of being wife, mother and daughter-in-law.

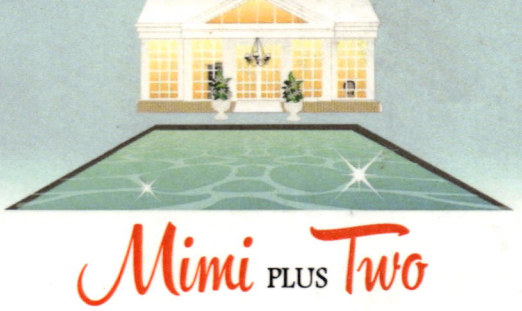

Mimi PLUS *Two*

WHITNEY DINEEN

While attending the University of Illinois in Chicago, Whitney Dineen was discovered by a local modeling agent and began an unexpected career as a plus-size Ford model. She modeled in New York City before moving to Los Angeles with her husband.

During "The Hollywood Years," Whitney was bitten by the writing bug and started creating characters inspired by strong women with a great sense of humor. In addition to writing romantic comedies, Whitney has also created a series of adventure books for girls. Whitney and her husband live in the beautiful Pacific Northwest, where they raise their children, chickens and organic vegetables.
For more on Whitney,
check out her website WhitneyDineen.com

ISBN 9781532766121